KT-549-941

LIBRARIES NI
WITHDRAWN FROM STOCK

LIBRARIES NI
WITHDRAWN FROM STOCK

The MIDNIGHT GUARDIANS

ROSS MONTGOMERY

WALKER
BOOKS

This is a work of fiction. Names, characters, places and incidents
are either the product of the author's imagination or, if real, used
fictitiously. All statements, activities, stunts, descriptions, information
and material of any other kind contained herein are included for
entertainment purposes only and should not be relied on for
accuracy or replicated as they may result in injury.

First published 2020 by Walker Books Ltd
87 Vauxhall Walk, London SE11 5HJ

4 6 8 10 9 7 5

Text © 2020 Ross Montgomery
Cover illustration © 2020 David Dean

The right of Ross Montgomery to be identified as author
of this work has been asserted by him in accordance with
the Copyright, Designs and Patents Act 1988

This book has been typeset in Adobe Garamond Pro, Agenda,
Bauer Bodoni, Berling, Frutiger, Helvetica Neue, Historical
Fell, New Century Schoolbook, Times, Times New Roman

Printed and bound by CPI Group (UK) Ltd, Croydon CR0 4YY

All rights reserved. No part of this book may be reproduced,
transmitted or stored in an information retrieval system in any
form or by any means, graphic, electronic or mechanical,
including photocopying, taping and recording, without prior
written permission from the publisher.

British Library Cataloguing in Publication Data:
a catalogue record for this book is available from the British Library

ISBN 978-1-4063-9118-3

www.walker.co.uk

For Nan, John, Kitty, Alan,
And all the Blitz kids;

And for Eve, Vera, Elsa,
And all the children of the Kindertransport.

Thank you for your stories.

21 December 1940

INVASION
MAY BE BY AIR

Despite three months of Nazi bombings, it seems many people in Britain have become lulled into a false sense of Christmas security.

The forces of the Third Reich are still only separated from us by twenty-two miles of water. There is growing evidence to support the belief that Hitler may be planning a new attack over the Christmas period. The threat of invasion is still very real.

T ONIGHT IS THE DARKEST NIGHT OF THE year.

It is so dark, you can barely make out the stone cottage sitting in front of you. It is the only building in the valley. A path runs right from the fields to a red front door, framed by the remains of a rose bush. In summer, when the days are long and warm, the roses flourish. But there are no roses now. It is the dead of winter and the dead of night. The door is surrounded by thorns.

The cottage is dark inside, even darker than outside. The windows are hung with heavy curtains, so that no light can escape and none can get in. There is a fireplace in the corner, but it has been a long time since anyone has lit it. The cottage is bone-cold, frozen from the inside out: even the floor stones are coated with frost. It is silent, and it is dark, and it is dead.

But not completely.

From somewhere in the attic, a light is glowing.

It comes from a single candle that rests in the centre of the floor. The light gleams off the rubbish packed high to the rafters: broken boxes, old rugs, furniture, all of it left and forgotten. The glow is small but strong – it feels like it could light the whole house, if it tried.

Three figures sit around it. They have been waiting for some time.

"This is stupid," says the first.

It's a knight in shining armour. He is much smaller than you'd expect – no bigger than a child. The candle-light shimmers off his breastplate and catches on the edge of his lance. A moustache pokes from his visor and dances when he talks.

"He's not coming! We're going to get in *heaps* of trouble and it'll all be for…"

"Quiet, Rogue."

The knight turns to the figure beside him – a badger. But this is no ordinary badger. He's smoking a pipe. He carries a club and wears a tweed waistcoat. Also, he can talk.

"I *told* you not to call me that," says the knight.

The badger bristles. "Oh! Your name! I can't call you your *name* now?"

"It's not *Rogue*," says the knight. "It's *the King of Rogues*. I've told you a thousand times! I don't call you

Noakes, do I? I call you 'Mr Noakes', because that's what *he* named you so…"

"Quiet, both of you."

The knight and the badger turn to the third figure – a Bengal tiger, towering over the room around them. Her head is lost to the gloom of the ceiling; her whiskers catch the cobwebs in the eaves.

"Col will come," she says. "Maybe not tonight, maybe not tomorrow, but he *will* come. We just have to keep calling him, that's all." She shuffles. "Now if you don't mind, I'd rather not do it listening to you two squabble like a pair of old ladies."

The badger grumbles and puts his club down. The knight sighs.

"Oh, Pendlebury … how can you be so *sure* that Col's coming?"

The tiger gives him a look that seems, at first, like anger. But it's not anger: it's fear. She is very, very scared.

"Because," she says, "he's the only hope we have."

22 December 1940

LONDON CROWDS BACK FOR CHRISTMAS

Thousands of evacuees arrived back in London this weekend for the Christmas holidays – despite the Ministry of Transport's "stay-put" appeal.

Trains arriving and leaving the big London terminals yesterday were packed, and the platforms at Euston Station were crowded with travellers.

Child evacuees who cannot return home for Christmas will have parties just the same.

In Bedford, there will be a free pantomime. Soldiers in Devizes will give an entertainment, and Macclesfield has promised "a really good party" for everyone evacuated there.

Since the war began, 2,100 children have been left orphaned and homeless.

The Evacuee

COL WAS IMAGINING THINGS AGAIN.

Are you there, Col?

Can you hear us, Master Col?

You must come back to the cottage, Col!

Col sighed. He'd been hearing the voices for days now, every time his thoughts drifted. It was strange: he hadn't thought about the Guardians in months, and now he couldn't seem to keep them out of his head.

But he didn't have time for imaginary friends – not now.

Not when Rose was waiting for him.

He raced down the empty streets, leaping over sandbags and skidding round corners. Blackout was about to start, and Buxton was deserted. The last of the Christmas shoppers had gone home, and the only people outside now were air raid wardens, wrapped up in scarves and camped out shivering in deckchairs.

The shop windows were all dark behind the strips of brown paper glued up to protect them from bomb blasts.

Not that any bombs would fall *here* – Buxton was a country town tucked in the valleys of the Peak District. It was the safest place in Britain, or so everyone kept saying. The only enemy planes you saw out here were the ones heading to bomb cities like Liverpool and Manchester. That was why Col had been sent up here in the first place. Buxton was safe. Safer than London, at least.

Col glowered. He was safe, all right: safe and miserable. He'd hated every minute of the six months he had spent here, over a hundred and fifty miles away from his home and everything he had ever known. Living with his Aunt Claire had been the darkest, loneliest and saddest time of his entire life.

But finally, all that was going to change. His sister was here: she had finally come. When he got back to Aunt Claire's, Rose would already be waiting for him. Col turned the final corner and saw the tiny crack of light beneath Aunt Claire's front door, where the blackout curtains didn't quite reach. His heart leaped. After months of being separated, he was finally back with his family – his true family. He threw open the gate…

And stopped. There was something waiting for him in the darkness of the garden. A crouched figure, its breath seething in silent clouds…

Col shook his head. He was just scaring himself, as usual.

"Mrs Evans?"

"Yes, dear?"

"What are you doing in the flowers?"

Mrs Evans glared at him from beneath her helmet. "Never you mind what I'm doing! It's a free country. Hitler's not here *yet*, you know."

No one in Buxton understood how Mrs Evans had been made an air raid warden. She was "an eccentric", "a real character", or "a raving lunatic", depending on who you asked. She was old – no one knew exactly how old – but she had the energy of a much younger lunatic, so no one ever made fun of her in case she hit them with her walking stick. She could usually be found putting neckties around the trees in the town square, having arguments with the garden moles at four in the morning, or – like now – crouching in Aunt Claire's geraniums in the middle of blackout.

"Who am I poking?" she said, giving him a jab with her stick. "Speak up, young man!"

"It's Col, Mrs Evans. From next door."

She nodded. "Ah, yes! The orphan boy."

Col's blood chilled. No one had ever used that word to describe him before – but it was true, wasn't it?

"I didn't recognize you, dressed like – *that*," said Mrs

Evans. "You look like a performing monkey at a funeral."

Col blushed. He was wearing a pair of black shorts, a black jacket, a bright white sash, and a pillbox hat with a little chinstrap.

"It's my uniform," he muttered. "I'm in the Boys' Brigade."

"Boys' Brigade?"

"It's like the scouts. Camping, making fires, that sort of thing. Aunt Claire thought it would help me make friends."

"Did it?"

"No."

Col had spent most of the last six months hiding in his bedroom. He'd always been a loner – and he didn't see the point in doing anything else, when blackout started so early and ended so late. Col had never known so much darkness.

He glanced at the crack of light under the door. He didn't have time for this – Rose was waiting for him.

"Can I help with anything, Mrs Evans? I still don't really understand why you're in our flowers."

Mrs Evans tutted. "If you must know, Col, I'm putting out salt for the little folk."

Col frowned. "Little folk?"

"Fairies! Pixies. Troopers. They're all over the countryside at the moment. The Midwinter King is in dominion, you see, and he's sent the fairies from the Spirit World to search for the Green Man. Good thing I had so much salt lying around!"

"Oh. Do they like salt?"

"No! Can't stand the stuff. Have to stop and count every grain, you see. That should keep the little runts out of my butter." She shivered. "Surely you've noticed the change in the weather, boy? That's *his* doing. He grows stronger every day."

Col had no idea what Mrs Evans was talking about – but she was right about the weather. Buxton was cold – iron cold, constant and brutal, coming up through the ground and clawing your ankles. No one had ever known a winter like it, and it was happening all over the country. By day, Britain was hammered by rain and blanketed in thick fog, stopping trains and stranding travellers. At night, the temperature plummeted: it cracked toilet bowls, froze sheep in their stalls, and cut off hundreds of houses with snowdrifts. The emergency services – already stretched to breaking point with the nightly raids – were forced to abandon the cities and cut paths through the snow to help cut-off villages.

That was the worst part of all. Despite the weather, the raids were still continuing. People were trying to stay cheerful and keep their spirits up, but things were becoming desperate. Rationing was getting worse, food supplies were running low, and the enemy was right on their doorstep. People said that they might stand a chance if America decided to join the war – but with each passing day, that seemed less and less likely. The end had never seemed so close before.

Col gazed at the sky. It looked like tonight was going to be worse than ever. The wind was beginning to pick up, and the sky was bare and black as sheet-ice, the moon a razor-sharp crescent that was almost too bright to look at. Raids were always bad on bright, cloudless nights like this, when enemy planes could make out the ground beneath them. People had started calling it Bomber's Moon...

Col snapped to attention. Mrs Evans was poking him with her stick again.

"Good grief! Are you deaf as well as stupid? I *said*, any plans for Christmas?"

Col's heart lifted at once. He'd been so distracted, he'd forgotten all about the plan.

"Yes!" he said. "My sister Rose is coming. She stayed behind in London to volunteer with the emergency services. It'll be the first time we've seen each other in six months!" Col glowed with pride. "She's a despatch rider – she bikes around during the raids, passing on messages for the fire service. Rose has always been brave like that."

Just for a moment, the cold and the dark disappeared – that always happened when he thought about Rose. Mrs Evans frowned.

"Really? And your aunt's OK with that, is she?"

Col grimaced. "She, er ... doesn't know we're doing it."

Col and Rose had been forced to keep their plan a secret for months – and with good reason. Rose and Aunt Claire did *not* get on, and everyone in Buxton knew it. His aunt badmouthed his sister every chance she got: *seventeen years old, and thinks she knows everything!* It was why Rose hadn't once been to visit – that, and the fact that trains were reserved for soldiers and war supplies, and tickets were so expensive, and then the terrible weather...

But tonight – finally – it had all come together. Rose was here, and there was nothing Aunt Claire could do about it. They were going to have the perfect Christmas together, just the way they'd always done it. The decorations, the presents, the food ... the cottage.

"We're staying in Darkwell End," said Col, his eyes shining. "It's where my dad grew up. It's the most magical place in the world! It's only half an hour away from here by train, but it's right in the countryside, with forests and fields and streams. We used to spend every Christmas there, before..."

Col stopped. He still didn't know how to finish that

sentence. The last of his words were left hanging in the air between them, like smoke from a snuffed candle.

"I should go," he muttered. "Rose will be waiting for me – her train got in an hour ago. Merry Christmas, Mrs Evans."

Mrs Evans nodded. "Merry Christmas, Col! Make sure the King's spies don't see you."

Col frowned. "What king?"

But Mrs Evans didn't answer – she just stayed where she was, fiddling with her salt and humming carols under her breath. Col considered getting her a blanket, then decided against it. He was late enough as it was. Rose would be explaining everything to Aunt Claire by now – she'd need his help.

He turned to the house, heart glowing. It was hard to imagine, after such a terrible year, that anything could ever be good again. The war had made everything so dismal. He and Rose had lost so, so much. But now, their struggles were all behind them. Just for a short while, the world didn't matter any more.

It was Christmas … and his family had come back to him.

He opened the door, and stepped into the light.

The Letter

THE LIGHT IN THE HALLWAY STUNG HIS EYES LIKE seawater. The darkness disappeared – the wind died. After being outside, the warmth of the house almost burned him. It felt like stepping from one world into another.

"Col! How many times? Close the door properly when you come in!"

He blinked. Aunt Claire was standing in the hallway, her arms folded. She looked tired and irritable, but then she always did. Col glanced around. There was no sign of Rose – she must be in the other room. He closed the door.

"Sorry I'm late," he said. "The Brigade meeting overran and—"

"That wind!" said Aunt Claire, cutting him off. "And you wearing shorts! Aren't you cold?"

"Yes," Col admitted.

"Well, mustn't complain, it's good for you." She thrust a shovel into his hand. "Now get back outside and bring in some coal! There's a storm heading this way tonight – the worst yet, they said. We'll need as much as we can!"

Col was thrown. There was no mention of Rose – no sign that she'd even arrived. No bags, no coat, nothing. Where was she? "But…"

"Stop arguing, Col, I'm not in the mood!" said Aunt Claire, shoving him back to the door. "I had to queue at the butchers for an hour, then work out how to make a Christmas pudding with vinegar instead of eggs, then I tripped over Mrs Evans in the garden…"

Col's mind raced. Why wasn't Rose here? What was going on? Her train was supposed to have arrived in Buxton at least an hour—

And then it hit him. The storm. Rose's train must be caught in it – it was stuck on the tracks, or rerouted to another station. She could be stranded in the middle of nowhere by herself, in the pitch dark and freezing cold.

"Wait!" Col cried. "Aunt Claire, listen…"

But Aunt Claire wasn't listening – she rarely did. She kept pushing him towards the door, cutting him off whenever he tried to speak. Col had to do something: Rose would be counting on him. He closed his eyes and steadied himself like someone preparing to lift a heavy weight.

"NO!"

Aunt Claire was shocked – Col never spoke back. He never even got the chance to. But now, he had to be brave. He turned to face his aunt, and swallowed.

"We need to go to the station. Rose is coming up from London. We're … we're spending Christmas together." He folded his arms. "That's right. We're going to Darkwell End, just like we used to. We knew you'd try to stop us, so we didn't tell you. We've had it planned for weeks. You can come too, if you'd like. Er… That's it."

He held the shovel up like a shield, steeling himself for the ear-clipping of a lifetime. But it didn't come. When he looked up, Aunt Claire wasn't angry, or even surprised. She looked … *sorry* for him. She let out a deep sigh.

"Oh, Col. Right. You'd better read it now."

She pulled a letter from her apron pocket and handed it over. Col frowned. He knew it was from Rose: you could tell by the beautiful patterns she drew on the envelopes.

"But…"

"Just read it."

Col didn't feel brave any more. He felt like something had shifted – like a curtain had been drawn back, revealing the true shape of the room. He opened the letter and read it in silence.

Dear Collie,

I'm so sorry to do this.

*By now, Aunt Claire will have told you the bad news.
I know you'll be angry. I know I promised we'd spend
Christmas together. I've wanted to tell you the truth for
some time, but you were so excited that I didn't know how
to be honest with you.*

*Things have been terrible in London – much worse than
I've said, and much worse than the newspapers have been
making out too. The bombings have been relentless and the
bad weather's made it so much worse. I'm helping at a nurses'
station during the day as well as doing all my despatch duties
at night. There are so many people here who desperately need
help, who've lost everything in the raids – their houses and
families, right before Christmas. Everyone has been so kind
since Dad's accident too. I can't leave them now.*

*I'm going to stay in London for Christmas, and you're
going to stay in Buxton. I know how much this will upset
you – I know how unhappy you've been living with Aunt
Claire, and it breaks my heart, but it means so much to
me to know that you're safe. I promise we'll see each other
soon. For now, we must both be brave, and do whatever
we can to help people – it's what Dad would have wanted.*

Don't worry, I'll send up your present!!
Rose

xxx

Col stared at the letter for some time. It felt like a sack of cold water had burst in his lungs. Aunt Claire stood and fussed at her apron, trying to keep her hands busy.

"I'm sorry, Col. She wrote to me the other day, asking for help," she said quietly. "The silly girl – raising your hopes like that, just before Christmas." She shook her head. "Honestly, Col, what were you both thinking? To come up here now, with everything that's going on? In weather like this!"

Col had told himself to be brave, that he wouldn't cry, but it was hopeless. Tears spilled down his face and onto his jacket.

"But... She promised. It's our first Christmas without him. Without Dad."

Aunt Claire winced, like something had stung her. It took her a while to answer. She reached out and placed a single hand on his shoulder. Col was almost shocked – it was the first time she had ever touched him.

"I know, Col. It's going to be a difficult Christmas for all of us." She swallowed. "We've all been finding life hard since ... the *incident*."

Incident. Col hated that word. Newspapers used it all the time. A bomb blast was an *incident*; a shelter collapsing on a family was an *incident*. What happened to Dad wasn't a disaster, or a tragedy – it was just an incident from six months ago, another entry in a list that grew longer every day. Aunt Claire quickly took the hand off his shoulder and used it to dry her eyes with her apron.

"I know it's tough, but there's a war on. Some people have lost their entire families, you know. Rose is right: your father would have wanted you here, where it's safe. You're just going to have to get used to it."

Something inside him suddenly boiled up. He held up the letter.

"No – I know what you're doing. This letter's a fake! You've always hated Rose, and now you're trying to keep us apart! You've got the *real* letter hidden somewhere…"

His voice trailed off. He knew it didn't make any sense – he just couldn't stand the truth. Aunt Claire rolled her eyes.

"Col, I'm sorry you're upset, but that is ridiculous. It's time you grew up and started living in the real world. This war is tough on everyone, not just you. You're twelve years old – you're not a little boy any more. You can't just shut yourself in your room and make up stories. You need to try to make the best of it. Like the rest of us."

Col clutched the shovel, burning with rage. "I never wanted to come here."

"Well, tough!" said Aunt Claire. "I never asked to be your guardian, did I? But do you hear me complaining?"

With that, Aunt Claire stormed out of the hallway and started slamming knives and forks onto the kitchen table. A belt of wind suddenly slammed the door open behind him and flooded the corridor with frozen air.

"What did I say? Close that door properly!"

Col spun round. The door was wide open, hammering against the wall. Outside was like another world, leading far away from all of this. A portal of deepest black stretched into nothingness ahead of him.

And there were the voices in his head again.

Come to the cottage, Col!

We need you, Col...

It's a matter of life and death!

"Col! Did you hear me? Close that door!"

Col dropped the shovel on the carpet. The wind wrapped around him, two frozen hands pulling him forwards.

"Col? *Col!*"

He stepped into the storm, and closed the door carefully behind him.

The Cottage

COL STOOD IN THE VALLEY, PANTING FOR BREATH. It had all been so easy. Nothing like the plan he'd made with Rose, of course – but the plan didn't matter any more.

Buxton had been so dark that he'd run straight to the station without being spotted. The trains were still running, thank goodness – there were porters on the platform with torches, but he'd managed to sneak past them in a crowd of drunk soldiers and onto a train. All the lights in the carriage had been turned off for blackout: hiding in a luggage rack and slipping off at the right station had been easy.

And just like that, there he was: Darkwell End.

Col shuddered, his knees knocking together painfully. It was even colder out here than in Buxton – but everything else was exactly as he remembered. The same fields, the same trees, the same stream. The same path leading to the same cottage.

An old stone cottage with a red door, framed by the remains of a rose bush.

Col's heart sang. The rest of the world might have changed, but Darkwell End was the same. It was like the cottage had been kept safe in a pocket: like the war had never happened.

Like Dad was still here.

Col knew it wasn't true. He knew that coming here was pointless. When Aunt Claire caught up with him, he'd be in so much trouble his life would barely be worth living. Things could never go back to the way they were.

But just for one night, he wanted to pretend.

Where are you, Col?

You have to come back to us!

Please don't shut us out, Master Col!

Col laughed bitterly. There they were again – his imaginary friends. His so-called Guardians. The ones he used to turn to whenever he was scared. So *that* was why he'd been hearing their voices over the last few days. Deep down, he knew the plan would fail, and it had terrified him.

When was he going to stop being frightened?

He'd always had a vivid imagination – *too* vivid, some might say – and he was too shy to make friends, so inventing his own came naturally to him. The Guardians had been his closest companions for as long as he could remember. First there was Pendlebury, a brave and noble tiger who could change size at will. In a snap, she could tower over the tallest trees or squeeze through the smallest mouse hole. Then there was Mr Noakes, a kind old badger with an amazing sense of smell – he could find buried treasure or track hidden enemies just by using his nose. Last came the King of Rogues, a gallant knight who was smaller than Col, but who was so courageous he could fight off a hundred dragons at once.

Col had lost count of the quests and adventures they had gone on together, defeating ogres and defending castles around Darkwell End or the backstreets of Herne Hill back home in London. But the Guardians were more than pretend friends. They had helped him overcome his fear of the dark. They had watched over him while he slept. Whenever he'd felt afraid, they'd been right beside him, giving him the strength to feel brave.

But that was a long time ago. Back when his biggest problems were bogies hiding under the bed. The world had changed completely now: there were actual terrors in his life, real-life ones, and Col had to face them himself.

What good were his Guardians now?

The wind roared; Col swung round. The storm was getting closer, he could *feel* it. The temperature was plummeting, the sky growing dull and heavy as stone. He didn't even have a coat: if he didn't get inside fast, he was going to freeze to death. He scrambled to the door and found the key hidden behind the loose brick, where it had always been, and let himself in.

He slammed the door and waited for his eyes to adjust to the dark. The cottage was silent: the only sounds he could hear were the pounding of his heart and the wind breathing down the chimney. When the room finally did emerge from the gloom, he saw at once that he was wrong. The cottage *had* changed. The cold had somehow got in the stones. The furniture was covered in old sheets and dust. It had been a long time since anyone had been in here. It was dead and dark and miserable.

It didn't feel *empty*, though. It felt like someone else was in here with him.

Like they had been waiting.

Col shuddered. He was scaring himself, as usual – he needed a fire, and fast. He fumbled his way to the fireplace while the wind rattled the windowpanes. He found a few pieces of coal inside the scuttle, and some old dry twigs for kindling, but nothing to get a fire started. No dry grass, no paper…

Col's heart clenched. He did have *some* paper.

He pulled Rose's letter from his pocket. He didn't need to reread it – he remembered every word.

What Dad would have wanted.

So she had lied to him. When he left London six months ago Rose had promised him – promised him – that they would be together again at Christmas. No matter how much he missed Dad, no matter how lonely he felt, no matter how much he hated Buxton, Christmas would be the same. Col had clung to that promise for months, like a shipwreck survivor to wreckage. And now, in a single letter, it was gone. After everything they had been through, Rose had decided that other people were more important than he was. She had abandoned him to help strangers.

How could she?

He screwed the paper into a ball and threw it into the fireplace. Then he took the lighting flint from his pocket – all Boys' Brigade members kept them to hand – and scraped the paper with sparks until it caught. He blew on the paper, arranging twigs on top to make a pyramid, until smoke plumed out and the pile *whoomphed* into flame. He watched the letter burn to ash, and then to nothing, and then he buried it in coal.

He and Rose had always been close – they'd had to be. Col's mother had left just after he was born and sent a letter six months later saying she'd moved to Australia and wasn't coming back. Dad had to work long hours at the store to make ends meet, so it was up to Col and Rose to run the household, cooking and cleaning and doing all the shopping together after school.

Christmas was the only proper time they spent together as a family: that's why they made the most of it. They would pile into the train at Euston, laden with presents and enough food to feed an army, and make the long journey to Darkwell End. When they arrived, Dad would head to the forest and find a tree and Col and Rose would cover the cottage with the same tattered decorations they used every year, shoving each other and giggling. The cottage didn't have electricity or hot water, so when it got dark Col would make a fire, and Rose would cover every surface with candles until it shone like a church.

"I think that's enough," Dad would say.

"Please," Rose would reply, rolling her eyes. "You can *never* have too many candles."

And that was all they needed. For twelve days, they would just … *be together*. They would listen to carols on an old wireless radio on Christmas Day, and "Children's Hour" in the evening – Dad's favourite. Rose would spend the days painting or sketching – she'd always been an amazing artist. Col would explore the valleys around Darkwell End while it was light and lie by the fire each evening, turning his day's adventures into stories for them.

"The Guardians and I went exploring in the forest! Mr Noakes found a secret tunnel under the trees, and the King of Rogues fought off the goblins guarding it. Then Pendlebury shrank down inside it and found a river, leading to an underground palace!"

And Dad would just listen.

Dad.

Col's eyes stung. He felt like he could see him now, drifting off to sleep in the armchair like he always did. His moustache, his thinning hair. His tired, gentle eyes. He'd be wearing one of the shirts that Rose made for him, stained orange or violet or – her favourite – a mixture of both. Rose did that with everything she touched. *Who wants boring old white?* she'd say, ruining yet another perfectly good tablecloth.

Other dads weren't like that. Other dads would have told Col to stop making up stories, or made Rose iron shirts instead of colour them. But that was Dad all over. He wasn't much of a talker. He couldn't spend as much time with his children as he wanted. Instead, he showed his love by making sure they had everything they needed to be happy. He worked his fingers to the bone, without complaining, so Col could run wild in his imagination and Rose could colour everything she touched with rainbows. Whenever Aunt Claire came to join them on Boxing Day she would tut disapprovingly and say that he was spoiling them, but it didn't matter. They were *happy*. Col couldn't believe how happy they'd been, now he thought back on it.

And then – the incident.

It had happened so fast that Col could barely follow it. One night – one split second. The ambulance, the funeral, the arguments between Rose and Aunt Claire... Suddenly Col was standing at Euston Station with his bags packed and his sister was hugging him, and he was powerless to do anything to stop it.

"You must be brave, Collie. It's only for a little while. I'll write every day. And we'll see each other at Christmas, won't we?"

He had watched his sister disappear out of the train window and understood for the first time that he was truly on his own. He had lost his mother, he had lost Dad, and now he had lost Rose. He was going to live on the other side of the country with a relative he barely knew. He still had his Guardians – but what good were they now? They hadn't protected him from what happened to Dad. They hadn't protected him from any of this. They had utterly, utterly failed him.

So just like that, he turned his back on them. He had sealed the door to his imagination, and shut out the only friends he'd ever known, and chosen loneliness.

But what did that matter after everything he had lost already?

Col gazed around the cottage. The fire was finally beginning to work its magic: bristling with the crackle and shift of firewood, the light was breathing life into the bricks once more. The wind raked at the walls, and flecks of snow were beginning to catch on the windowpanes: but it didn't matter. The cottage felt safe.

"Col, please!"

"Can't you hear us?"

"We're running out of time!"

Col sighed – there they were again, right on cue. His Guardians. Why couldn't they just leave him alone? Why couldn't they—?

"If you're there, my liege… Oh, stuff this! He's not listening."

Col paused. The voices sounded different. They didn't sound like they were inside his head any more.

They sounded like they were coming from inside the cottage.

Col peered over his shoulder – and froze. A thin trickle of light was coming down the stairs. It came from the wooden hatch that led to the attic.

"We have to face facts – he's not coming!"

"He's close now, I *swear* I can smell him…"

Col's stomach lurched. He'd been right: the cottage *wasn't* empty. There were people in the attic. He could hear three of them, arguing in the room above him. But who was going to be hiding out here in the middle of nowhere? Homeless people, sheltering from the storm? Black market thieves hiding stolen goods? *Nazi spies?*

But they didn't sound like any of them. In fact, they sounded just like…

Col shook his head. No, it couldn't be. It was his imagination again. The wind must be warping the sound of their voices – that was why the people hadn't heard him come in either.

He got to his feet and crept towards the front door, praying that the wind would cover the sound of his footsteps. He had no idea how he was going to get back to Buxton in the middle of blackout and with a storm already well on the way, but whatever happened—

"We're doomed! He's forgotten us! We might as well give up now!"

"If he don't stop his whining, Pendlebury, I'm gonna thump him."

Col stopped.

"What? How dare you!"

"One little bop on the head – please. Just to shut him up."

"Mr Noakes, you will do no such thing!"

"I can't help it if I'm naturally eloquent…"

"*Enough*, Rogue!"

"*KING – OF – ROGUES!*"

Col stood locked to the spot. There was no mistaking what he'd heard. The names were the same. The voices were identical. It couldn't be a coincidence.

It's not real, he told himself. *I'm dreaming.*

But he wasn't dreaming. The cold buzzed at his lips and fingertips. His heart jackhammered in his chest. His breath plumed out in frozen gusts. He was awake and alive and this was really happening.

But how?

Col turned to the attic hatch, shining in the darkness. The argument behind it was in full flow now.

"KING – OF – ROGUES! Can't you remember *anything* longer than one syllable?"

"That's it, I'm thumping him."

"Mr Noakes, no!"

Col walked to the staircase, and climbed the steps towards the attic.

"Let's see how brave he is without that armour on."

"Unhand me, oaf!"

"Mr Noakes, put him down!"

Col pressed his hands to the wooden hatch. The sounds behind it were growing louder and louder. He could hear feet scuffling on the floorboards, chairs being pushed back, vases toppling over.

"Moron!"

"Gasbag!"

38

"Reprobate!"

"STOP!"

Col pushed open the hatch and gazed into the light.

The attic was just as he remembered it. The smell of dust, the ancient furniture, the clutter of a hundred years. Nothing had changed.

Except for the knight and the badger, who were lying in the middle of the floor and strangling each other.

They both turned and saw Col at the same time.

"M-Master Col!" cried the badger.

The knight leaped up. "He's here! Pendlebury, he's—"

"Just in time," said a voice above them.

Col looked up. Resting along the rafters, her body filling the attic from end to end, was a Bengal tiger.

"Oh Col," said Pendlebury. "I knew you'd come back to us."

The Return
of the Guardians

COL STARED AT HIS IMAGINARY FRIENDS.
The Guardians were exactly as he'd always imagined them. Pendlebury was sleek and mysterious, a creature woven from stars and midnight. Mr Noakes was moth-eaten and burly, like an affable old man in a country pub. The King of Rogues was all bug-eyes and wonky limbs, more of a puppet than a person.

But now they weren't imaginary: they were *real*. They were talking and moving in front of him like real people. And their *colours*. Since the war began, the world had been all ration-book greys and blacks, weak tea and burnt toast. Winter had drained the life from everything. Yet the Guardians were so bright, so *vivid*, they seemed almost to shimmer in the air. Col was utterly speechless.

The King of Rogues suddenly threw himself to the floor in front of him, sounding like a stack of tin cans being chucked down a staircase.

"My liege! I never once doubted you would come!" He bowed his head over his sword. "We, your loyal Guardians, have returned to our place of making to fulfil our sacred duty and…"

Mr Noakes bustled him to one side.

"Oh, leave off! Poor lad can't understand a word you're saying." He stood in front of Col and beamed furrily. "What an honour to finally see you in the flesh, Master Col! You've become quite the gentleman. Look at you, all dressed up in your fine monkey suit!"

Pendlebury poured herself down from the rafters.

"Boys, please! Give Col some room. This must be a lot for him to take in – after all, he's never seen us like *this* before. Have you, Col?"

Col yelped. The tiger's tail had reached behind him and was tickling him on the cheek.

"What's going on?" he cried. "What's happening?"

The Guardians' smiles dropped.

"Is he … frightened?" said the King of Rogues.

"He doesn't *seem* very happy to see us," said Mr Noakes.

Col shook his head like a dog trying to dry itself. This was all too much. There was no way, no *way* that his imaginary friends were standing in front of him in his attic.

"This isn't happening – it's not real! I'll close my eyes, and when I open them you'll be gone!"

He closed his eyes, counted to five, and opened them again. His Guardians were still standing in front of him, looking even more confused than before.

"Aaaargh!" said Col.

"He *is* frightened," said Mr Noakes.

"Of course he's frightened!" snapped the King of Rogues. "You're standing two inches in front of his face, and *she's* the size of a dragon! For heaven's sake, Pendlebury, make yourself presentable."

The tiger raised an eyebrow. The knight gulped.

"Er… I mean, if you wouldn't mind," he added.

There was a short, sharp sound like the ripping of stitches, and then Pendlebury was the size of a regular tiger, without anyone knowing quite how she'd done it.

"Better?" she said.

"Maybe a *little* smaller," suggested the King of Rogues.

"No," said Pendlebury.

Col stared at the tiger in shock. He could see every strand of her fur shifting and swaying in the candlelight. There was no doubting it: she was as real as he was. She turned to face him, and spoke.

"Do not be frightened, Col. It is us, your Guardians – your lifelong friends and protectors. We have broken all the laws of our kind to come to your world, and bring you dire news. There is much that will shock you – much that you will struggle to believe. But you *must* believe, Col. If you do not … then all is lost."

She raised herself to her full majestic height, her eyes shining down like amethysts.

"Are you ready, Col? Are you ready to hear the most important news of your life, and discover *why* we have travelled from another world to find you?"

The Guardians waited expectantly for his reply. The attic was so quiet you could hear snowflakes settling on the roof.

"Not really, no," said Col.

There was a long silence. Pendlebury shifted on her paws.

"Sorry – did you just say *no*?" she asked.

Col sighed apologetically. "Look – I've had a lot of bad news today. I'm not sure I can take much more. Especially from – and I don't mean to be rude – my imaginary friends come to life." He held out his hands. "You can understand that, can't you? This is an awful lot to take in at once. I don't understand *how* you're here in front of me, let alone why. I feel a bit overwhelmed." He shuffled his feet. "Sorry."

The Guardians looked at each other.

"He never used to be so difficult," muttered Mr Noakes.

"I *told* you he'd be like this," said the King of Rogues.

Pendlebury was somewhat deflated. "Er… I suppose this *is* a lot to take in. But we have an awful lot to explain, Col, and we're sort of … running out of time." She gazed at him pleadingly. "Is there *anything* we could do that would help you listen?"

Col put the teapot on the table.

"There's no milk. Or sugar. Sorry."

The Guardians sat around the kitchen table while Col poured the tea. It was all very civilized. He'd taken the best cups from the cabinet and even put down a tablecloth.

"This is ridiculous!" snapped the King of Rogues. "Every second counts, and here we are having a *tea party*, like—"

"Shhh!" said Pendlebury. "We are Col's Guardians. Whatever he asks for, we will do."

Col blushed. "Sorry. I just thought doing something normal might help."

Old habits die hard. It had always been Col's job to make tea when Dad or Rose needed to sort out their problems. That was the rule in their house: no matter the crisis, big or small, you put on the kettle and chewed through it together.

Col sat down and took a sip of tea. It was almost a year old and stale as sawdust, but it helped instantly. He gave a weary sigh.

"Right. Let's start at the beginning." He leaned forward. "You're not imaginary – you're real. How?"

Pendlebury blinked. "What do you mean?"

"You're not inside my head any more, doing stuff I make up," said Col. "You're actually in front of me, doing things I don't expect like—"

Mr Noakes sprayed out a mouthful of tea like a fountain.

"*BLIMEY* that's hot! Owowowowow!" He scrabbled at his tongue with his paws. "Oof! Better leave that for a bit, everyone…"

He trailed off. The rest of the table stared at him, dripping with tea. He coughed into his paw. "Do carry on."

Pendlebury shook herself and turned back to Col.

"We've *always* been real, Col. You created us. You made us, with love and purpose. You gave us thoughts and feelings. And when you make something like that, you bring it to life."

"We just don't live in *this* world, that's all," said Mr Noakes, blowing on his tea.

Col was staggered. "Wait – I actually *made* you? You actually *live* somewhere?"

"The Spirit World!" said the King of Rogues. "Where all imagined creatures like us live. Monsters, giants, fairies… A million years of magic and history and fables, all in one place."

Col tried to get his head around this and failed. "I – I don't understand."

Pendlebury sighed and held up her teacup. The liquid swirled and glistened in the candlelight.

"Look at this tea. You can only see the surface – but there's more beneath it, *much* more. It is the same with your world. Another world lies right beneath it – a hair's breadth away, beyond where your eyes can see. A place where all imagined things must go – a place for everything that cannot live in your world. The Spirit World."

She placed the cup back down.

"There was a time when all kinds of imaginary creatures could cross the barriers between each world … but not any more. There is far less magic in your world than there once was: our kind cannot survive here for long. It is why we had to come to Darkwell End to wait for you. The three of us cannot survive in your world unless we're close to you. And this cottage is filled with memories of you. It's where you made us."

She ran her paw across the table, where Col had scratched his name into the surface with a fork years ago. Col looked at her in shock.

"Is that why I've been hearing your voices inside my head for the last few days?" he asked.

Pendlebury nodded. "The four of us share an unbreak-able bond, Col. You are the reason we exist. We might not have been beside you on your adventures, but whenever you thought of us, we heard it in the Spirit World. We've been calling you for days, to try to bring you back to Darkwell End." She swallowed. "You arrived just in time – a few more hours, and the power of the cottage alone would not have been enough to protect us any more."

Col blinked. "Protect you from what?"

The wind howled. The candle flickered. It was as if a shadow had passed over the table. When Pendlebury next spoke, her voice was much quieter.

"We are not supposed to be here, Col," she said. "We have put ourselves in terrible danger to break over the barrier and talk to you like this. But we had to warn you. Even if it meant defying … *him*."

Col looked at his Guardians. They were terrified.

"Who?" he asked. "Who are you talking about?"

Pendlebury looked at the Guardians – they nodded. She cleared her throat, and turned back to him.

"The Midwinter King," she said. "He is in dominion once again – but this time, everything has changed. He has driven the Green Man from the Spirit World and—"

"Hang on." Col stared at her in disbelief. Now he realized where he'd heard someone mention the Spirit World before. "The Midwinter King – the Green Man. Those were the things Mrs Evans was talking about."

Pendlebury nodded gravely. "They are two of the

most powerful beings in existence, Col. Our whole world hinges upon their actions – and so does yours."

She sat up straight, the candle casting her shadow on the wall behind her.

"The Midwinter King is the lord of all darkness – the prince of night. For half of each year, he rules over the Spirit World – and when he does, life dies. It brings winter into your world. Our two worlds are closely connected, Col – what happens in one affects the other."

She gazed at the flickering candle and smiled.

"Then, six months later, the Green Man rises back up and defeats him. He is the lord of life; the bringer of light. The balance is restored: it brings spring into your world. It is a cycle that has been repeated since time began."

"Until now," said Mr Noakes quietly.

Pendlebury turned to face Col.

"Your war has tipped the balance, Col. There has never been so much darkness in your world; so much threat and fear and danger. The Midwinter King *feeds* off darkness – it made him more powerful than ever before. This year, he didn't just imprison the Green Man until spring, as he has done every year since time began: he set out to destroy him utterly. To cut him from existence and claim the Spirit World for himself, once and for all." Pendlebury shuddered. "He did not succeed, thank goodness. The Green Man escaped into your world and is hiding here now, weak and wounded. The Midwinter King has filled the land with spies to seek him out and drag him back to the Spirit World. The fairies, the goblins, the trolls…"

"And not just his usual creatures, either," said Mr Noakes, bristling with disgust. "All kinds have now started switching sides to serve the Midwinter King. Even the enchanted trees have sworn allegiance to him!"

"Except the oaks, of course," said the King of Rogues. "And the giants are too busy fighting among themselves, as usual."

Pendlebury nodded. "The Midwinter King is using his newfound power to crush all resistance and frighten the rest of the Spirit World into switching allegiance to him. He has blocked all the barriers between the worlds so that no allies of the Green Man can break over to try to help him. With each passing day, the Green Man becomes weaker and the King grows stronger. Now he has even started seeing visions of the future, and he's using them to…"

She paused. Col wasn't listening to her any more. He was resting his head on the table.

He was *laughing*.

Pendlebury frowned. "Was that … funny? I don't think I said anything funny."

49

"I don't think you've *ever* said anything funny," said the King of Rogues.

Col sat up, wiping his eyes. "Let me make sure I heard you correctly. You're saying that everything Mrs Evans told me – about the Green Man and fairies – is real." He looked at the Guardians. "*Mrs Evans.* The one who thinks her beehive can intercept Nazi messages."

Pendlebury was dismayed. "Col, the fight against the Midwinter King is real! It is more important than you can possibly imagine! If the Green Man is cut from existence… "

"Sure," said Col sarcastically. "And I'm the only one who can stop him, I suppose? Me – a twelve-year-old boy. Just like one of my old adventures." He leaned back and shook his head. It was finally all clicking into place. "I understand now. None of you are really here – this is all in my head! The news from Rose hit me harder than I thought and I've totally cracked!"

Col sighed with relief. He was a little concerned that he'd cracked, but it made more sense than what Pendlebury was saying. After all – what on earth did the Green Man and the Midwinter King have to do with him?

He turned to Pendlebury … and was shocked by what he saw. Her eyes were closed. Her poise, her bravery – it was all gone. When she opened them again, he could see at once that this was the moment she'd been dreading since Col's return.

"It's no use," she said. "We have to show him."

The effect on the Guardians was electric. The King of Rogues leaped to his feet.

"*No!* We can't! We're not even supposed to be here! If anyone finds out what we're doing…"

"There's no other way," said Pendlebury, shaking her head. "Col has to see. He has to understand what's at stake."

Col's eyes widened. "See what? What are you talking about?"

Mr Noakes sighed. "She's right, Rogue. We haven't come this far to fail him now."

He held out his paws. Pendlebury took one. The King of Rogues slumped his shoulders in defeat, and took the other.

"Take it," he said, holding out a hand to Col. "You must complete the circle in order to see."

"But remember, lad," said Mr Noakes, holding out a paw. "We don't do this to hurt you."

There was something in the kindness of his voice that frightened Col more than anything else. A part of him didn't want to know what they were talking about – but he only had to take one look at the expression on Pendlebury's face to know how important this was. He took the warm leather paw of Mr Noakes in one hand, and the cold metal glove of the King of Rogues in the other, and the four of them joined as a circle around the table. The Guardians closed their eyes and bowed their heads. The room fell silent.

Nothing happened.

Col swallowed. "What are we waiting f—?"

The image ruptured in his brain all at once, surging like waterfall from rock.

He was flying through the night sky, gazing down over London. The entire city lay beneath him, a vast tapestry of rooftops and rivers and bridges and buildings, stretching out as far as the eye could see.

It was all on fire.

The Vision

*L*ONDON IS A RAGE OF FLAMES,
A silhouette beneath a moonless sky
Lit by green-white chandeliers that plummet down
To shatter on the rooftops
And spread a sea of fire
That feeds
And grows
Into something bigger,
Something worse,
Until
It'
s
…
Nothing.
A cloud of dust.
A heap of rubble where a city once stood.
And lining the silent streets like autumn leaves…

"No!"

Col wrenched himself out of the circle and back into the kitchen. The Guardians sat in front of him, wide-eyed. Outside, the wind had risen to a shriek, making the candle flame shudder and writhe on the table.

"Hear that?" the King of Rogues cried. "It's *him*! He must have discovered us! Oh, we shouldn't have shown him, we shouldn't have shown him!"

"We had to show him!" cried Pendlebury. "Col had to see! He *has* to believe us!"

Col's head spun. He didn't want to believe what he had seen – but the vision had been as clear as a film reel. London on fire – the whole city destroyed. There was no way anyone could have survived it. Pendlebury grabbed him and held him steady by the shoulders.

"Col, listen to me: the vision does not lie. There is going to be a terrible raid on London – the worst one yet. It will raze the city to the ground and fill this land with more fear and despair and pain than ever before. That will give the Midwinter King all the power he needs to find and destroy the Green Man. This is why he showed this vision to all the Spirit World: to prove that it was futile to stand against him."

Col couldn't believe it. Her words drew like ice water up his backbone.

"But … but what about Rose?" he whispered. "She's in London right now!"

Pendlebury nodded. "Yes, Col. And she is in terrible, terrible danger."

Col's mind reeled. Rose would be cycling outside during the raid, carrying messages when the bombs were falling. There was no way she would survive what he'd just seen. Suddenly all he could see was her body lying on the road, or trapped inside a burning building, or crushed beside her bicycle as fire rained down from the sky around her…

"H-how long do we have?" he said. "How long until it happens?"

Pendlebury turned to the kitchen window. It was almost completely covered by snow now … but you could still make out the crescent moon cutting through the clouds above them, a high white sickle in the stars. Her voice was eerily calm. "In the vision," she said, "the sky is moonless. That is how long we have. Until the next new moon."

Col's stomach dropped. "But that's…"

Pendlebury nodded. "Six days. Seven at the most."

Col looked at his Guardians in horror. "Then what are we doing here? We have to tell everyone what's going to happen! We have to stop it!"

He raced to the kitchen door, but Mr Noakes grabbed his arm.

"Master Col – don't you understand? If you tell people about the raid, the Midwinter King will find out and stop you! Our only hope is that he doesn't know we're here!"

Col stared at him in disbelief. "So that's it? You're just going to let it happen?"

The King of Rogues stepped towards him. "My liege – there is nothing we can do to stop the raid. We're sworn to protect *you*..."

"A little late, aren't you?"

The Guardians were silenced. Col laughed bitterly.

"I mean it. If you wanted to protect me, where were you when Dad died? Why didn't you come to life and warn me about *that*?" Col's eyes were stinging now, filling with tears he thought he'd finished crying out long ago. "Now Rose is going to die too ... and there's nothing you can do about it?" The words came boiling out of him. "No – I won't let her die! If you're not going to stop the raid, I'll do it myself!"

He tore his arm free and raced out of the kitchen, throwing open the front door...

"Col, wait!"

The wind came at him like a thing with teeth, cutting straight to his bones. He flung his arms over his face. The storm had arrived ... and it was more powerful than any he had ever seen before. The world had been bled white, filled with blinding sheets of snow that piled into drifts on every side. He couldn't even see the paths that led out of Darkwell End any more. The fields, the trees, the streams ... they were all completely covered. There was no way the trains would be running now – no way the phone lines would be working. It was like another world.

"Look – his power grows even stronger," said Pendlebury behind him, her voice filled with dread. "He has brought all this already, and it is not even midnight."

Col gazed around in horror. "The storm? This is all *him*?"

Mr Noakes nodded. "And it will only get worse, lad. Once the King cuts the Green Man from existence, it will be like this always. A winter that never ends. A darkness until the end of days."

The realization hit Col like a punch to the stomach. There was no way he could get to Rose in this. He was stranded in the middle of nowhere, and the weather was only going to get worse. Even if he did find someone and told them everything he had just heard ... why on earth should anyone believe him?

So that was it. Rose was going to die, and there was nothing he could do about it. In six days, he was going to lose the last true family he had. Col sank to his knees in the snow.

"N-no. I can't lose her too. I *can't* lose Rose..."

He felt a paw on his shoulder. He turned, and met the warm brown eyes of Mr Noakes.

"No, Master Col," he said gently. "You will *not* lose her. Not if we have anything to do with it."

The King of Rogues stepped beside him. "This is why we've come into your world, Col. After what happened to your father, we swore to each other that we would never let you face something like that alone, ever again. No matter the risk."

"That's right," said Pendlebury. "We can't stop the raid – we can't stop the Midwinter King. But we *can* save Rose. We're going to take you to London, and get her out of the city before the raid hits."

Col stared at his Guardians in disbelief. They weren't joking. He shook his head.

"But ... haven't you looked around you?" He turned back to the raging storm. "We're trapped! London's over a hundred and fifty miles away. The trains aren't running. There are no cars on the road any more. I have no idea how to get there! Even if the weather was normal, to walk a hundred and fifty miles in six days..."

There was a sound, like a ripping of stitches, and the world fell still. There was warmth where there had been cold, and calm where the storm had been. Col turned around and almost fell back in shock. Pendlebury had grown twenty feet tall, the last of the moonlight gleaming in a halo around her. She smiled down at him.

"Who said anything about walking?"

The King of Rogues clapped a hand on Col's shoulder. "Don't you understand, my liege? We're travelling by tiger! Twice the speed – twice the power! And you made Pendlebury the best navigator in two worlds – she'll find the way to London in no time!"

Col made to argue – and stopped. The King of Rogues was right: in their imaginary quests, Pendlebury had always known which way to go.

"But we can't ride around on a giant tiger," he protested. "People will see us!"

"Not *all* of them, Master Col," said Mr Noakes. "Some people see magic – some people don't. How do you think the Green Man has been able to hide in your world for so long? Someone could be standing right in front of the lord of light and life, and have no idea!" He tapped his snout. "Besides – you know me. I'll sniff out anyone who gets within a hundred feet of us!"

Col's skin began to tingle. Mr Noakes had always been able to smell when trouble was close – it was his special power. "But – but what if the Midwinter King's spies see us? You said they're all over the countryside. And you're not meant to be here!"

"Ha!" said the King of Rogues, brandishing his sword. "I'll make mincemeat of anyone who tries to stop us!"

Pendlebury nodded. "This is what you made us for, Col. To carry you. To protect you. To fight for you. And without you beside us, we can't step a foot out of this cottage. If you want to save Rose, we have to do it together."

"That's right!" said the King of Rogues. "The old Guardians, together again, on our greatest adventure yet! What do you say, my liege?"

Col's heart started to pound. It was like a candle of hope had been lit inside him. For a moment – just a moment – the impossible felt possible. Maybe they could do it. Maybe they *could* make it to the other side of the country, through the worst storms of the century, and save Rose from a clash between two wars and a god of darkness…

And just as quickly as it was lit, the candle was snuffed out. He was just one boy and his imaginary friends. He turned back to the storm. The darkness was vast, insurmountable, unstoppable. What chance did they have?

"We can't. It's impossible. How can we possibly win against so much…?"

He trailed off. Pendlebury had picked him up in her

jaws and placed him on her back. The warmth of her fur was incredible: the coldness in his legs melted instantly. Until that moment, Col hadn't realized how cold he had been.

"Col," she said, "I think it's time you started using your imagination."

Col gazed out over her shoulders. And right away, he saw the truth: that from up here, the world was different. The storm was vast, but it had edges: the darkness ended somewhere. Col had spent months gazing out at that darkness in his bedroom in Buxton, listening to the sound of bombers droning over the rooftops. He had never in his life felt more small, more weak, more powerless.

He was still frightened now – terrified, in fact. But for the first time in a very long time, he could finally do something about it. He couldn't stop the war – he could never bring Dad back. But he could fight for the thing he loved. He could save Rose.

"Let's do it," he said. "Let's go home."

The Guardians cheered. The King of Rogues performed an elegant backflip, landed behind Col, and raised his lance.

"Onwards – to adventure!"

"To London!" said Mr Noakes, clambering up beside him.

"To *Herne Hill*," Pendlebury corrected.

"To Rose," said Col.

They leaped across the drifts of the valley, out of Darkwell End, to the point where the moonlight shone through a crack in the clouds.

The Burnt Throne

T HE FOREST WAS DEAD FOR MILES IN EVERY direction.

The trees were dead; the ground they stood on was dead. Nothing had grown here for as long as anyone could remember. There were some who believed that a terrible crime had been committed here centuries ago, and cursed the land. *That* was the reason, they said, why nothing grew here.

Others said it was worse than that. They said that a monster lived in this forest. *That* was the reason, they said, for the fear you felt in the pit of your stomach when you walked among the dead trees. Others said this was nonsense. They were just stories made up to frighten people, and people believed them so much that they felt true. *That* was the reason for the sickness you felt in your heart when you even so much as thought of the forest.

They were all wrong.

If they could somehow look *through* the forest – to the world that lay beneath it, just a hair's breadth away – they would understand.

They would watch the trees shift and disappear, to be replaced by a black blasted clifftop, rising hundreds of feet above a world of darkness. They would see the throne, vast and desolate, bursting from the stone and spreading into the sky like an abomination. They would see the man sitting inside it.

It was wrong to call him a man. There was only where he was, and where he was not.

The Midwinter King opened his eyes.

They were not really eyes. They saw much, much more than simply what lay ahead of them. They could see inside thoughts, over walls, under stones. From his throne, the Midwinter King could search the minds of every single one of his subjects – even the ones he had sent into the world beyond to search for the Green Man.

The Midwinter King had never known power like it. He had more control over the Spirit World than ever before. In the world beyond, he was bringing the worst storms he had ever created. His powers were growing stronger with every passing moment, and nothing seemed to be stopping them…

Until now.

The Midwinter King felt it like one feels a draught

beneath a door. Something had altered in the world beyond. The change was small – almost insignificant – but he had felt it. The slightest shift in his fortunes. The Midwinter King paused for a moment, gazing at the dark world below him. His mind calmly worked.

Barghest, he said.

At his command, a dog appeared in the shadows beside his throne. Her body was covered in scars, many of them new. She had been fighting a lot these last few days.

"Your Majesty," said his general. She did not need to bow: her curling spine already pushed her head close to the ground, like a snake.

The Midwinter King did not turn to face her. *Did you block the barrier out of the Spirit World, like I asked?*

It was not a normal voice. It was swept into your head and stayed there, cold as cave water. Barghest had grown used to it, in a way.

"Yes, my lord. No spirits will be able to break over the barrier and enter the world beyond to aid the Green Man."

Really? said the Midwinter King.

Silence fell like black stone. Barghest nodded, with the unhappiness of someone who realizes that they have already wandered into a trap. The Midwinter King continued to gaze ahead.

I have just felt a change in the world beyond. Someone is trying to interfere with my plan. To alter what will pass in the vision.

Barghest was shocked. "The Green Man?"

The Midwinter King shook his head. *This is not the work of a god. It is smaller than that. I just counted how many are in the Spirit World ... and there are three missing since my last count.*

Barghest looked horrified. "But that's not possible, my lord…"

She stopped. She had felt something inside her. An ice-cold hand, closing around her guts. The Midwinter King turned to face her – and she finally saw his eyes. It was wrong to call them eyes. They were like two dying stars, coming from somewhere far beyond him.

You told me that no more creatures would escape. You told me you had closed the barriers. You told me all my enemies were imprisoned. And yet three spirits have defied my orders and broken into the world beyond, and now I cannot even find them. What do you have to say to that?

Barghest swallowed. She knew there was no point trying to lie to her king: he always knew when you were lying and when you were not. It was why none of his other generals had lasted long. She tried to ignore the frozen grip, tightening like a noose inside her.

"It … it took some time to block the barrier, my

lord. There is a chance that some spirits who are still loyal to the Green Man could have broken through before we were finished, but there is no chance they could possibly—"

Are you lying to me, Barghest?

She gasped. The grip in her guts was moving: she could feel icy cold tendrils sliding into her brain, prising between her thoughts, searching her mind for lies. Barghest let it happen. Fighting only made it worse.

You tell the truth, said the King after a while. *You are still loyal to me, at least.*

The tendrils let go, and Barghest sagged with relief. The Midwinter King sat back on his throne, the worst of his temper calmed.

Double the guards along the barrier. Make sure no other spirits break over. I will send word to my spies in the world beyond and tell them to keep their eyes peeled for three spirits. They will lead us to the Green Man.

She bowed down. "V-very good, my lord."

And Barghest?

She met his gaze, and cowered. It was like an iron stake, pinning her to the stone.

Never fail me like that again.

She bowed quickly, and twisted away through the shadows.

The Midwinter King turned back to the Spirit World. There was not a single part of it he did not now control. Darkness filled every corner of it. And yet there were still spirits who were prepared to defy him. And the worst part was that whenever he tried to search for their minds … he could not find them. They were hidden from his view, just like the Green Man.

But it did not matter. His spies would quickly locate the three miserable creatures and bring them back kicking and screaming to the Spirit World. The Midwinter King would make them reveal where the Green Man was hiding, and then he would finally cut the god of life from existence. And even if his spies did not find them, the raid in the vision would come soon: it would make him more powerful than ever before.

That was the beauty of his plan. It was the very dead of midwinter: it was his time. The world beyond had never been so dark, so pitiful – and it was getting darker every day. No matter what happened, his powers would grow and grow and grow. No one could stop him now.

The Midwinter King sat in his throne, and waited.

23 December 1940

INFORMATION FOR THE HOUSEHOLDER TAKING ON UNACCOMPANIED CHILDREN

When you receive unaccompanied children into your home, you will be expected to control and care for them as if they were your own.

You will receive 10s. 6d. a week for one child or 8s. 6d. a week for each child if you are taking more than one. This will cover full board and lodging, but not clothing or medical expenses.

If you can spare the time to do so, you are strongly recommended to attend any Home Nursing or Child Welfare Lectures that may be available.

Do not forget that the children will be in strange surroundings and may be homesick. You should therefore watch them carefully.

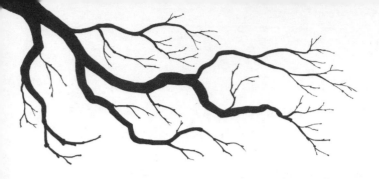

The Enchanted Forest

DAWN HAD ARRIVED, AND THE WORST OF THE storm had finally passed. Sunrise was gracing the horizon, turning the snowdrifts into sparkling mounds of crushed glass. Col gazed around the forest: it was absolutely beautiful. The air was filled with sparse winter birdsong, and the trees were gradually waking up around them, stretching their limbs. He wondered, once again, if he was dreaming.

A handful of wet snow fell down the back of his neck, and helpfully reminded him that he *wasn't* dreaming. He really had spent the night racing through the storm on the back of a giant tiger. He really was in a race against time to save his sister from a raid that was going to destroy London with his old imaginary friends. Col had spent the whole night breathless with fear, wondering at every turn if they were going to be spotted by spies of the Midwinter King, his mind filled with thoughts of Rose…

And yet he could barely stop his heart from pounding. He had never been so excited in his life. It was his greatest fantasy come true. He was on a real-life quest with his Guardians, and it was just like he'd always imagined it would be.

Sort of.

"Take that! And that!"

"SHUT. UP!"

Col sighed. The Guardians had been arguing for the last hour. Despite riding all night through gruelling weather, they weren't in the slightest bit tired. The King of Rogues was somersaulting through the snow beneath them, jabbing his lance into the trees, and Pendlebury was shouting at him to stop.

"STOP IT!" she bellowed for the hundredth time. "You're going to blow our cover! There could be any number of the King's spies in this forest!"

"Exactly!" said the King of Rogues, twirling his lance. "And I want to be ready for them when they show up. I'm the one who's going to fight them, aren't I? Unless you want to try *boring* them to death or—"

He was pinned to the snow by a giant paw in less than a second.

"I must have misheard you," said Pendlebury, leaning over him with a bland smile. "Please, do repeat what you said about me being boring."

"Oh, for heaven's sake, it was a joke! A *joke*!" said the King of Rogues, struggling feebly. "Just because you wouldn't know a joke if it slapped you in the face!"

Pendlebury frowned. "Yes I would."

"Ha! Tell ONE joke."

Col groaned. Being with the Guardians in real-life was different to how he imagined it would be. It turned out they liked arguing – a lot. It was the last thing he needed. His nerves were at fever pitch after a sleepless night worrying about Rose. "Maybe we should…"

"Quiet!" cried Mr Noakes. "Master Col wants to talk!"

The fight stopped at once. The Guardians stared at him eagerly.

"Yes, my liege?"

"Shush, let the master speak!"

Col grit his teeth. He'd always thought having friends that followed his every command would be a dream come true – it turned out it was actually quite annoying.

"Maybe we should … stop for a while," he said evenly. "I think we could all do with a break."

Pendlebury glanced at Mr Noakes. "Is it safe?"

Mr Noakes sniffed the air. "Hmph – can't smell nothing but trees. *Something's* not right, though."

The hairs on Col's arms stood up. He'd noticed it too: the sense that something was watching them. It didn't

72

help that this forest was so different to the ones around Darkwell End. They must have travelled at least ten miles by now: the trees here were twisted and decrepit, their trunks creaking like masts in the wind.

Mr Noakes sniffed the air again, whiskers twitching … and then shrugged. "Nope! No spies that I can spot. No fairies, no grindylows, no bogies…"

Col's blood turned cold.

"B-bogies? Those monsters that hide under your bed? They're real?"

"Yep!" said the King of Rogues. "And they're with the Midwinter King now." He shuddered. "Trust me – we do *not* want to bump into one of those."

Col turned pale. The news that they might bump into a monster from his childhood nightmares was doing nothing for his nerves. "On second thoughts, maybe we should keep going – we've got a lot of ground to cover today…"

"Ahem."

Mr Noakes was blushing as much as a badger could blush.

"I might need to … stop for a bit."

Pendlebury groaned. "Again?"

"I *told* you not to drink all that tea," said the King of Rogues.

Rrrrrrip

The sensation was bizarre. One moment, Col was sitting high on Pendlebury's back and gazing out through the trees: the next he was knee-deep in snow. He had no idea how it had happened, except that his stomach was doing backflips and Pendlebury was now the size of a normal tiger. Mr Noakes leaped off her back and scampered behind the nearest trunk.

"Don't go too far!" called Pendlebury. "Remember, we have to stick near Col at all times if we want to stay hidden from the King!"

Col shivered. His Guardians might be needy and argumentative, but he was grateful they had to stay close. "Can the Midwinter King really not see you if you're near me?"

Pendlebury nodded. "He's connected to all his subjects – just like we're connected to you. But being near you hides us from him. It's like we're protected in a pocket of love."

She gazed at Col affectionately. He turned away, embarrassed. He didn't feel capable of protecting anything at the moment, especially not from a god of darkness. Besides, all this clinginess was starting to get a bit much. Pendlebury saw him ignore her and huffed, clearly a little put out.

"Light helps hide us too. We'll be safe in daytime, but at night we'll need to make sure we have a fire nearby.

The Midwinter King's powers are always strongest at midnight – after all, he's the god of darkness." She cleared her throat. "In fact, you could say that instead of a *deity*, he's a … *night-ity*."

A cavernous silence filled the forest. Col gazed blankly at Pendlebury. She looked extremely pleased with herself.

"See?" she said. "I told you I could make jokes."

"*That* was a joke?" said the King of Rogues.

Pendlebury frowned. "Of course it was! A 'deity' is a god, so I took the 'day' part…"

"Please don't explain it," begged the King of Rogues. "You're just making it worse."

"And 'night' is the opposite of day…"

"Stop, it burns," the King of Rogues cried, writhing on the ground.

Mr Noakes finally reappeared from behind the tree. Col turned to him gratefully, keen to get going before another argument started … and frowned. There was something hovering in the air behind the badger, just over his shoulder. It looked like two spider webs, floating in mid-air beside each other.

"What are those?" said Col, pointing.

Mr Noakes looked at the spider webs – and the spider webs looked back. They blinked.

They weren't spider webs, they were eyes.

Mr Noakes spun round. "The trees! Quick!"

Before he could run, a branch whipped down out of nowhere and bound him to a tree trunk – another pinned the King of Rogues to the ground. Five more grabbed Pendlebury and fastened around her legs and neck, holding her in mid-air and tightening their grip whenever she tried to change size. Col had just enough time to gurgle with surprise before something grabbed his ankle and lifted him twenty feet into the air.

He dangled upside down above the forest floor, arms flailing, and searched left and right for their attackers … but there was no one. The clearing beneath him was empty.

"Good work, lads! Four in one fell swoop!"

The voice was low and creaky, like a house shifting in the wind – and it came from behind him. Col turned his head and gasped. The tree holding him was *alive*. It had spider webs strung between its branches for eyes and a knothole for a mouth that moved when it talked.

"Nice one, Keith!"

"Good timing too, that *night-ity* joke was just awful."

"Did everyone see? That badger just peed on me!"

Col was speechless. *All* the trees in the clearing were alive. They had beards made from ivy and tattoos where people had carved love hearts into their trunks. They looked like a gang of shabby wooden pirates.

"It's an enchanted forest!" Mr Noakes groaned. "Oh, I should have known…"

"Ha! But you didn't, did you?" said the tree called Keith. "*No one* suspects the trees! We waited for just the right moment, and then – bam! We got you!"

"We heard you coming from miles away," said another tree. "You lot are *really* loud."

Keith dangled Col from his branch like a prize fish. "And now you're our prisoners! Looks like we've got ourselves a tiger, a badger, a knight and a … er … performing monkey of some kind."

Col groaned. They didn't have time for this – every minute wasted was a minute closer to the moment he lost Rose. They couldn't let anything slow them down. "Sorry, could you put me down, please? I'm a human, not a monkey…"

"Sure you are," said Keith, unconvinced. "The Midwinter King told us to keep our eyes peeled for any rebel spirits wandering this world. He *said* there'd be three of you – imagine how delighted he'll be with us when we bring him back four!"

Col's stomach dropped. "The – the Midwinter King?"

"That's right!" said Keith. "He's told all his spies about you – and now you're going to lead us to the Green Man!"

Col turned to his Guardians in despair. The look on their faces said it all. They had already been caught by

77

the King – their quest was over before it had even started. He couldn't let this happen – he couldn't let Rose die. He had to make the trees understand.

"Please – let us go! We don't want anything to do with the battle in the Spirit World. We don't care about the Green Man!"

But Keith just ignored him. "This is it, lads – we've hit the big time! From here on out, us enchanted trees will be the pride of the Midwinter King's army!"

The King of Rogues heaved with rage against the branches holding him. "You should be ashamed of yourselves! Turning against the Green Man now, when he needs you more than ever! You – you treacherous stumps!"

A leaf slapped around the knight's mouth, muffling him.

"Don't say that word!" cried Keith.

Col frowned. "What? Stumps?"

The trees lurched as if hit by a belt of wind, their leaves fluttering to the ground.

"Stop it!" Keith shrieked. "Don't you know what that word *means*? Barry's best friend is a stump now!"

"The things these humans do to trees," sobbed the tree called Barry. "I've seen five more cut down today already! Oh, the humanity!"

The trees wept thick, sappy tears. Col was surprised:

the trees might *look* tough, but they were surprisingly sensitive. They might be fighting for the Midwinter King, but the mere thought of a tree being cut down was enough to shake them to the roots.

An idea suddenly formed in his mind.

"Sorry!" he said. "We won't mention anything unpleasant again. Like … lumberjacks."

The trees screamed.

"Aaargh!"

"Where?!"

"There's not one here *now*, is there?"

Col smiled. "Or … woodpeckers?"

"Eeek!"

"Oh, those horrid little beaks…"

It was working. The trees were cringing so much that their grip on the Guardians was slipping. Pendlebury caught his eye – she'd worked out what he was doing.

"What about … bonfires?" she added.

"Noooo!"

"Treehouses?" said Mr Noakes, catching on.

"Stop!"

"Dutch Elm Disease?" the King of Rogues mumbled behind the leaf.

"STOP IT!" cried Keith. "STOP, STOP, STOP!"

The moment had come – the trees were so distracted,

they weren't even paying proper attention. Col nodded at Pendlebury, and she shrank to the size of a mouse and shot out of their grip. The trees shrieked with surprise and tried to grab her, but only succeeded in tangling up their branches. The King of Rogues wrenched himself free and drew his sword in one graceful movement, effortlessly slicing through the branches that were holding down Mr Noakes.

"Ah ha! Have at you! Take that, and that!"

Col gasped. The King of Rogues was an even better fighter than he'd imagined. He watched in awe as the knight kicked one branch away, slashed over his shoulder to cut another, dodged a third with an elegant backflip ... but no matter how good he was, he was still hopelessly outnumbered. Cutting off the trees' branches seemed to make no difference to them – for every branch that the knight hacked off, five more seemed to take their place. How on earth was he going to defeat a dozen enemies that were ten times his size?

Before Col could worry about it too much, Keith lunged for the King of Rogues and let go of Col's ankle. He suddenly found himself hurtling headfirst towards the ground.

"Pendlebury, help!"

Rrrrrrip

She grew back to her regular size and threw herself

beneath Col right at the last second – he landed on her back like she was a great furry mattress. She swept up Mr Noakes and the King of Rogues and shot across the forest floor, weaving between the trees like liquid silk and leaving the clearing far behind them. Mr Noakes shook his paw at the circle of trees.

"Ha! So long, sap-bags! Sorry you can't join us!"

The enchanted trees tore themselves out of the ground and scuttled after them on their roots like spiders.

"Oh, yeah – I forgot they could do that," Mr Noakes muttered.

Col gasped in terror. The enchanted trees were chasing after them, and they were fast – *very* fast. Their branches crashed against the canopies, sending out great explosions of snow, but they showed no signs of slowing. Pendlebury couldn't possibly outrun them. "They're catching up!"

"Don't worry, I've got a plan!" cried Pendlebury. "Hold on tight…"

Col had just enough time to grab the tiger's fur before she twisted to the left and flung herself over the edge of a sheer drop, soaring over a little stream in the forest floor below and landing gracefully on the other side. Then she simply sat down and faced the oncoming trees, without any apparent concern.

"What are you doing?" Col gasped. "They're right behind us!"

Sure enough, the trees were tearing towards the ledge above them.

"Keep going, trees!" Keith shouted. "Victory is ours! Nothingwillstoptheriseofthe—*OHGODIT'SASTREAM!*"

He tried to stop himself, but his twisted root legs weren't strong enough to hold his weight and he fell, screaming, over the edge. He landed on the snow in front of the Guardians – and all life left him instantly, with an audible *pop*. His face froze, his branch arms hardened into place, and he fell silent. In less than a second, he was just another fallen tree in the forest.

Col was bewildered. "What just happened?"

Pendlebury nodded at the tiny stream weaving its way through the snow in front of them.

"Enchanted beings can't cross running water," she explained. "It washes the magic off them."

Col was confused. "Then how come you three can cross it?"

The Guardians gave him a withering look. They almost seemed embarrassed for him.

"We're not *enchanted*, lad," said Mr Noakes. "We told you – we're *imaginary*."

"You've got a lot to learn," muttered the King of Rogues.

Meanwhile, the enchanted trees stood at the edge of the drop above them, unable to take another step further. They shook their branches with fury.

"You – you monsters!" cried Barry. "You won't get away with this! We'll make you pay for what you did to Keith!"

Col gazed at the dead tree on the ground before him, and the realization suddenly hit. This wasn't imaginary any more: this was really happening. Because of him, Keith wasn't coming back. From now on, every decision that he made had consequences. He couldn't just stop playing along when he'd had enough. The thought made him feel sick to the stomach. In a single instance, the path to Rose had become longer, harder, more dangerous.

"Do they really mean that?" said Col. "Are they going to keep coming after us?"

Mr Noakes snorted derisively. "Ha! Don't listen to them, Master Col, it's classic tree talk. All mouth and no trousers!"

"Yes," said Pendlebury. "You could say their *bark* is worse than their *bite*."

No one said anything.

"Bark – trees have bark," said Pendlebury.

"You thought NOW was the time for a joke," said the King of Rogues.

Pendlebury blushed. "I thought it would lighten the mood."

"Wait – that was a joke?" said Mr Noakes. "I don't

get it. I thought jokes were supposed to be funny."

Pendlebury threw up her paws in exasperation. "It *was* funny! And clever! Wasn't it, Col?"

Col opened and closed his mouth several times, trying to work out the nicest thing to say. "It was a very, very good joke, Pendlebury. Perhaps if you worked on it for a bit longer…"

"You're lucky I'm sworn to protect you," she muttered, racing out of the forest before he could say anything else.

The Unexpected Guest

THEY RODE SOUTH FOR THE REST OF THE DAY. The snowfall made progress slow, and soon the rain and fog that had plagued the countryside for weeks began once more and made progress even slower. It was made worse by the fact that every sign they found had been painted white to confuse the enemy. Most of the time they had to trudge through empty fields, following the telephone lines that hung covered in an inch of snow.

But Pendlebury was an amazing navigator, just as Col had always imagined. He would have been lost a hundred times over in the distance she covered, charging over snowdrifts and riding the hills like waves. She seemed to know by instinct when to avoid towns and villages, when to wait for showers to pass, and when to use the cover of fog to press on. Col was grateful to have her on his team, even if her jokes were terrible.

Finally, as sunlight was beginning to fade, they came to a lone farmhouse at the edge of a forest, with lights at the windows and smoke winding out of the chimney. Beside it stood an old wooden barn stacked high with hay bales.

"That's far enough for today," gasped Pendlebury, her breath clouding out like a steam train. "Let's rest here for tonight."

Mr Noakes sniffed the air. "Hmmm – I can smell humans. Maybe we should keep going…"

"Humans are the least of our worries," Pendlebury snapped. "We need to hide before nightfall. Besides, I've done twenty miles today. I'm – I'm not going any further."

Col's stomach churned with worry. Twenty miles wasn't enough. If they wanted to get to London in time, they had to go nearly twice that distance every day. Part of him wanted to insist they press on too, to forget about sleeping and get to Rose as soon as possible… But there was a note of worry in Pendlebury's voice that he hadn't heard before. She was tired, and she was trying to hide it from everyone. Col quickly stepped in before Mr Noakes and the King of Rogues could start protesting.

"Pendlebury's right – it's going to get dark soon, and the storm will be back. We need to make sure we're protected. Besides, no humans are going to come in the barn until morning, and we'll be long gone by then."

Mr Noakes saluted. "Excellent plan, Master Col!"

"Genius, my liege!"

Pendlebury give him a grateful look. Col smiled – at least he was doing the right thing by her, even if it did slow them down. His stomach groaned.

"We should eat too. If we don't keep our strength up, none of us will make it halfway to London." He didn't want to think about what that would mean for their quest. "Mr Noakes – have a look around the farm and see what you can find."

The King of Rogues practically exploded. "*Him?* Why him? I should get the food!"

Col blinked. "But Mr Noakes can sniff it out faster than any of us…"

"So?" said the King of Rogues. "I can do *cartwheels*!"

Col sighed. The King of Rogues might have the heart of a warrior, but he also had the temper of a toddler. He wished he'd imagined someone less difficult.

"We need to be … subtle," said Col, choosing his words carefully. "You said some people can see magic, right? If someone *does* see Mr Noakes, they might think he's just an ordinary badger." He turned away before the King of Rogues could argue. "Remember, Mr Noakes, don't go too far. If anyone *does* see you…"

"Yes, Master Col!" He drew his club. "I'll give them a quick bop on the head and come right back!"

Col pushed the club back down. "NO! No bopping! We're being subtle, remember? Subtle."

Mr Noakes tapped his snout. "Ah, *subtle*! Of course, Master Col! I'll be as subtle as subtle can be!"

He scampered off, snuffling with excitement. Col slumped with exhaustion. He was used to spending time in his own company: after almost twenty-four hours with his Guardians, he was beginning to lose patience. He supposed this was what having children was like.

He led the others into the barn, the King of Rogues grumbling and kicking over tools in a sulk along the way. It was dim and draughty inside, but at least it was dry. It was warmer than outside too: Col's bare legs had started to turn the colour of rhubarb. He found a hidden spot at the back and spread some hay over the floor.

"Here! We'll sleep on this for tonight."

Pendlebury needed no encouragement – she collapsed onto the floor, panting for breath. Col looked at her with concern. She looked utterly exhausted – and she was the one who was supposed to carry them all the way to London. What would happen if she couldn't make it? Was *that* why she was trying to hide that she was tired from the others?

"King of Rogues," he said, "can you do me a fav…" He stopped – that was *never* going to work. He lowered his voice to a stage whisper and span round with jazz hands. "How would you like to go on a *quest*?"

The King of Rogues gasped. "A quest, my liege?"

"Yes!" said Col breathlessly. "A daring, perilous quest to … get more hay! From over there!"

The King of Rogues saluted. "To the death, my liege! I shan't fail you!"

He bounded away, jabbing his lance into bales and shouting "Ah ha!" every now and then. Col nodded with satisfaction – he was still way out of his depth, but at least he was getting good at handling his Guardians. He was finally alone with Pendlebury too. He crouched beside her, stroking her chest.

"Pendlebury – is everything all right?"

Her eyes snapped open at once. "What? I'm fine! Absolutely fine!"

Col winced – he was clearly on a sensitive subject. He tried to remember what worked whenever Rose or Dad needed to talk about their problems.

"Would you like a sweet?" he offered.

Pendlebury's eyes lit up. "You have sweets?"

Col reached into his pocket and held one out.

Pendlebury frowned. "That looks like a twig."

"It's liquorice root. It's the only sweet that hasn't been rationed."

She ate it.

"It tastes like a twig too."

"I think that's why they haven't been rationed." He stroked her chest again, feeling her heartbeat hammer like a kettle drum. "Pendlebury, you need to tell us if you're too tired. I don't want you to hurt yourself."

Pendlebury's face flickered with shame.

"I'm fine, Col, really. I'm just … a little drained, that's all. I had to push myself to put some distance between us and those enchanted trees. They're going to tell the Midwinter King about us – that means there'll be lots more spies looking for us soon." She sighed. "So much for keeping a low profile."

Col glanced nervously out of the barn windows. It had become pitch-black in a matter of minutes, and the wind was already picking up. It wouldn't be long before the storm returned. The crescent moon in the clouds was thinner than it had been the night before. Soon it would be gone completely, and then the raid would raze London to the ground. They only had five days left to get there, and more than a hundred and thirty miles to go. So much was stacked against them already – how on earth were they going to deal with an army of spies as well?

There was another worry too, front and centre in his mind. It had been there all day, and easy to ignore when they were travelling, but now they had stopped there was no avoiding it.

"Pendlebury – what's going to happen when we get to London?"

She glanced at him. "What do you mean?"

"How are we going to find Rose and get her out of the city? Tell her that we've seen a vision of a raid and that she has to come with us?"

Pendlebury frowned. "Col, you don't need to worry about any of that. We'll make sure no one sees us. Mr Noakes will be able to sniff her out wherever she is, and the King of Rogues can fight off any…"

Col shook his head. "I don't mean that. I mean, how am I going to convince her to come with me? She might just think I'm making up some stupid story. She might not be able to see any of you – she might not understand." Now more worries reared up, riding in the wake of the first. "W-what if the raid starts before we can get her out? What if we're trapped in the city when it's burning to the ground? That fire – I've never seen anything like it."

Pendlebury reached out and placed a paw on his shoulder.

"Col – I don't know what's going to happen. I haven't thought that far ahead. But whatever happens, you won't face it alone. We're going to work it all out together, just the four of us. The way it's always been."

Col smiled. The Guardians might not be exactly how he imagined them, but one thing was exactly the same at least. They were on his side, no matter what.

"Thank you, Pendlebury."

"For what?"

"For helping me."

Her voice rumbled with pleasure. "You're welcome, Col."

He paused. "Did you just *purr*?"

"No," she said, far too quickly.

"Aaargh!"

The cry had come from the other side of the barn. Col spun round.

"King of Rogues? Was that you?"

There was a long pause.

"Er, yes," he replied. "I've … found someone. Hiding in one of the hay bales."

Pendlebury leaped to her feet, all exhaustion gone in a second. "Another spy?"

There was another pause.

"Er, no," said the King of Rogues, his voice a higher pitch than normal. "A human. They've been here the whole time."

Col and Pendlebury shared a look of dismay.

"What do we do?" whispered Col. "We can't just run – they've already seen us! Our cover's blown!"

Pendlebury's eyes grew cold and hard. "Leave them to me. I'll deal with it."

Col gulped. "You're not going to *hurt* them, are you?"

Pendlebury didn't reply. She shifted her weight on her paws and gazed ahead. "Rogue – bring them out."

There was another, much longer pause.

"I'm afraid that's not going to be possible," he replied, at an even higher pitch than before. "I'm sort of ... being held prisoner."

He stepped out from behind a hay bale with his hands above his head.

"She grabbed it while I was doing a cartwheel," he muttered. "It's, er ... never happened before."

Col gawped. Standing behind the knight was a girl his own age, with one arm wrapped around his chest and the other holding the sword to his neck. She was wearing a pair of dungarees and a battered raid helmet, which she'd covered with hay to camouflage herself. She almost looked funny – but Col only had to take one look at her face to know there was nothing funny about this, whatsoever. She had, without a doubt, the most serious face Col had ever seen in his life.

"First," said the girl, "you will explain what you are doing here. Then, you will explain about the tiger and the knight, and how it is that they are both somehow talking."

She looked Col up and down with distaste.

"Then perhaps you can explain why you are dressed as – *ach*, how to say – a monkey at a funeral."

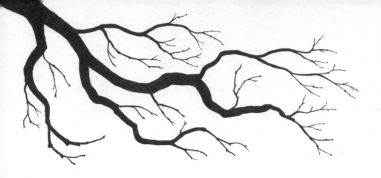

Ruth

COL STARED AT THE GIRL IN HORROR. SHE WASN'T one of the Midwinter King's spies ... but in many respects, she was just as bad. Even if Col and the Guardians managed to escape, the girl would tell everyone about what she'd seen. By now, Aunt Claire would have told the police that Col was missing – they'd be on the lookout for a boy his age, wearing shorts in the middle of winter. If the police recognized the girl's description of him and managed to catch up with them, it would all be over. Col would be taken back to Buxton and they'd never make it to Rose on time. Suddenly the entire future of their quest hung in the balance.

It was Pendlebury who finally broke the silence.

"You moron!" She glared at the King of Rogues. "How could you let her catch you? She's a six-year-old girl!"

"I am eleven," said the girl, affronted. "Now tell me what it is you are doing here!"

Col frowned. The girl's accent was hard to place. It was like she was picking each word carefully and balancing it in her mouth before saying it.

"Ha! We make the rules here, missy!" said the King of Rogues. "Isn't that right, Pendlebury?"

He nodded at the tiger. On cue, she gave a menacing growl and started creeping forwards. The girl gasped, clutching the King of Rogues tighter against her.

"S-s-stop! Do not come closer!"

"Let – him – go," Pendlebury growled.

She was growing as she walked, ripping and ripping until she practically towered over the girl. The girl waved the sword in wild swipes and knocked off her own helmet in terror. Col was taken aback: suddenly, he saw the girl for what she really was. Not a threat, but a frightened child, backed into a corner by a giant tiger. He remembered how frightened *he* had been when his Guardians first appeared in front of him – and they were his oldest friends. What must they look like to her?

"Stop it!" said Col, grabbing Pendlebury's tail. "You're frightening her!"

Pendlebury looked at him in surprise. "Col, I'm trying to—"

"I *order* you to stop."

Pendlebury hesitated. Then, with a weary sigh, she

shrank back to her normal size and sat down beside him. The girl gawped in amazement.

"See?" said Col. "They're not going to hurt you. They're my friends."

The girl swallowed. "And the rat?"

Col frowned. "What rat?"

The girl searched for the right words. "The big, fat rat with black-and-white fur."

"Oh – you mean Mr Noakes," said Col. "Yes, he's my friend too."

It felt weird, hearing a stranger talk about his imaginary friends. He'd never shared them with anyone else before.

"Big fat rat!" howled the King of Rogues. "Just wait until he gets back, that's classic…"

Col shushed him. "Please – let the King of Rogues go."

The girl glanced between Col and Pendlebury, and after a moment's hesitation shoved the King of Rogues away. He shot her a filthy look and scampered to Col's side, muttering something about not playing fair. The girl stayed where she was, holding out the sword with trembling hands. She was making a concerted effort to look commanding, despite being clearly terrified – Col thought she was doing a good job of it, all things considered. It wasn't every day you saw a giant tiger in your back garden.

"Thank you," he said. "Now, let me explain. My name is Col – these are my Guardians."

The girl frowned. "Guardians?"

"My imaginary friends," said Col. "Er … I mean, they *were* imaginary, but now they're real. It's sort of hard to explain. You see, there's this place called the Spirit World, and it's where all imagined things go, and there's this thing called the Midwinter King…"

He clearly wasn't explaining this very well. The girl was staring at him blankly.

"Didn't you have imaginary friends when you were younger?" he asked.

The girl snorted. "What? No. This is childish."

"Oh. Um … yes, I suppose it is a bit," said Col, turning bright red.

"This is taking too long," snapped Pendlebury. "Let's find Mr Noakes and get out of here."

"Agreed!" said the King of Rogues. "I'll tie her up."

Col was appalled. "You can't tie her up!"

"Why not?"

"Because … because it's rude, that's why!"

"No one is tying me up!" barked the girl. "From now on, you are going to do whatever I say! I am in charge!"

Col's face fell. "I beg your pardon?"

The girl took a deep breath and stood tall. "I hear *everything* you say to the tiger. About a big raid that is happening in London in a few days' time, and that you are going there for someone called Rose." She held the sword steady. "You will take me with you! I will not take no for an answer!"

Col groaned. This was the last thing they needed. "We can't take you with us!"

"Fine!" said the girl. "Then I am telling *everyone* what I have seen!"

"I'll get the rope," said the King of Rogues.

"We're not tying her up!" Col repeated.

"But she's going to tell everyone about us!"

"She can still do that if she's tied up!"

"Ha! And who's going to believe her?" Pendlebury gave the girl a withering glare. "Who's going to listen when you say you saw a knight and a giant talking tiger in your barn, little girl?"

"Mr Wilkes," said the girl.

Col blinked. "Who's Mr Wilkes?"

She pointed over their shoulders. They turned around. Standing behind them, wide-eyed with shock, was a farmer in pyjamas.

"R-Ruth?" he said. "What the hell is going on?"

Col froze – his Guardians froze too. There was nowhere to run, nowhere to hide. They'd been caught red-handed. The look on the farmer's face said it all. He shook his head in disbelief.

"I – I don't believe it," he said. "You're with … a *boy*!"

Col glanced at the Guardians in confusion – and in a flash, he understood. The farmer couldn't see Pendlebury or the King of Rogues: he couldn't see magic. All he saw was Col and the girl, standing together in an otherwise empty barn.

"I've been looking everywhere for you!" the farmer shouted. "And where do I find you? Hiding in here, smooching with your boyfriend!"

Col nearly choked. "What? We weren't…"

He trailed off – Pendlebury and the King of Rogues were silently shaking their heads at him. Col gave a groan of resignation. They were right – this was their only chance to get away.

"Yes – that's correct, sir," he said wearily. "We were smooching."

The girl looked horrified. "Mr Wilkes, do you not see the tiger? The knight? They are standing straight in front of you!"

The farmer grabbed her arm roughly. "That's enough from you, missy – this is the last straw! Get inside! You're in *big* trouble!"

The girl turned to Col, her face desperate. "Please! You must help me!"

Col gasped. The farmer was hurting her – he was practically pulling her arm out of her socket. Col knew what was happening was wrong ... but this was their only chance to get away. The farmer would never believe anything the girl said – the Guardians could escape without anyone knowing they'd even been there. Col couldn't let anything come between him and his quest to save Rose. So instead of helping, he did nothing. He watched as the farmer dragged the little girl away.

"You've been nothing but trouble since you got here!" the farmer ranted. "A right little madam, and now a thief to boot! To think, after all we've done for you, I walk in the house to find you've ransacked the kitchen and given Mrs Wilkes a terrible bop on the—"

BOP!

The farmer stayed upright for a second longer ... then collapsed like a cut puppet. Col's heart sank. Standing behind the farmer was Mr Noakes, waving his club and clutching a handbag full of food.

"I did it, Master Col!" he beamed. "I found food, and I did it like a subtle, just as you asked!"

"*A* subtle?" Col's face fell. "Mr Noakes, do you know what the word 'subtle' means?"

Mr Noakes nodded. "It's a type of fish, isn't it?"

Col put his head in his hands. This was getting worse and worse by the second. Right on cue, his Guardians started arguing again.

"Hopeless!" said Pendlebury. "You're all hopeless!"

"I told you I should have got the food!"

"Shut up, Rogue!"

"KING – OF – ROGUES!"

They squabbled furiously while Col looked on, too exhausted to try to stop them. Suddenly he wished he'd spent his childhood playing tiddlywinks instead of making up imaginary friends. The girl stood beside him, rubbing her arm.

"They do this a lot?" she asked.

"All the time." Col sighed.

There was an awkward silence. Col glanced at the girl, his chest heavy with shame. She wasn't being hurt any more, but it was no thanks to him. He would have let her get dragged away *and* take the blame for Mr Noakes too.

"I'm sorry for not helping you," he said. "And for lying. And for … *that*."

He pointed to the unconscious farmer on the ground. The girl sneered.

"Mr Wilkes? I do not care for him, nor Mrs Wilkes either. They are just two nasty, horrible people I am made to live with."

Col put two and two together. "Wait – you're an evacuee too? Where are you from?"

The girl shook her head. "This is not important. What is important is that you take me to London. If there is to be this raid, I must get there before it happens."

Col groaned. "Look, we can't take you with us…"

The girl refused to give in. "You said you are sorry, yes? This is how you show me! The tiger says you need a place to hide – I know a place nearby. No one knows but me. I will show the way!"

Col shook his head. "I'm sorry, but … I just can't. I've only got five days to save my sister. If Pendlebury has to carry an extra person…"

The girl's face changed. It cracked like an eggshell, and for a moment it seemed as if something small and desperately sad was peeking out from inside her. Suddenly she didn't look commanding any more. She looked terrified.

"Please," she begged, her voice barely a whisper. "Do not leave me here."

Col was torn. He understood that face. It was the face of someone fighting to save something they loved. The girl had been sent away from her home – just like him. She wanted to get back home – just like him. She had something she needed to protect. His Guardians had thrown him a lifeline: was he going to use it to help her, or was he going to pull it in after him, and let her suffer?

What would Rose do?

He gave a long, weary sigh.

"Look – it's not going to be easy," he said. "We've got a hundred and thirty miles left to go. You're going to see plenty more strange things on the way too. We got attacked by trees earlier."

The girl nodded firmly. She still clearly had a lot of questions to ask, but she wasn't going to turn down a lifeline when it was offered. "Th-that is fine. Just, please, keep me safe from … *them*."

She pointed at the squabbling Guardians. Col frowned.

"Wait – you're scared of them?"

"Of *course*!" said the girl, her eyes wide. "The knight, he is nothing. But the other two … it is a giant tiger and a *huge* fat rat!"

"Badger."

"What?"

"Never mind." He held out his hand. "Ruth, isn't it?"

She nodded. "And you are Col."

They shook hands. Col turned back to his Guardians, who were still arguing.

"Right!" he said. "Enough – we're going, and Ruth's coming with us."

The Guardians were rendered speechless – almost.

"*WHAT?*" bellowed the King of Rogues. "We can't take her with us!"

"We have to!" said Col. "She knows somewhere we

can hide. And frankly, after today, I think we need all the help we can get…"

There was a sudden groan from the floor. Everyone spun round. Mr Wilkes was waking up, feebly touching the lump on his head, which was now the size of a hot-cross bun.

"Quick – we don't have time for this!" Col gasped. "We have to go, now!"

Mr Noakes bowed, his eyes wide with concern. "Master Col, we can't take the girl. If she slows us down…"

"No."

Everyone turned to Pendlebury. She was gazing at Col, her face weary but determined.

"I can carry her. Col is our master. Whatever he asks, we will do."

The King of Rogues was horrified. "But…"

"We are his Guardians," said Pendlebury steadily. "We don't do what's easy – we do what we must. No matter how difficult it is."

Col glowed. He loved Pendlebury more than anything at that moment. Right on cue, the farmer started trying to push himself up off the floor.

"Right – let's go!" said Col. "Don't worry – I've told Ruth how important this quest is. I'm sure she won't be any problem and…"

He trailed off. Ruth had shoved past him and was mounting Pendlebury's back, hands shaking slightly.

"What are you waiting for, tiger? I am in charge now! We go! Onwards! Obey!"

She pointed ahead like a sultan, pulling Pendlebury's whiskers and kicking her flanks. The King of Rogues and Mr Noakes winced. Pendlebury glared at Col with absolute fury.

"Um … maybe don't kick her," said Col.

The Hideout

THE HIDING PLACE WAS EXACTLY WHERE RUTH described it. After a couple of miles they came to a stream that curled around the back of a rock face, and on the other side was a cave, stretching into darkness like a stone throat.

"Is it safe?" asked Pendlebury.

Mr Noakes sniffed the air. "Hmph. I suppose."

He was obviously annoyed that Ruth's suggestion was a good one. In fact, all the Guardians seemed annoyed – they hadn't said a word since leaving the barn. They didn't need words to show how much they disapproved of Col's decision to bring Ruth with them. He shuffled awkwardly – it was weird, being given the silent treatment by your own imaginary friends.

"How did you find this place?" he asked Ruth, glancing inside the cave.

"I come when I wish to be alone," she replied

haughtily. "Now, inside! You four talk too much. Everything is talk, talk, talk!"

With that, she jumped off Pendlebury and marched into the cave. The Guardians shared a glance.

"Last chance to tie her up," offered the King of Rogues.

Col watched Ruth go, bristling with irritation. He had put himself on the line to help her – gone against the advice of his Guardians, risked his own quest – but she wasn't even trying to be polite, let alone grateful. Worse still, she was trying to take control of the quest and boss them all around – and it was *Col's* quest, *Col's* Guardians. As if he didn't have enough to deal with already.

"We'll camp here tonight and leave first thing tomorrow," he muttered. "I'll get some firewood. Pendlebury, you get some rest…"

"I won't get much rest with *her* around," Pendlebury grumbled.

Col ignored her. "Mr Noakes, you're in charge of dinner…"

"We'll need even more food now there are five of us," he muttered.

Col grit his teeth. "King of Rogues, you can…"

"Don't worry, I'll keep a close eye on her, my liege!" he answered immediately. "She might have fooled *you*, but she won't pull the wool over my eyes, no siree! I know a traitor when I see one. Turning up out of nowhere, taking my sword... Mark my words, the moment we turn around she'll stab us in the..."

Col walked away before he could finish the sentence.

It took him ages to find any branches dry enough to burn. By the time he had gathered enough for the night, the temperature was plummeting and a vicious wind was already howling through the trees. The storm was coming again, even faster than the previous night. Col gulped. He wasn't looking forward to spending a night outside – especially after everything the Guardians had said about the King's spies searching for them. He hoped the light from the fire would be strong enough to hide them from the eyes of the Midwinter King.

When he got back to the cave, Pendlebury was stretched across the floor, snoring like a faulty radiator. The others were sitting as far away from each other as possible. The cave was filled with a sour, silent atmosphere.

"Everything OK?" he asked.

"What would I know?" said Mr Noakes, hacking away at a stack of vegetables. "I'm just a big fat rat!"

Col groaned. "Rogue, did you have to tell him?"

"*King* of Rogues," said the knight, trying to hide a smile.

Ruth sat at the back of the cave by herself, clutching a canvas kitbag to her chest. Col frowned.

"Where did that come from?" he asked.

Ruth reeled back instantly. "Hands off! It is mine!"

Col finally lost patience with her. Frankly, he'd had enough of people being difficult for one day.

"For heaven's sake, I don't want your bag. You didn't have it with you when we left the barn, that's all!" He folded his arms. "You don't have to be so rude. I'm letting you come with us, on the most important quest of my life, and I don't even know anything about you! Why should I trust you when you don't tell me anything?"

Ruth thinned her eyes, keeping her hands clamped to the kitbag.

"These are my private things," she said begrudgingly. "I hide them in here for safety."

Col frowned. "Hiding them in a cave doesn't sound very safe."

Ruth's face darkened. "It is safer than at the farm. Mr and Mrs Wilkes are paid money to take care of me, but they say it is not enough to pay for the food I am eating. They sell many of my things when I first arrive too. My clothes, my books. A locket from my mother."

Col was shocked. No wonder Ruth was so suspicious of everyone. He'd heard of people taking in evacuees and treating them unkindly, but he'd never heard of anyone stooping so low as to sell their belongings. It made living with Aunt Claire seem like paradise. She might be annoying and overbearing, but she wasn't cruel. He felt a sudden pang of guilt – Aunt Claire must be worried sick about him. She'd still have no idea where he was.

"That's terrible," he said, brushing away the thought.

Ruth shrugged. "I told you, Mr and Mrs Wilkes are not nice people. They make me work like a slave all day, and then they do not want me in their house so I must walk outside until it is dark again. That is how I found this cave, yes? And why I was hiding in the barn when you found me." She shuffled uncomfortably on the cold stone floor. "It is always the same in this country. *Ich habe genug um die Ohren…*"

Col knew he'd recognized her accent from somewhere. "Ahhh, you're German!"

He'd met lots of Germans in London over the last few years – many had fled to Britain before the war began, trying to escape from the Nazis. There had been dozens of young German men working in the stockrooms at Dad's work – he said they worked harder than anyone. When war was declared, every single one had been arrested as an enemy alien and taken away to prison camps. Dad said he never saw them again.

Ruth frowned. "This does not frighten you? The

110

children around here, they say that because I am German, I am a Nazi spy."

Col shook his head. "So, are the rest of your family still living in London? Is that why you need to get there?"

That was too many questions. Ruth closed up again, like a bear trap.

"That is – how do you say here – *none of your beeswax.*"

Col sighed. After twenty-four hours of no sleep, no food, and an ambush by enchanted trees, the last thing he needed was another argument. If Ruth didn't want to tell him anything, that was her problem. Right now, all he cared about was warming his legs up.

He set to work making a fire until the cave was warm and flickering with shadows around them. Mr Noakes cooked over the embers, boiling sliced turnips in a pan stolen from the farm and mashing them into paste with his paws. Pendlebury woke up and wolfed down her portion in a single mouthful. Ruth managed a few small bites of her own before catching sight of Mr Noakes' filthy paws and pushing it away in disgust.

Afterwards they sat in exhausted silence, passing around a tin of condensed milk that had warmed by the fire and taking swigs until it was gone. Col glanced out the cave entrance: the storm had fully arrived now, and the forest outside was lost to a spiralling whirlwind of snow. He shuddered. Any number of the King's spies could be out there, hiding in the darkness.

"Are you sure we'll be safe in here?" he asked nervously.

Pendlebury stood up groggily. "Like I said, the fire will help protect us from the eyes of the Midwinter King. I'll block the entrance, so no one sees the light. You can sleep next to me if you're frightened, Col."

Mr Noakes gasped. "No, I'll look after Master Col!"

"Nonsense!" said the King of Rogues. "I'll protect you, my liege!"

Col turned bright scarlet. It was mortifying, hearing them talk like this in front of Ruth. "I'm fine, really. I'll sleep over here."

"But my liege—"

"Master Col—"

"Would you mind just calling me Col?" he snapped.

The Guardians were taken aback. Col cleared his throat.

"Look, I'm twelve. The whole 'master' and 'my liege' thing – it's a bit childish." He smiled apologetically. "Maybe you should just call me 'Col' from now on. OK?"

Col had never seen a knight or a tiger or a badger look so offended before.

"Of – of course!" spluttered Mr Noakes. "Whatever you say, Mas— Col."

"Yep. Sure. No problem," said the King of Rogues, shooting Ruth a filthy look, as if it was all her fault.

Pendlebury said nothing at first. She just gave Col a look that he'd never seen before – one that was somehow sad and hurt and proud, all at the same time.

"As you wish," she said.

She lay at the entrance – *rrrrrrip* – and grew to fill the space, blocking it like a plug and making the cave as warm and safe as a burrow. Col huddled beside the fire and folded his jacket into a pillow. He felt guilty for snapping at the Guardians – after all, they were only trying to protect him. But he couldn't keep letting them treat him like a baby. If he was going to save Rose, he had to be brave. This wasn't imaginary any more – this was real life.

He didn't have time to worry about it – he was too exhausted for that. The rock beneath him might as well have been a king-size feather bed in The Ritz. He didn't so much fall asleep as plummet.

"And, remember, missy," he heard the King of Rogues say, "I'm watching like a hawk! One wrong move…"

"You have said this already, many times," said Ruth wearily. "You do not need to keep saying this."

"Ha! You'd like that, wouldn't you? Well, I'll remain vigilant! I won't sleep a wink! I…"

"Shut up, Rogue," mumbled Mr Noakes.

"King of Rrrrrrr…" His voice drifted into a snore, and within a few seconds everyone in the cave was fast asleep.

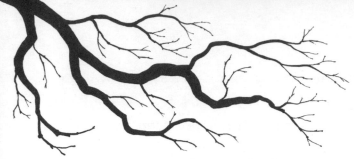

Rise of the
Midwinter King

YOU LET THEM GET AWAY.

The Midwinter King glared at the trees cowering before the burnt throne, trembling and whimpering.

I gave strict orders. I told you to bring the three spirits to me.

Barry looked up. "W-we tried, Your Majesty!"

"Silence!" cried Barghest. "How dare you interrupt the King?"

She stood in the shadows, flanked by her troops: a mass of black dogs. There were hundreds of them, their eyes throbbing hungrily in the dark. Barry cowered in terror.

"They … they tricked us, Your Majesty! It all happened so fast! And besides there were four of them, not three, and—"

Four?

Barry stopped. The King was staring at him, his eyes flared in surprise.

"Y-yes, Your Majesty. Four. A tiger, a knight, a badger and a human boy."

The King gazed ahead in amazement. Suddenly it was all falling into place. The reason why he could not find the three spirits when he tried to look for them.

It is a human and his imaginary friends. They are protected from my gaze whenever they are near him. That is why I cannot see them.

Barghest was shocked for a moment – then she gave a pitiful laugh. The other dogs joined in, until they were a howling, baying mob in the dark.

"Then we need not concern ourselves with them, my lord – they are a child's imaginary friends! The lowest of the low! There is nothing they can do to stop the raid, or help the Green Man, or…"

Her words froze to a choke in her throat. The Midwinter King turned to face her, his eyes like two boiling furnaces.

Yes, Barghest. That is correct. Three of the lowliest creatures in the Spirit World were able to break through your "impenetrable" barriers. And you tell me this makes no difference?

The Midwinter King stood to his full height. He was over ten feet tall, thin as dead twigs, with a high black crown and long, flowing robes that curled at the edges like smoke. It was impossible to be sure of any part of him. He was darkness cut from the world.

You have failed me again.

Barghest collapsed on the stone. The black tendrils were inside her again, spreading into her mind like thorns. But the King wasn't trying to read her thoughts this time – he wanted to hurt her, and he could do that as easily as breathing. The other dogs fled into the shadows, as did the trees. No one wanted to be around to see this.

You have made me look weak. You have shown everyone that I can be defied by even the lowliest of creatures.

"They … they couldn't have broken over the barriers by themselves, Your Majesty!" Barghest cried. "They must have had help!"

Precisely. They had help. So others will be able to break over too. Who knows how many?

The Midwinter King could not allow this. If word got out that a few spirits were able to defy him, it could give the Green Man's allies the belief they needed to keep fighting. It could show that the Midwinter King could be beaten. It could undo everything he had achieved. If the Spirit World was not afraid of him, what power did he have?

It was time to show them what a god of darkness was capable of.

He let go of Barghest, and she gasped in agony on the stone.

Take charge of my armies while I'm gone. I want all the Spirit World to prepare for my return.

Barghest looked up. "R-r-return?"

I am going into the world beyond. I will find these imaginary spirits and bring them back myself. I will show all the Spirit World what happens to those who defy me.

The Midwinter King smiled: but it was wrong to call it a smile.

I will make an example of them.

Barghest looked horrified. "Your Majesty, no! You cannot leave your throne! We have already sealed the barriers into the world beyond, to open them now…"

You do not need to open anything.

The Midwinter King shut his eyes and drew deep from his powers. In a single instance, he flew a million miles and a single hair's breadth…

And when he opened his eyes, he stood in another world.

The Midwinter King smiled again. He had never tried such magic before – and it had worked even better than he had expected. His powers truly were greater than ever. He had transported himself into the world beyond, simply by wishing it. He stood in a valley that was filled with snow. A single building lay nestled in the centre, in a sea of unbroken white.

An old stone cottage with a red door, framed by the remains of a rose bush.

The Midwinter King's eyes flared. *This* was it: the

place where he had felt the shift in his fortunes. This was where the imaginary creatures had come to defy him.

He would find everything he needed here.

He walked to the cottage, the snow blackening beneath him with every step. The door slammed itself open as he approached. He stepped inside and made his way up the attic stairs without stopping. Had anyone been there to watch, they would have noticed that his feet never quite touched the steps.

The Midwinter King stood in the attic and gazed at the pitiful room around him. Little more than a closet, filled with old rubbish. A guttered candle sat in the middle of the floor. It was silent, and pathetic, and empty.

But not completely.

The Midwinter King breathed in. He understood at once why the spirits had come here: the cottage was *filled* with memories of the boy who had made them. The very dust in the air held his thoughts, his fears, his dreams and desires.

The Midwinter King opened his mouth, and ate them.

The change was instantaneous. The moment he ate the boy's memories, they appeared inside him. The boy. His father. His sister. His home in Herne Hill.

His name.

Col, said the Midwinter King.

He had done it. Now he was connected to the boy, just like he was connected to all his subjects. The Guardians might be protected by Col's love – but Col was different. Once he was asleep, his mind would be unprotected. The King would be able to reach inside it and find whatever he needed.

And now, it was his time. It was midnight: his powers were beyond reckoning.

The Midwinter King closed his eyes, and reached across the world.

The Invasion

I T WAS MORE OF A MEMORY THAN A DREAM.

"Collie, quick! He'll be home soon!"

"Just one more minute."

"Oh, for heaven's sake…"

The war was only a few months old. They were still at their house in Herne Hill. It was before France fell, before the raids … before the incident. Back when the worst thing they had to deal with was food rationing and carrying around their gas masks all the time.

"Don't rush me!" said Col. "I want to get it right."

"Well, it'd better be right soon," said Rose. "He's here."

She pointed out of the blackout curtains. Sure enough, a thin strip of coloured light was wheeling around the corner. You could spot Dad's bike lamp a mile off – it was orange and violet, where Rose had stained the glass with rainbows. Dad said it made him look a total plank and he'd get a new one someday, but he never did. They all knew he secretly liked it.

"Just in time!" said Col, bringing a bowl to the table. "It's ready."

Rose glanced at it dubiously. "*That's* ready?"

"Don't be rude!" said Col. "It's the *Good Housekeeping* recipe of the month."

At that moment the door opened and Dad walked in. Col and Rose held out their hands.

"Happy birthday!"

They'd spent all day getting the house ready – it wasn't easy, with money tighter than ever before, and rationing making the queues at the shops even longer. But they'd done a great job. The fire was crackling, the table was set, and they'd made Dad's favourite food – sort of.

Col proudly held up a bowl filled with steaming grey paste. "It's called Mock Banana! It's made from boiled parsnip and banana essence. They say it's just like the real thing!"

Dad gave a weak smile. "What a treat. Thank you, Col. Thank you, Rose."

Something was wrong. Dad was trying to hide it with his voice, but the smile-lines had gone from his eyes.

"What's the matter?" asked Col.

"Nothing's the matter!" said Dad, shaking his head. "Let's tuck into this and…"

"Dad." Rose gave him The Look. Dad often did this – tried to fix problems by himself, not wanting Col and Rose to worry. But there was no getting away from The Look. "For heaven's sake, just *tell* us."

"You haven't been sacked, have you?" said Col nervously.

Dad looked at him, surprised. "No – no, it's not that." He ran a hand through his hair and sighed. "Fine. Put the kettle on, Col."

That *was* serious. Col sorted out a pot and soon they all sat around the table, each with a cup and a steaming plate of Mock Banana. They ate in silence for a while, waiting for Dad to start talking. Finally, he put down his spoon, folded his hands, and explained.

"Your Aunt Claire wrote to me today. She doesn't think it's safe for you two to live here any more." He rubbed at his knuckles, worrying the skin. "She thinks you should move up to Buxton and live with her until the war's over."

Rose's eyes rolled into the back of her head. "Oh, please! Dad, I'm seventeen. I'm not being evacuated."

"Me neither!" said Col.

Thousands of children had been evacuated from the city when war was first announced – you saw them wherever you went, lined up at train stations and tagged up like baggage. But since then, there'd been no bombings, no gas attacks – nothing. Every air raid was a false alarm: most shops didn't even bother closing when the sirens went off any more. Within a few weeks, every child who'd been evacuated in Col's class came back home, complaining about the food and the outside toilets. Dad shook his head.

"I … I don't know. Maybe your aunt's right. No one knows what the Nazis will do next. We could all be gassed in our beds while we sleep." He swallowed. "You two don't know what war's like – I do. If the Nazis get over here, it's going to be very, very bad."

Col was shocked. Dad never talked about the last war – and he never looked scared like this, either. Col had no idea what to say to make him feel better… But Rose did. She always did.

"Exactly." She took Dad's hand. "No one knows what's going to happen. That's why we need to stick together. If the Nazis do invade, then we'll see it out together. Just the three of us – the way we always have." She glanced over the table. "Right, Col?"

Col took Dad's other hand. "Right."

Dad looked at them with something like wonder. The laughter lines came back around his eyes. "You're sure you don't want to live with Aunt Claire?"

"I think I'd rather be bombed," said Rose.

Col snorted with laughter. Dad gave them a look.

"Don't say that. Your aunt's been kind to us – more than you know. You'll be grateful to have her one day." He sighed. "I mean, let's face it – no one knows what could happen tomorrow, especially when there's a war on. I might not always be around to look after you both."

"Dad!" Col hated it when he said things like that.

"He's right," said Rose. "If the bombs don't finish us off, this Mock Banana will."

Col kicked her under the table. "Shut up!"

Dad tried not to laugh and gave up. "God, it's awful! Parsnips and banana essence! What were they thinking? I'm sorry, Col, it was so nice of you."

Col tried to look hurt, but he couldn't help himself. "It's really horrible, isn't it?"

Dad cackled and dragged him over the table, rubbing his head – Col *loved* it when Dad did that. Rose threw her arms around them both and they held each other, giggling about how strange and ridiculous it all was, and when they'd finished laughing they just stayed there for a while, holding each other for longer than they needed to.

Col had never felt safer than he had at that moment. A hundred planes could have dropped a thousand bombs on them and blown the house apart like balsawood, and when the dust cleared the three of them would still have been sat at the table, holding each other. It was one of the last true happy memories that he had before the night everything changed. Before—

He felt it at once.

The air had turned to rotten ice. Something was in here with them – something bad and wrong. He pulled away in confusion.

"W-what's going on? What's—?"

Dad and Rose weren't moving. They were locked in place, smiling like a frozen film reel. Col gasped. This wasn't a memory any more – this wasn't even a dream. This was something else, something much worse. He turned around – and the scream froze in his throat.

Something was forcing its way inside the house, prising beneath the doorway and the cracks around the windows. It was darkness – pure, living darkness, forming the shape of a black tongue in the centre of the room. Col watched in horror as it started scrabbling in the corners, smashing the furniture, searching for something...

"G-get out!" Col cried. "Get out of my house!"

The darkness *heard* him. It lunged like a viper and grabbed him by the throat, lifting him off his feet and dragging him out the door.

"No!" Col screamed.

But it was no use. His street wasn't his street any more: it was a black chasm with no walls and no boundaries, and the darkness was dragging him through it at indescribable speed towards something at the centre, getting faster and faster and faster...

And there in the heart of the darkness, something was waiting for him. Two eyes, looking right at him. Two eyes like dying stars.

There you are.

Col felt ice-cold tendrils shoot inside his brain. There was no stopping it, no fighting it – it was pointless even to try. Col watched as his most private memories were wrenched out of him and discarded, like someone tearing the pages from a book. Dad lying on the street. Rose being held down at the police station. The funeral. Rose on the platform. London on fire, Dad lying on the street, the funeral, Rose at the station, London on fire...

"NO, NO, NO..."

"NO, NO, NO!"

Col fought and kicked against the hands holding him down.

"Col, you're safe! You're here! You're with us!"

Col leaped to his feet and scrambled back to the cave wall, heaving for breath. The Guardians stood in the last of the firelight, their faces filled with shock and concern. Ruth was pressed against the far side of the cave, staring at him with wide eyes.

"Your – your hands," she said quietly.

Col looked at his hands. They were cut and bleeding, from where he'd been fighting the stone floor. Pendlebury leaned in close.

"Col, what happened? What did you see?"

Col reeled, trying to calm his breathing and stop his heart pounding. "It was ... it was a nightmare. It was the worst nightmare I've ever had."

The Guardians gave each other a look. Pendlebury spoke calmly and carefully.

"Col – what happened?"

He closed his eyes and tried to stop himself from shaking. The feeling of the darkness reaching inside him still felt so raw, as if it was just a hair's breadth away. He had to think clearly – he had to remember what happened, even though he didn't want to. The very thought made him feel sick.

"It – it was a memory, but then it all changed. It was Dad's last birthday. Then something got inside the house and dragged me out and pulled me towards it. Like it had found me." He swallowed. "It was ... darkness. Darkness with eyes."

Mr Noakes cried out. The King of Rogues staggered back. Pendlebury sagged with horror.

"No," she whispered. "No, no, no, it can't be."

"I told you," said the King of Rogues. "I said he'd find us! I *knew* he'd find us!"

"But *how?*" said Mr Noakes. "He's never been able to do that to humans before! How could he possibly…"

"His powers grow stronger every day," said Pendlebury. "Look."

She pointed to the cave mouth. Outside, the storm was worse than ever: the wind had risen to a relentless scream, tearing between the trees like blades.

"W-what is going on?" demanded Ruth, her voice high and frightened. She was still frozen to the wall, staring at Col and his bleeding hands like he was a monster. "Tell me what is happening!"

"Quiet!" the King of Rogues shouted. "This is all your fault! We let you join us, and now look what happens!"

"This has nothing to do with her!" snapped Pendlebury. She turned Col to face her again. "Col, I need you to listen to me, this is very important. What happened when the darkness found you?"

Col didn't want to talk about it – he didn't want to think about it ever again. But he could tell by the look on Pendlebury's face how serious this was. He closed his eyes, remembering the darkness, the ice-cold tendrils prising into his mind…

"It – it went through my memories. Like it was looking for something."

Pendlebury nodded gravely. "Did it see anything about us? About today? About where we are?"

Col shook his head. "N-no. It was all about Dad. About his accident."

His eyes stung. He thought he had forgotten the details of that night – now he realized that they were all still inside him, hidden just below the surface, fresh and raw as the day it happened. Suddenly he was crying. Pendlebury held him close, pressing his face into her fur.

"We need to go," she said to the others. "Now. We can't be sure he hasn't heard us."

"But it's midnight!" cried the King of Rogues. "It's the height of his powers! How are we going to travel in that storm?"

"We don't have a choice!" said Mr Noakes. "He could be sending his spies this way right now. We have to keep moving!"

Col's mind reeled. "That – that was the Midwinter King, wasn't it? He got inside my head. He's coming after me!"

Pendlebury hushed him. "You have enough to worry about already, Col. You focus on Rose, and we'll—"

"NO!" he shouted.

Pendlebury was shocked. Col took another breath. A part of him didn't *want* to understand what had just happened – but he had to know. It was too serious to pretend.

"I'm not a child any more. You can't protect me from everything. You have to tell me what's going on, even when it's bad." He swallowed, chest heaving. "If that really was the Midwinter King, then … then I need to know. I need to understand what it means."

Pendlebury looked at him for a while. Her tail flickered. Then she sat down.

"Yes, Col," she said quietly. "That was the Midwinter King. He's using you to try to find out where we are. And now that he has done it once, he will be able to do it again. Whenever you sleep and your defences are down, he will try to get inside your head."

Col's stomach heaved. The thought of that ever happening again filled him with dread. His most personal, private memories had been sorted through and burgled.

"But … why?" he asked. "I'm not trying to stop him. I'm not even trying to stop the raid. I just want to save Rose!"

"It doesn't matter to him," said the King of Rogues. "We've defied him. And there are terrible consequences for that. Consequences worse than death."

Col looked at him. "There's nothing worse than death."

"Oh, there *is*, Master Col," said Mr Noakes. "Much,

much worse. To be cut from existence. To be wiped from this world and all others. To be nothing, with neither death nor life for all eternity."

"No one would even remember that we existed," said the King of Rogues quietly. "Not anyone – not even you."

"It is the Midwinter King's greatest power," said Pendlebury. "And if he catches us, that is all we can expect."

Col stared at them in horror. He'd had no idea what the Guardians were facing by taking on this quest. If the Midwinter King found them, the Guardians wouldn't just die – they would never have existed. The quest would fail, he wouldn't save Rose, and he would never see his Guardians again. He would lose them all. For a moment, as the darkness had taken hold of him, he had felt what it was to be utterly powerless – to be nothing. It had been beyond imagining. To face an eternity of that...

No one spoke. Fear had filled the cave like hot smoke.

"Let's go," said Pendlebury. "We're leaving the girl. She's too much of a risk."

Ruth looked at them in desperation. "N-no! You will not leave me here! I must come with you!"

Pendlebury ignored her. "Come, Col. If we leave now, we might be able to cover another ten miles by dawn."

Col looked outside at the howling storm. Ten more miles. They'd have another one hundred and twenty miles left to get to London, in weather like this, with the god of darkness tracking them at every step...

And suddenly the hopelessness, the sheer hopelessness of what they were doing hit him like a wall of black water. They had so far left to go. They were up against so much. Even if by some miracle they made it to London, the Midwinter King would never stop coming after them. His Guardians would be caught and slaughtered and Col would lose them for ever. No matter what happened, no matter what they did, they had already lost.

He slumped against the wall and sank to the floor.

Pendlebury looked confused. "Col? Col, what are you doing?"

"I'm not going," he said weakly, clutching his knees to his chest. "I – I can't do it. I'm sorry."

The Guardians were horrified.

"My liege, we must go!" said the King of Rogues. "If we don't get to Rose in time..."

"We can't save her," said Col. "Look at us. Look at what we're up against. It's impossible."

It was true. There was no way they could possibly win – he just had to accept it. To go out there now, and fight it with everything he had, and to *still lose*...

"You three should try to hide while you still can," said Col. "There's nothing I can do for Rose. I have to—"

"No."

Col looked up. Ruth was marching towards him.

"Enough! *Das reicht schon.* Stand up." She grabbed his arm and started trying to heave him off the floor.

Col shook his head. "Ruth, what are you…"

"Come! Your sister is waiting for you."

She kept pulling his arm. Suddenly Col was angry with her. He snapped his arm away. "Ruth, you don't understand! I felt him get inside me, I *know* we can't beat him…"

"Do you want to find out that you were wrong?"

She held out her hand.

"*Come.* If you stay here, this thing – this Midwinter King – he has won already."

She stayed, staring down at him, waiting with her hand outstretched.

"I am not going until you say yes," she said. "It is a miracle that I found you. I am not giving up now."

Col was speechless. He had never met anyone as single-minded as Ruth. She had accepted everything that had happened that night – the Guardians, the quest, the nightmare – and kept her sights set on the one thing she needed the entire time. She was going to get back to London even if it killed her.

"You honestly think we can still make it," said Col, "after everything that you've just heard."

"We might," said Ruth.

"But it's impossible."

"No, no, it is just hard."

And just like that, it was as though a single candle was lit inside him.

Col looked at Ruth – he looked at his Guardians, waiting for him. He took her hand and got to his feet.

"Ruth is ... right," he said. "We should keep going."

The Guardians looked as shocked as he did.

"Are you sure?" said Pendlebury.

Col thought about him and Dad and Rose, holding each other at the table.

"I'm sure," he said.

The King of Rogues just about managed to pull himself together. "Well – off we go, then!" he said. "Nothing can stop us Guardians, eh? The four of us, together again…"

"Five."

They spun round. Pendlebury was gazing at Ruth.

"There are five of us now," she said.

Mr Noakes placed his paws on her shoulders. "Anyone who helps Col is a friend of ours, Miss Ruth."

The King of Rogues looked as if he'd just been slapped. Even Ruth was shocked. Pendlebury turned to the cave mouth before either of them could respond.

"Come on," she said. "We've got a long way to go."

They stepped into the forest, bowed low against the razorblade wind, and climbed onto Pendlebury's back. Col peered at the sky. The night was at its darkest, the storm at its very worst – but he could see where it ended. There was a point on the horizon where the moonlight hit the hills, making them shine like glaciers. The way home was still there. It was hard, and it was fraught with danger, but it was there.

And he wasn't facing it alone.

The Guardians rode out of the forest together, on towards the sun.

The Coming Storm

THE MIDWINTER KING OPENED HIS EYES.

He had done it. He had found the boy's mind. Col had been right in his grip.

Then he'd been torn away, just when he'd got his hands on him.

The floorboards began to blacken and smoulder beneath him.

These spirits – these *Guardians* – were cleverer than he'd thought. They had woken Col before the King could find what he needed. He hadn't been inside Col's mind long enough to know where they were hiding. But he knew where they were heading, at least.

London.

So that was it. The Guardians had shown Col the vision of the raid: they were taking him to London to save his sister. That was why the Midwinter King had felt such a small change: they did not want to stop his plan. They had nothing to do with the Green Man. They wanted to save one death among thousands. He need not waste any more time on them. He could return to his throne now and his rise to power would continue.

No.

He had told Barghest to gather all the Spirit World for his return. What kind of message would it send if he came back empty-handed? That the Midwinter King ignored those who defied him? That the god of darkness was outsmarted by even the lowliest creatures of the Spirit World?

He could not allow it. The boy and his imaginary friends might not be helping the Green Man, but their one small act of rebellion could upset everything. It could show the Spirit World that the Midwinter King could be defeated. It could swing the balance, right when it mattered the most.

A single match could burn down a forest, if you let it.

The Midwinter King could risk nothing now. He had never been so close to absolute power before. He could not let the Guardians get away. He would drag them back screaming, for all the Spirit World to see.

The Midwinter King stepped outside the cottage and gazed towards the horizon. The Guardians would not get far. The land between here and London was filled with his spies: there was no way anything could get past them undetected.

All he had to do was catch up with them.

He raised his arms, slow and incontestable, like the hands of some dreadful clock, and waited.

Nothing happened at first. Then, the snow melted beneath him. The soil began to turn. Worms writhed from the ground at his feet, like a tongue in a gagging mouth. Something was rising out of the undergrowth, tumbling from the darkness like foam.

Bones – hundreds of them, dragged from the earth and forming a shifting cloud in the valley. They came together, scraping and rasping against each other, creating something new and terrible in the last of the moonlight.

It was a horse, and it was made of bones. All four legs ended in a human skull, their teeth clamping into the earth. Its face was a cluster of ribs and fingers. It turned to face its master, and it waited.

The Midwinter King mounted the horse and glanced at the sky. He only had a few hours of riding left. He could not stay outside like this when daylight came: the power of the sun would burn him like acid. But he could not go back to the Spirit World, either. He would have to find a way to hide himself until night returned.

But it did not matter: it would not take long to catch up with the Guardians. They could not outrun him now.

For who can outrun darkness?

The Midwinter King rode south out of the valley. He took the storm with him.

24 December 1940

UNEXPLODED BOMBS

Air Raid Wardens have issued a warning to the public about the dangers of venturing near bomb craters, or of picking up any metal container found in the ground. These articles may be unexploded bombs and are extremely dangerous to anyone touching or interfering with them.

We remind the public that extra care should be taken when walking through fields, as enemy planes often jettison their leftover bombs in the country before making home.

Creature in the Fog

"I JUST DON'T UNDERSTAND WHY *I* HAVE TO GO at the back!"

The Guardians had been riding all day. Ruth sat at the front, crouched low over Pendlebury's shoulders. Mr Noakes was behind, holding her steadily in place. Then came Col, with the King of Rogues at the very back. He had been complaining about this fact for the last two hours.

"Because someone has to hold Col," said Mr Noakes for the hundredth time.

"But why is *she* at the front?" he whined. "She's not even a proper Guardian! I've been doing this for years and I've *never* got to sit at the front! Far be it from me to complain, but..."

"I'm not sure I can take much more of this," Pendlebury groaned.

"He *is* being annoying," Col agreed. Pendlebury and

Mr Noakes had finally come to accept Ruth, but the King of Rogues still refused to trust her. He had spent the whole day finding reasons to accuse her of betrayal, duplicity and – on one memorable occasion – sorcery.

"I meant the mud," said Pendlebury.

She held up her sodden paws. The heavy snow had given way to hammering rain and freezing fog once again, and Pendlebury's pace had been reduced to an agonizing crawl. They'd been trudging through marshland for the last hour. Col could just about make out the pale sun through the fog – it was already past midday, and they couldn't have covered more than ten miles. It still wasn't enough – they were falling further and further behind.

And that wasn't his only worry. Sunset meant darkness, and darkness meant the Midwinter King could leap into his mind again. Col had spent all day trying not to think about it, but now his nerves were like a faulty switchbox. Keeping an eye out for spies was bad enough – now he had the god of darkness to worry about too. It didn't help that he couldn't see anything in this fog. He kept expecting to look up and see those sightless eyes at any moment, glowing ahead of them...

"Let's stop and get our bearings," he said, pushing away the thought. "The sooner we find a way out of this marsh, the better."

Pendlebury found a small patch of dry land and shrank down to regular size. It was little more than a hump of mud with a single rotten tree stump poking out the centre.

"Yowch!" said the King of Rogues, rubbing his backside. "Can't you shrink a little slower next time?"

"I'm freezing," said Mr Noakes.

"And this island is disgusting," said Ruth, curling her lip at the mud. "Can we not find somewhere clean?"

Pendlebury took a long, deep breath. "If one more person complains about a single thing, I am going to eat them."

Col's stomach groaned. "Speaking of which – have we got any food left?"

Mr Noakes shook his head. "Nope – we've had everything I took from the farm. Plenty of salt left, though!"

He held up the handbag of food he'd stolen from Mrs Wilkes and produced an enormous cotton sack from inside, beaming with pride. The King of Rogues scowled.

"What did you bring that for? If you left that out, you could have doubled the food we could carry!"

Mr Noakes spluttered. "And cook without proper seasoning? Be my guest! I might be a badger but I'm not a savage."

Pendlebury sighed. "Right – I'll look for something to hunt. King of Rogues, make yourself useful and look that way."

The King of Rogues pointed at Ruth. "Me? Why can't *she* do it? She never does anything!"

"Fine," said Ruth, holding out her hand. "Give me your sword."

He laughed. "Ha! Nice try, missy! You must think I was born yesterday!"

The King of Rogues marched into the fog – Pendlebury shook her head in exasperation and padded off in the other direction.

Col looked around nervously. "Er … should we really be splitting up now?"

Mr Noakes clapped a paw on his shoulder. "Never fear, lad! It's still daylight – the King can't try to get inside your head for hours yet. You have a rest, and I'll keep watch for bogies!"

All the blood drained from Col's face. Mr Noakes sat on the stump, humming merrily to himself.

"Bogies?" said Ruth. "What is this word, please?"

"They're monsters that live under your bed," said Col quietly. "Apparently they're real and we might bump into one."

"That's right!" said Mr Noakes. "Col's always been afraid of bogies, haven't you? You wet the bed once, thinking there was one in your wardrobe!"

Col turned bright red. "I just spilled a glass of water, actually…"

Mr Noakes shuddered. "Trust me, the *last* thing we want is to run into a bogie. Well, that or—"

There was a sudden flash of light in the fog.

Col swung round. "What was that?"

"I saw it too!" said Ruth. "A green glow, yes?"

Col swallowed. "It … it came from where Pendlebury just went. Pendlebury?"

There was no answer. The fog lay still and silent. Mr Noakes sniffed the air – and his eyes widened.

"Rogue! Get back here – we're not alone!"

"KING – OF – ROGUES!" came the reply. "How many times do I have to—?"

There was another green flash, followed by a yelp of pain – and then nothing.

Col gasped. "King of Rogues?"

No reply.

Mr Noakes leaped to his paws. "Stay where you are! Don't move!" He paced the island with his club held steady, a low growl building in his throat.

Ruth stepped closer to Col. "I do not like this," she whimpered. "Do you think it is bogies?"

That was the last thing Col wanted to think about. "I – I don't know. Let's just be ready to run, OK?"

He was trying to sound brave, but the tremble in his voice was unmistakable. He turned to heave Mr Noakes' handbag off the ground – he could barely lift it with all the salt inside – when there was another green flash, right behind them this time. They both screamed and spun round.

The island was empty. Mr Noakes was gone.

"Mr Noakes?"

There was nothing but bright white silence on every side. Col's heart pounded. He felt as if he was trapped inside another nightmare – that at any moment, a set of hands were going to come flying out the fog and clasp around his neck and…

Crack.

The sound was unmistakable. It was the sound of a very small footstep stepping on a very small twig, and it was right behind them. Col and Ruth turned … and stared in disbelief at the thing that was standing on the island.

"Meine güte," said Ruth. "What *is* that?"

Col frowned. "It – it almost looks like…"

There was a final flash of green, and Col saw nothing else.

The Underground Fortress

COL OPENED HIS EYES.

He was ... well, he had no idea where he was. But it was cold, it was dark – and it stank.

He looked up, head throbbing. He was in some sort of dark, wide chamber, with a low black ceiling and thick black walls. He could hear squeaks and scratches in the darkness all around him, like a cavern teeming with rats. There were movements too: queasy green lights, hundreds of them, glowing and fading…

He heard a groan close by and snapped round. Ruth and the Guardians were stretched out on the floor beside him.

"Pendlebury!" Col cried. "What's going on? Where are…"

He tried to reach for her, but his hands were tied. And not with rope either. With … weeds?

"Well, well, well! The prisoners are finally awake!"

The voice was harsh and squeaky – like how a fly would sound if it could talk. It was followed by a chorus of high-pitched giggling from every side. Col gasped. The green lights were moving.

They weren't lights – they were tiny, glowing people.

They were, in fact, the ugliest people Col had ever seen in his life. They had squashed heads and gummy eyes and jagged teeth, and clothes made from cobwebs and apple rinds. Some had acorn helmets and maces made of swung conkers; others were riding armoured squirrels. Every single one of them had a set of mangy moth wings poking out their backs.

"Oops," said Mr Noakes blearily. "Er … looks like we were standing on a fairy fortress."

"Oops?" said Pendlebury. "How could you miss a thousand fairies right beneath us?"

"It's not my fault!" the badger protested. "All that bog stench confused my nose! I'm not a miracle worker!"

Ruth blinked. "Wait – fairies? I was thinking fairies were pretty."

"No," said Pendlebury. "They're like rats with wings."

"Or angry slugs," said Mr Noakes.

"Or wasps," said the King of Rogues, "but not as friendly."

"Silence!"

They looked up. In the centre of the room was a throne made of twisting wood, stretching from the floor to the ceiling. Col finally understood where they were: they were underneath the island in the swamp. The black walls were made of slimy earth, and the throne was built inside the roots of the rotten tree.

Sitting inside the throne was the smallest, ugliest fairy of the lot. He was wearing a pine-cone crown and mangy moss robes, and he was being hand-fed earthworms and fanned with nettles by a pair of unhappily shackled toads. A fairy guard suddenly flew down and whacked Col with a handful of thistles.

"Bow down before King Buttercup, Ruler of the Fairies!" the guard shouted.

"Ow!" said Col. "That hurt!"

Thistles were the least of his worries. Fairies were spies for the Midwinter King – even Mrs Evans had mentioned that. And now he and the Guardians were trapped inside one of their fortresses. What was going to happen to them? King Buttercup slurped down another earthworm and gave them a leer.

"So! Thought you could sneak past us without being spotted, did you? Well, you thought wrong! *No one* gets past the fairies!"

Pendlebury got unsteadily to her feet, balancing awkwardly on her bound paws, and cleared her throat.

"Your Fairiness, this is all a terrible misunderstanding. My friends and I are also King's spies, searching for the Green Man! We must have stumbled on your fortress by accident. If you let us go, we'll happily forgive the mistake and…"

She trailed off. King Buttercup was laughing. All the fairies were tittering along with him, like a cave of smelly bats.

"Nice try, traitor!" snapped King Buttercup. "We know exactly who you are. The Midwinter King has informed all his spies to look out for a boy travelling with a tiger and a knight and a badger. And he has given us *very* clear instructions about what to do when we find you!" He gave them another leer. "That's right! He's coming here himself, to take you back to the Spirit World and make an example of you!"

The Guardians' faces fell in horror. Mr Noakes leaped to his feet.

"You – you filthy beggars! Let us go!" He struggled at the bindings on his wrists. "When I get out of these stupid weeds…"

King Buttercup cackled. "Try all you like, badger! Those weeds around your hands are enchanted bindings of my own making – quite inescapable!" He glanced Ruth and Col up and down. "As for these two – I'm sure the Midwinter King will allow us to keep them once we've handed you over. It's been thousands of years since fairies were last allowed to have human slaves. It'll be just like the old days, when fairies ruled this land from end to end!"

He leaped to his feet.

"Fairies! For too long, we have been forced out of our rightful home by humans and made to live in the Spirit World – but not any more! When the Midwinter King is made ultimate ruler of the Spirit World, we can finally restart our ancient war against humanity!"

The chamber filled with a high-pitched war cry. King Buttercup shook his fists.

"That's right! It'll be just like the old days. We'll make their cakes go flat! We'll spook their dogs! We'll move their things to different places so it's really annoying!" He raised a filthy finger. "Mark my words – soon, there won't be a single milk pail in the land that hasn't been tipped over!"

The fairies cheered. King Buttercup pounded his tiny fists against his puny chest. "And then … ALL THE BUTTER SHALL BE OURS!"

The fairies bellowed with triumph and swarmed around the chamber, sending out a firework of green sparks.

Col glanced at Pendlebury. "That's it? All they want to do is annoy people and steal their butter?"

"Don't get me started," she muttered.

Col felt sick. The fact that the fairies were doing all this for something so stupid somehow made everything worse. They had to find a way to stop the fairies from summoning the Midwinter King. But how? There were thousands of them – Col had nothing on him except his lighting flint and the handbag he'd taken from Mr Noakes. *Think, Col, think!*

"You morons!" the King of Rogues snapped at the fairies. "You don't stand a chance against the humans. The last time you fought them was over two thousand years ago – they've got guns and tanks and planes now!"

King Buttercup snorted. "For your information, puny tin man, we've been arming ourselves in preparation for weeks!" He turned to the others. "Guards! Show him the weaponry we've already stolen from the humans!"

The guards carried in the loot and dumped it in front of the Guardians. There was an old picnic basket, some dirty glass bottles, a bent fork, a deflated bicycle tyre and a wet slipper.

"Taken from right under their noses!" cackled King Buttercup. "They didn't even try to stop us! And now for the greatest weapon of all— Bring in … *the thingy!*"

The fairies rolled something huge across the chamber floor towards them. It took at least a hundred of them to do it: the thingy was the size and shape of a boiler and seemed just as heavy. It took Col a moment to recognize what it was – after all, he'd only seen photographs in newspapers before.

"C-Col?" said Ruth, turning pale. "Is that…"

"Yes," said Col weakly. "Yes it is."

There was no mistaking the unexploded bomb in front of them. They watched in horror as King Buttercup jumped on top of it.

"That's right! It fell from one of the humans' big metal birds, and they didn't even bother coming back to get it!" He gave the bomb an experimental kick. "With this in our hands, we'll finally bring humanity to its knees! Once we work out what it does, and so on."

Col spun round to Pendlebury in horror.

"We have to get out of here!" he hissed. "That's a bomb – a hundred kilos at least! It could go off at any moment!"

Pendlebury held up her bound paws in dismay. "We can't – you heard what King Buttercup said. These magic bonds are unbreakable! We'll have to wait until he's asleep or distracted…"

"I don't think we have that long," Col whimpered as the fairies took it in turns to hit the bomb with sticks.

King Buttercup waved a grubby hand at them. "Guards – take the prisoners away! Search them for any weapons and prepare me a frogspawn bath!

I wish to beautify myself before summoning the Midwinter King."

At his command, the guards grabbed the Guardians and started rifling through their pockets. Col panicked – now was their only chance to get away. There had to be some way to escape, there *had* to be...

Suddenly one of the fairies tried to take Ruth's kitbag, and she lashed out wildly. "No! Get off, you horrid creatures! It is mine!"

King Buttercup gasped. "She's hiding something! Quick! Check all their bags!"

A dozen fairies instantly descended on Ruth and started scratching and biting her, but she fought them off with everything she had. Another guard suddenly tried to grab Mr Noakes' handbag from Col and opened the top, pulling the cotton sack of salt from inside.

"For goodness sake, there's nothing in there!" cried Col. "It's just..."

And all of a sudden he remembered Mrs Evans, crouched in the darkness of Aunt Claire's garden.

Salt! Can't stand the stuff. Have to stop and count every grain, you see. That should keep the little runts out of my butter...

Col acted fast. He pointed at the cotton sack. "No! Not *that* bag! Torture us all you want – enslave us if you have to – but please, *please* don't touch our sack of precious butter!"

The sound of a thousand fairies gasping at the same time was something to behold. King Buttercup's eyes widened with glee.

"Butter? Did you just say *butter*?"

He grabbed the cotton sack from Col and raised it high above his head, salivating down himself like a water sculpture.

"Hahahaha – bad move, prisoners! Now your delicious, creamy, melt-in-the-mouth butter is all mi—"

He tore open the bag and salt exploded everywhere, covering the chamber from end to end like snow.

There was a very long, very loud silence. Several thousand eyes fell onto the tiny white grains covering every inch of the dirt floor. The fairies took in a deep breath – and screamed as one.

"SAAAAALT."

Within seconds, the chamber was madness. The fairies swarmed over each other like flies, scrambling across the floor to count every grain.

"One, two, three…"

"Twenty-seven, twenty-eight…"

"Gah, now I have to start over! One, two, three…"

King Buttercup waved his hands feebly. "No! Don't count them! Fight the urge, fairies! Fight … the…"

His eyes were slowly, uncontrollably, dragged towards the floor. His teeth clenched – his brow dripped sweat – then, with a wail of resignation, he threw himself to the floor and started counting alongside them. "Out of my way – kings first! One, two, three…"

With King Buttercup finally distracted, the magical weeds around the Guardians' hands snapped apart. Col leaped onto Pendlebury's back, pulling Ruth behind him, and Mr Noakes quickly followed. Only the King of Rogues lingered.

"King of Rogues! Come on!" snapped Pendlebury.

The knight had managed to reclaim his sword and was waving it around his head like a helicopter. "Ha! You think I'm leaving now, after what he called me? PUNY! The nerve!" He stood his ground. "You cowards can run if you like – I'm not leaving until I've cut off that little squirt's beard to wipe my—"

Pendlebury picked him up by the plume of his helmet and carried him out of the chamber in her mouth, like a cat with a kitten. The King of Rogues kicked furiously.

"Stop it! Put me down! This is an outrage!"

Pendlebury calmly made her way out of the fortress and back onto the swamp. Col looked around in surprise. The fog had finally cleared.

"The weather," he said, confused. "It got better."

"Perfect!" said Pendlebury. "Those fairies will be

counting for hours before they can tell the Midwinter King about us. That's enough time to find another shelter for the night and…"

She trailed off. The King of Rogues had struggled free of his helmet and was charging back into the fortress.

"King of Rogues! Get back here right now!"

"NO!" He swung round. His hair was dishevelled and his eyes were desperate. He was a knight on the edge. "I will NOT be humiliated like that! Being made to sit at the back is one thing, being ordered about by a six-year-old girl is another, but being insulted by a fairy…"

"I am eleven," said Ruth.

"I – DON'T – CARE!" bellowed the King of Rogues. He pointed to the tunnel. "Give me one good reason why I shouldn't march back into that fortress right now and—"

KABOOM!

The ground erupted, sending a column of mud a hundred feet high. There was a short pause – then swamp rained down in every direction. The air was filled with the sound of a thousand screaming fairies, a thousand tiny bodies hitting the mud, a thousand bleary groans – and then, after a short pause, the sound of steady counting.

Pendlebury had managed to grow at the last second, shielding the rest of the Guardians from the worst of the explosion.

She turned back round. "You were saying?"

The swamp directly behind the King of Rogues was now a vast crater. The knight hadn't moved an inch the entire time. He was covered from head to toe in filth and pondweed. He opened his mouth and spat out a handful of frogspawn.

"On second thoughts," he said, "let's just go."

"You're sure?"

"Absolutely."

"You're sitting at the back."

"Yes, very good, whatever you say."

He jumped onto Pendlebury's back and didn't say a thing for the next two hours.

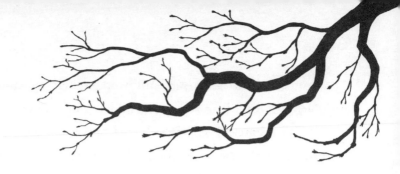

Shelter

B Y THE TIME THEY FOUND A FOREST TO HIDE IN, the swamp was long behind them and the sun was setting. This time, there was no helpful cave to use as shelter. The best they could find was a hole in the ground where an old oak tree had toppled in the snow, its roots jutting from the ground like ribs and forming a crude roof over the top.

"This will have to do," sighed Pendlebury. "We'll be protected when it snows, at least."

Ruth looked at the hole in horror. "In *there*? But it is filthy!"

"So are we," said Col.

They were still caked in slime after their run-in with the fairies. Ruth shook her head firmly. "No! I am not sleeping in a mud pit! I am cold, I am tired, I am dirty…"

"I can lick you clean if you want," Pendlebury offered.

Ruth stared at her, waiting to see if she was joking.

She wasn't. Ruth glowered and hunkered down under the tree roots. "I hate the countryside," she muttered.

Col leaped off Pendlebury's back. He was trying not to think about what lay ahead, but it was no use: the memory of the Midwinter King prickled at the back of his mind. "R-right. I'll gather some firewood…"

"I'll go with you!" said the King of Rogues, jumping beside him.

Col shook his head. "Actually it would be better if you—"

The King of Rogues grabbed his arm before he could protest and dragged him away through the trees. He kept going until they were well out of sight of the others, and then he suddenly stopped.

Col blinked. "What's the matter?"

"Nothing's the matter!" said the King of Rogues. He folded his arms and looked down at his feet, as if there was something very interesting there.

Col cleared his throat. "King of Rogues? Is there something you want to say?"

"What? No! I'm fine! Everything's fine!"

"Are you sure?"

There was an extremely long pause. The King of Rogues opened his mouth, then closed it, then looked at the trees for a bit, then looked at his sword, then looked at his feet again.

Col sighed. "Fine – suit yourself. I'll start getting some…"

It all came out at once.

"Look, she turns up out of nowhere and all of a sudden everyone thinks she's amazing and we have to listen to her ideas and she gets to sit at the front like she's just as important as any one of us and you like her much better than you like me even though *I've* been around right from the very beginning and my ideas are just as good as anyone else's, and I can do cartwheels."

It took a while for Col to piece all this together.

"You mean … Ruth? You're jealous of Ruth?"

The knight's helmet almost popped off. "Jealous? Me? Of her? How funny! That makes me laugh! Aha ha ha ha, ha ha ha ha, ha ha ha, ha ha ha ha ha, haha, ahahahaha, ha ha ha ha…"

Col felt a pang of guilt. It wasn't the King of Rogues' fault that he was so proud and difficult – after all, that was how Col had made him. He'd wanted a Guardian who was the exact opposite of himself: someone who was never afraid, who would always fight back, who would never back down. Col was beginning to understand that that kind of strength came at a price.

"You don't need to be jealous of Ruth – no one could ever replace you," said Col. "You're one of my oldest friends! I'll never forget everything you've done for me…"

"Well you forgot before, didn't you?" the King of Rogues snapped.

Col was shocked. The King of Rogues regretted what he'd said immediately.

"I – I'm sorry, I didn't mean that. But after what happened to your dad…" He shook his head. "We wanted so much to help you, Col, to protect you. But you just blocked us out. You forgot us."

Col shook his head. "I didn't forget you."

"You tried to." The knight scuffed his feet on the floor. "Our kind always get forgotten eventually. That's just how it is. They make you, they love you, and then one day – they grow out of you." He looked up, and Col saw that his eyes were red. "But *we* never grow out of you, Col."

Col had no idea what to say. It had never occurred to him that the King of Rogues could have his feelings hurt. He was so loud, so confident, so courageous. But it turned out that underneath all that armour, the King of Rogues was more vulnerable than anyone. Maybe that was why he wore it.

"I'm sorry," Col whispered. "I never meant to upset you."

The knight smiled sadly. "I know you didn't. And I don't blame you for being angry with us, I really don't. But it was awful, watching you go through it all alone.

If I could have fought it for you, Col, I would have done. Fighting's easy. It's… It's letting you go that I can't do."

They stood for a while in silence as the forest grew dark around them, and the first flakes of snow began to filter down through the trees. Col could make out a trail of searchlights along the horizon, scanning the skyline for planes. Then, just like that, the King of Rogues snapped out of it.

"Right!" he said, clapping his hands. "No point going on about it. Let's find some food!"

Col blinked. The King of Rogues was trying to pretend that their heartfelt conversation hadn't happened. He suddenly realized who the knight reminded him of: it was Aunt Claire.

He felt yet another stab of guilt. He'd left her without so much as a backward glance. He pushed the feelings down. He couldn't worry about that – he had enough things to worry about as it was. He looked around the empty forest. "I don't think we'll find any food here before it gets dark. I think we might have to go hun—"

There was a splash behind him – Col swung round. The King of Rogues stood knee-deep in a stream, half a dozen fish already stuffed flapping in his breastplate.

"Col," he said haughtily, "I have had *quite enough* of being insulted for one evening, thank you very much."

They returned to camp laden with food and firewood. Col got a blaze going while Mr Noakes gutted and scrubbed the fish, stuffing them with forest herbs and roasting them over the fire on twigs. The smell was so good that even Ruth emerged from the hole under the tree. She was still wearing her raid helmet, but her mud-caked dungarees had been changed to a green velvet dress with pearl buttons. Even in the firelight, Col could tell it was expensive.

"Where did that come from?" he asked.

Ruth shifted, as if deciding whether or not she should tell him. "It is my last dress from home."

"Is that what you were hiding in your kitbag?"

"None of your beeswax."

Col smiled. He wished Ruth wasn't still being so secretive with him, but after everything she had done for him in the last twenty-four hours, he supposed that she had earned the right to privacy.

They ate like kings – even Ruth ate a fish with her bare hands, after checking it over and muttering something under her breath in German. By the time they were done it had started snowing again, and coldness was settling on the forest like stone. Col's legs began to throb. They were OK during the day, when he was riding Pendlebury and they were covered by her fur, but at night they were absolutely freezing. Their colour had now turned from rhubarb to beetroot.

"We'd better get inside," said Pendlebury. "The storm will be here soon."

Col swallowed. He had been dreading this moment all day – the moment when he would have to go to sleep, and his mind would once again be prey for the Midwinter King. Pendlebury saw the look on his face and understood immediately.

"Maybe it would be best if you stayed awake tonight, Col. You can sleep during the day while we're travelling – the King's powers will be less strong then."

Col nodded silently. Pendlebury looked so concerned for him. She was always watching out for him.

"Remember, Col – it's us he wants, not you. The Midwinter King can't harm you: our kind are forbidden from harming a human. It's our most sacred law. He'll try to frighten you into giving up information about us, but that's all."

Col appreciated her saying it, but it didn't make him feel any better. The thought that he wasn't even safe inside his own head any more made him feel sick.

Pendlebury turned to the others. "We'll take it in shifts to keep the fire burning," she said. "We'll need all the protection we can get to shield us from the King's eyes. Mr Noakes – you're on first watch. King of Rogues – you're on second. I'll stay close to Col and make sure he stays awake."

Col frowned. "Mr Noakes can't stay out here in the storm..."

Mr Noakes chuckled. "Don't you worry about me, lad, I'll be right as rain!" He waved his club. "If any of the Midwinter King's spies try their luck, I'll make sure they regret it!"

Col felt a huge rush of affection for him. The badger was giving up so much to protect him – all the Guardians were. How could Col be frightened in the face of such bravery?

They settled under the roots of the tree and Pendlebury grew to fill the hole, wrapping them in her fur and hiding them from view. It was deliciously warm and close – after such a long and exhausting day, the King of Rogues fell asleep in seconds. Despite everything Pendlebury had said about staying awake, her eyes soon drifted shut as well. Col couldn't blame her: she'd carried them fifteen miles today in gruelling weather on just a few hours' sleep. She must have been exhausted.

Col shuffled. Fifteen miles. They had four days left and over a hundred miles to go. If they didn't speed up, they were never going to make it to London in time.

Soon, the roots were filled with the sound of quiet, steady breathing. Col sat in silence, his mind churning with thoughts of Rose and the raid and everything that lay in-between. The ground beneath him was frozen hard, and tiny draughts of ice-cold air kept pushing inside the trunk and up his spine. That was fine – he needed to stay awake. He had to be strong. He had to turn his mind into a fortress. The Guardians were counting on him. But all he could think about were those gleaming eyes in the dark, waiting for him to fall asleep…

"You are shaking," said Ruth.

Col nearly leaped out of his skin. "I'm not scared! Just cold!"

Ruth sounded surprised. "This is perhaps because you are wearing short trousers."

"It's my uniform," said Col quickly. "I'm in the—"

"Yes, yes, I know."

They sat in silence while Col waited for his heart to stop pounding. There was no chance of him going to sleep now. "You're awake too."

Ruth nodded. "Yes. I am thinking about this raid." She shuffled. "This sister of yours – this Rose. She is very lucky, I think, to have someone who is coming to save her."

Col frowned. "Well … I have to. She's the only family I have left, apart from Aunt Claire. My mum left after I was born, and Dad…"

He stopped. He'd never told a stranger about what happened to Dad. Everyone in Buxton had already known about it. How would the words sound, coming out of his mouth?

"Dad died in an accident a few months ago," he said quickly, wanting to get it over with. "It's just me and Rose now."

The words hung in the air, just as they were – just a fact.

Ruth nodded. "Yes. I heard you say this, after your nightmare. I am sorry. It is terrible, to lose a parent like this."

Col nodded. "It was."

It was strange: he'd thought that talking about something so serious would make Ruth feel uncomfortable, but she didn't seem to mind at all. The silence between them felt different this time – less cold. It was like the two of them had moved a little closer. Asking the next question felt like the most obvious thing in the world.

"What about you?" said Col, turning to her. "What are your parents like?"

Ruth didn't reply for a long time. Col could almost *feel* her decide whether or not to answer him.

"Mama is a famous singer," she said eventually. "She performed in many big concerts in Berlin. Always she is the centre of attention. She does not like cooking, and she cannot mend clothes… But she makes everything exciting, even boring things."

Col nodded. He could well imagine that. Ruth was so elegant, almost stately, with a touch of high drama thrown in for good measure. Having a performer for a mother made sense.

"Papa is a journalist," Ruth continued. "*Was*, I mean. He wrote many articles, telling everyone about the terrible things that the Nazis were doing. When Hitler took over they made him leave his job. He is very brave. This happened to many other people also, when the Nazis were in charge."

She stopped talking, so Col risked a question. "Is that why you left Germany?"

"Yes."

"When?"

Ruth shuffled. "Two years ago."

Col could almost sense her closing up again. He was going to stop – but then he realized something.

"Hang on a second. You've only been speaking English for two years?"

Ruth nodded. Col was speechless. Ruth spoke English almost as well as he did – certainly a lot better than he could speak German. He suddenly had a vision of her at the front of her class, putting up her hand for every question, always knowing the right answer.

"That's amazing!" he said. "How did you learn so fast?"

Ruth shrugged. "I did not have a choice. I did not want anyone to know that I was German."

He could understand that. He thought about the German men at Dad's work who'd been arrested as enemy aliens when the war started, even though they had nothing to do with the Nazis. He thought about the children who accused Ruth of being a spy. No wonder she wanted to hide where she came from.

"Col," she suddenly said, "can I ask you a question?"

Col nodded. "Sure."

"Do you think we will make it to London before this raid?"

Col gulped. He didn't want to lie to her – but he didn't want to think about how behind they were, either.

"We're going to have to speed up if we want to stay on track. I think we've managed twenty miles a day since we left, and we left on the twenty-second so…"

It was like being struck by a lightning bolt. Col sat in stunned amazement. Ruth glanced at him.

"What? What is it?" she said.

"It's December twenty-fourth!" said Col. "It's Christmas Eve!"

Ruth blinked. "And?"

Col looked down at himself, covered in mud in a tree stump, and started giggling. He couldn't stop. He laughed until tears rolled down his face and snot came out of his nose and the Guardians grumbled and shuffled in their sleep. It made him feel a hundred times better.

"What is so funny?" said Ruth.

Col sighed. "Sorry. It's just that I've spent months thinking about what I was going to be doing for Christmas. I never thought I'd be in a hole under a tree in the middle of nowhere."

Ruth shivered, and shuffled closer. "Yes, well, I never thought I'd ride a tiger."

They fell asleep like that, leaning on each other.

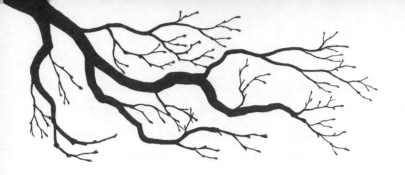

The Bone House

THE MIDWINTER KING CROUCHED IN THE darkness, waiting.

The bones formed a tight shell around him, blocking out the daylight. They were the very same bones that had made his horse: they had done a fine job of hiding him in darkness. The Midwinter King had spent hours patiently waiting for midnight to return. And now, here it was. The height of his powers.

It was his time.

The bones split apart like an eggshell and the Midwinter King stood up, gazing at the world ahead of him. Winds whipped across the hills like a pack of wild dogs. Snow threw itself in tidal waves against the land. Wherever he turned, the world was cowering, frightened, desolate. Those who slept, slept uneasily; even their dreams were restless.

The Midwinter King smiled. It was a pleasure to

see first-hand what his powers had wrought. He was bringing the worst storms ever seen, travelling between worlds, controlling humans for the first time. His powers were growing greater every day. Once the raid had come, and the Green Man was destroyed, there would be no telling what new powers he might be capable of. Perhaps he might even rule over both worlds, the spirit and the human, controlling everything in existence.

Was that not worth a little patience?

He gazed across the world of darkness, and focused all his power. This time, he would not let the boy's mind get away from him. He would be fast: he would scare Col before he could respond and clamp inside his mind. He would find out where the Guardians were hiding, and then he would send everything he had after them. He had seen enough of the boy's memories to know what he feared the most, what was most precious to him.

Making a nightmare for him would be easy.

25 December 1940

CHRISTMAS DAY
Radio Broadcast by
King George VI

REMEMBER this. If war brings its separations, it brings new unity also, the unity which comes from common perils and common sufferings willingly shared. To be good comrades and good neighbours in trouble is one of the finest opportunities of the civilian population. We must go on thinking less about ourselves and more for one another, for so, and so only, can we hope to make the world a better place and life a worthier thing.

The Trap

COL STOOD IN THE RUBBLE OF LONDON. There was nothing left: the raid had destroyed it utterly. The streets were hung with smoke, strewn with shattered glass. Col was alone. Everything was rubble and dust and silence. This was a world where the sun never shone, and the sky was always black, and everything was dead.

He walked the empty streets until he came to Euston Station. Suddenly there was Rose, standing at the very spot on the platform where he had last seen her. Col ran to her and saw that she was clutching a canvas kitbag to her chest. Only it wasn't a bag – it was a bomb. She was cradling it in her arms like a baby.

"It's just for a little while, Collie," she was saying. "Just for a little while."

"Rose, we have to go!" he cried. "The Midwinter King is coming and—"

It happened. The ceiling tore open and darkness gushed into the station, swallowing everything it touched, pounding down the platform towards them. There was no fighting it – no stopping it.

Col cried out. "He's found us! We have to—"

But when he looked round Rose was gone. So was the train station. He was standing in a dark street, facing a set of black metal railings. A man was lying beneath them, crumpled beside his own bicycle. The cracked bike lamp was flickering orange, violet, orange, violet...

"Dad?" said Col.

The man's head snapped up. It wasn't Dad. His eyes were gone. In their place were two dying stars, coming from somewhere far beyond him.

There you are, said the Midwinter King.

Col screamed. *"NO!"*

"NO!"

Col woke with a start.

It was dawn. He was still in the shelter beneath the tree trunk. Ruth and the Guardians were snoring peacefully beside him.

Col sat still, heart pounding. He hadn't imagined it – something had dragged him out of the nightmare at the very last second, before the Midwinter King could get inside his mind. Col had even *felt* something pulling on his shoulders ... but there was no one that could have done it. Everyone was asleep. Pendlebury and Ruth and the King of Rogues...

Col frowned. The King of Rogues was supposed to have taken over from Mr Noakes by now, but he was still here, snoozing and mumbling.

"Mr Noakes?" said Col.

He clambered out of the roots and looked around. The fire had burned down to ashes – Mr Noakes was nowhere to be seen. The forest around him was like a Christmas picture postcard: calm and white and muffled in snow. A set of paw prints led straight from the fire and out of sight over a nearby slope. Col could hear voices coming from the other side.

"For the last time, there's *nothing there*..."

"Nev, I know a badger when we see one!"

"I told you, it's not *A* badger. It's *MY* badger."

Col gasped. He scrambled over to the nearest tree and peered down the slope. What he saw turned his stomach to stone.

A gang of men stood in the clearing below, wearing helmets and long cloaks. They were Home Guard soldiers: local men who'd signed up to protect their villages in case of an invasion. They had a selection of homemade weapons – garden forks, knives tied to broomstick handles, cudgels and clubs – that made them look more like scruffy gardeners than soldiers. The one at the front had a shotgun in the crook of his arm and was beaming from ear to ear.

"Talk about luck!" he said. "I was *livid* about doing duty on Christmas morning, but looks like I've hit the jackpot! Roast badger, here we come!"

Col's blood turned cold. Strung to the tree in front of the soldier was Mr Noakes, his back paw caught in a snare. He was thrashing wildly to try to escape, but the more he thrashed, the more the wire tightened around his paw. His waistcoat lay on the ground beside him, next to a scattered pile of sticks. Col quickly pieced it together: Mr Noakes had gone for more firewood, got caught in the snare, then torn off his clothes to try to look normal when he heard the men approaching. Col had to do something – but what? How was he possibly going to stop these men by himself?

"For the last time, Gary, you can't roast a badger," said one of the soldiers. "The meat's tough enough as it is."

"That's right!" said another. "You have to boil it. Tail makes a lovely gravy."

"Boil it? I've been snaring badger since before you were born, mate, it's smoking or nothing."

"Who's got time for that?" said Gary. "I told Mrs Digby she'd have a Christmas roast, and she's getting one!"

"Lads," said one of the others, "for the last time, there's *nothing there*…"

Everyone groaned.

"*Shut up,* Nev!"

"We can all see it!"

"Well, *I* can't!" said Nev, now furious. "If this is another stupid joke about my glasses…"

Col's heart sank – this was even worse than he'd feared. Every single one of the Home Guard soldiers could see magic, except for Nev. The odds of it happening were astronomical – but then, statistics were the least of his worries now. The men were going to eat Mr Noakes – and there was no way Col could warn the other Guardians in time. He had to think of a way of getting rid of the men and saving Mr Noakes himself, fast – but what?

Meanwhile, Mr Noakes was lashing out desperately at the man with the shotgun.

"Careful, Gary!" one of the other men shouted. "He'll take your leg off if you get too close!"

"That's right," said another. "It's bad luck, being bitten by a badger."

Gary turned and stared at them. "Bad luck? Of course it's bad luck! You've just been bitten by a badger!"

"Wait – bad luck?" said another. "I heard it was good luck."

Gary threw up his hands. "How could it possibly be good luck?!"

"Seriously, lads, joke's over, you've all had a laugh…"

"SHUT UP, NEV."

"*All* of you, shut up!" said Gary, raising the shotgun. "You're putting me off my aim…"

"NO!"

Col was racing down the slope before he knew he was doing it. The soldiers stared at him in amazement.

"Oi!"

"Where'd *he* come from?"

"Are those *shorts*?!"

"Blimey, I've never seen legs that colour…"

Mr Noakes' face lit up with relief, then quickly replaced it with horror when Col leaped between him and the shotgun.

"Don't shoot – please! He's mine!"

Gary frowned. "*Your* badger? Who the hell are you?"

Col froze – he couldn't use his real name when the police might be looking for him. He needed a fake name, fast – Ben? Bill? Bob?

"Bulb," he said, before he could stop himself.

He saw Mr Noakes wince out of the corner of his eye. There was a heavy silence. The soldiers stared at him.

"Your name is Bulb," said Gary.

Col wracked his brains for an explanation. "I'm from London."

The soldiers all *aaaahhhh*ed at the same time.

"*That* explains the clothes!"

"Went down there once, you wouldn't believe the price of a pint, no idea what all the fuss was about…"

"Seriously, guys, if this is all part of the joke…"

"SHUT UP, NEV."

Col sighed with relief. It was a good lie. If there was one thing he'd learned from living in Buxton, it was that the rest of the country thought Londoners were weirdos who ate chips all day and had no idea what a cow was. The only one who didn't seem convinced was Gary. He narrowed his eyes and took another drag of his cigarette.

"If it's your badger," he said suspiciously, "what's it doing in my snare?"

Col thought fast. "He's … my pet! I've raised him myself, ever since he was a baby badger. I've taught him tricks!" He turned to Mr Noakes. "Er … what's two plus two?"

Mr Noakes glared at him with indignation, then held up four fingers. The men were amazed.

"Would you look at that!"

"A counting badger!"

"Right, that's it, I'm going home."

"SHUT UP, NEV."

"Well, thanks for looking after him!" said Col, trying to sound breezy. "I'll take him back home and put him in his, er, little hutch."

He turned to release Mr Noakes – and felt a hand press down on his shoulder.

"Not so fast, sonny."

Col gazed up. Gary's cold, unblinking eyes were staring down at him, the cigarette dangling from his smirking lip.

"My snare," he said quietly. "My badger."

The others groaned with protest. "Ahhh, Gary, come on!"

"It's Christmas!"

"You can't eat a counting badger."

Gary spun round. "*Shut up!* Mrs Digby and I haven't had a proper meat ration in months – I'm not spending another Christmas choking down Mock Banana! Got it?"

The men backed off. Gary thrust Col to one side and raised the shotgun, fixing Mr Noakes in its sights…

"NO!" cried Col.

The shot never came. Gary's gun was whipped from his hands and flung across the clearing. He had just enough time to look up before something huge and hairy landed on him from above and pummelled him to the ground. All the men screamed – except for Nev, who was beaming from ear to ear.

"WOW! All right, I take it back, I don't know how you did that but it's actually pretty g—"

The thing leaped up and knocked out Nev with a single punch. The others fumbled with their weapons while the thing flung itself at them in turn, knocking each one out cold. One of the soldiers managed to grab Gary's shotgun from the ground and aimed it at the thing, but the thing kicked up the barrel just as it fired with a terrific *BANG*. The soldier was still reloading when the branch he'd blasted off the tree landed on his head.

Col stared as the thing unfurled itself to its full height in the centre of the clearing. It was as scrawny as a scarecrow, covered from head to toe in coarse hair, with six arms and legs that bent in the wrong direction. It had teeth like bear traps, claws like kitchen knives, and one enormous, blood-red eye that stared directly at Col.

It was also wearing a Father Christmas hat.

"Hi!" It held out a hand. "Leonard the bogie. Pleasure to meet you."

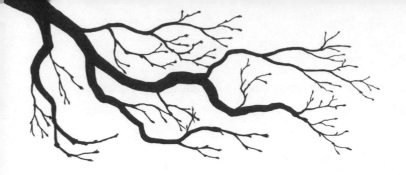

Leonard the Bogie

COL WAS FROZEN TO THE SPOT. IT WAS A BOGIE – the monster of his childhood nightmares. The most feared of the Midwinter King's spies. It was standing right in front of him, more terrifying than he could possibly have imagined … and it wanted to shake his hand.

When several seconds had passed and Col still hadn't moved, the bogie patted him on the head instead.

"Sorry for scaring you! I thought you could do with some help. I hate bullies, don't you?"

He unfurled a claw the size of a scimitar and used it to cut the wire holding Mr Noakes to the tree. Mr Noakes rubbed his back paw. "Th-thank you."

"You're welcome! We have to look out for each other, don't we? I'm Leonard! You're naked, by the way."

Mr Noakes looked down at himself, yelped with embarrassment, and raced behind a bush with his waistcoat. Leonard turned to Col and clapped his six hands together.

"So! What shall we do now?"

Col blinked. "W-we?"

"Sure! It's a beautiful day – no point wasting it! We should go for a walk. Or have a chat! I love chatting!" Leonard's face dawned with delight. "Oh wow – we could walk and chat *at the same time*!"

"Col!"

Pendlebury and the others appeared at the top of the slope and were racing towards them. Col had never been so happy to see his Guardians – surely they could protect him from this terrible monster?

"We heard the gunshot!" cried Pendlebury. "What on earth—?"

"Hi! I'm Leonard!"

They came to a screeching halt. The King of Rogues' face fell. "Oh, no, not..."

"A bogie, yes!" said Leonard, holding out a hand. "Leonard! Nice to meet you!"

Mr Noakes emerged from the bush, now fully dressed.

"Leonard, er ... saved my life," he muttered.

The bogie waved a hand. "Nothing to it! Talk about luck! There I was, thinking I'd be spending Christmas Day all by myself, and who do I bump into but..."

Quick as a flash, the King of Rogues drew his sword and held the tip to Leonard's throat.

"Right, you – cut the act! Where are the other spies? Waiting around the corner to ambush us?"

Leonard beamed at the sword like he'd just been offered a bag of sweets.

"Wow, what a great sword! I love swords. There's no need to stab me. I'm not a spy! I want to help you!"

The King of Rogues snorted. "Oh, please! We all know the bogies are allied to the Midwinter King."

Leonard shook his head, suddenly serious.

"Not all of us. Lots of bogies didn't want to fight for the Midwinter King, but he forced everyone into doing it. My family are loyal to the Green Man – that's why we snuck over the barriers before Barghest closed them off, to try to find him again. There are dozens of us over here, fighting for the resistance!"

Pendlebury frowned. "Hang on… Resistance? There are more creatures loyal to the Green Man on this side?"

Leonard nodded. "All kinds! Elves, hobs, brownies … we've even got some goblins and fairies fighting for us, if you can believe that."

"What about the giants?" said the King of Rogues. "Have they chosen a side yet?"

Leonard shook his head. "They're still too busy arguing with each other. We could do with them on our side – we've been searching for weeks for the Green Man, but there's been no sign of him. We know he'll be trying to heal himself somewhere, but we can't find where he's hiding. That's what I was doing when I ran into you!"

Pendlebury frowned. "Hang on – how are all of you hiding from the Midwinter King?"

Leonard leaned in secretively, as if the unconscious men on the ground might somehow hear him.

"Get this. There are places on this side where even *his* eyes can't reach. We call them sanctuaries – ancient places, where the old magic still flows. There are dozens all over the country, and we're finding more every day. We think the Green Man must be hiding in one of them – that's why no one can find him. It's how us rebels have been able to hide from the Midwinter King too! My cousin and I are staying in one that's just over a day's walk from here – I can take you to it right now!"

The King of Rogues looked suspicious. "Why do you want to help us?"

Leonard leaned in even closer, his eyes widening. "Well, you're *them*, aren't you? The ones the Midwinter King is looking for. The whole Spirit World is talking about you! They say that he left his throne to bring back three spirits, and he *still* hasn't found you! Everyone's saying he must be losing his powers!" Leonard shook his head. "It's incredible – three imaginary friends, beating the lord of darkness! How did you even manage to break over the barrier by yourselves?"

The Guardians suddenly looked alarmed.

"No reason!" said Mr Noakes quickly.

The others glared at him. Col frowned – Mr Noakes was lying, and he was terrible at it too. But why? What was he trying to hide?

"Well, the sanctuary's twenty miles away," Leonard said. "It's just outside a place called Leicester. We can make it there by nightfall if we leave now…"

Col gasped. "Leicester's only a hundred miles from London!"

His heart lifted. If they could make it there by nightfall, they'd be back on track – and he'd be able to sleep without the Midwinter King getting inside his head too.

"Exactly!" said Leonard. "And we can have a lovely chat on the way too! I love chats. They're almost as good as hats! I don't know which I like better – chats or hats! Speaking of which, do you like my hat? I found it in a ditch and…"

Col smiled. The more Leonard talked, the more harmless Col could see he was. He might look like a monster from your worst nightmares, but underneath it he was more like an eight-foot-tall, annoying younger brother. The Guardians weren't quite so charmed by him.

They turned away in a huddle while Leonard continued talking, oblivious.

"What do you think?" said Pendlebury. "Do we go with him?"

"No," said Mr Noakes.

"Absolutely not," said the King of Rogues.

"Not in one million years," said Ruth.

Col frowned. "Why not? He seems nice." He pointed at Leonard, who had stopped talking and was now chasing a feather. "I don't get it. I thought bogies were terrifying monsters that hid under your bed."

The King of Rogues laughed. "Oh, they hide under your bed all right! Then they wake you up in the middle of the night to ask you what your favourite type of dog is, or whether you prefer the sun or the moon. Most people are too busy screaming to notice how annoying they are."

Pendlebury sighed. "But if those sanctuaries mean that we're hidden from the Midwinter King ... they might be our only hope of getting to London safely. The King's going to be searching for Col's mind harder than ever now."

Col nodded. "He got into my dreams again last night. It was even worse this time – it was like he'd created a nightmare for me to walk into. I only just woke up in time."

A shard of guilt cut across Pendlebury's face – she clearly felt terrible about falling asleep when she was supposed to be protecting him. Col considered mentioning the hand that he had felt on his shoulder, pulling him out of the nightmare at the last second ... but decided against it. He didn't want to give Pendlebury any more to worry about.

"Then that settles it," she said. "We head for the sanctuary."

"Are you sure you can cover twenty miles before nightfall?" asked Col, concerned.

"I have to," said Pendlebury grimly. "It'll be easier with Leonard showing us the way. I think we can trust him. No matter how ... *eccentric* he might be."

She turned back to Leonard, who was calmly eating a leaf.

"Leonard – we would like to take you up on your kind offer, please. Can you show us to your cousin's place?"

Leonard gasped for joy. "Of course! We can have a chat on the way! I love chats! I haven't had one in ages because people keep running away and screaming whenever they see me, but you can't have everything, can you?"

He leaped onto Pendlebury's back and Col perched behind him. The others reluctantly joined, trying to sit as far away from Leonard as they possibly could.

"No," said the King of Rogues. "*I* want to go at the back."

"No," said Ruth. "It is my turn."

"I insist," said Mr Noakes.

"*I* insist!" said the King of Rogues.

Col gazed at the sky. The sun had risen fully now, casting pink stripes across the clouds. Once again, he felt like a candle of hope had been lit inside him. He and Leonard might be from different worlds, fighting different battles, but just knowing creatures like him existed somehow made everything feel easier.

And besides – it was Christmas.

"Right! We've got a long journey ahead of us," said Leonard. "Anyone know any jokes?"

"I do!" said Pendlebury.

"Great!" said Leonard. "We'll take it in turns to tell our favourite ones! I know hundreds of them! Hundreds and hundreds and hundreds and…"

"Kill me," whispered the King of Rogues as they tore through the trees.

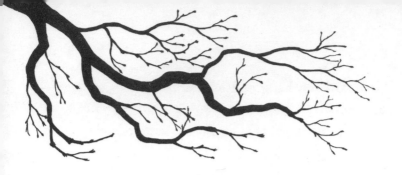

The Bunker

"LEFT AT THIS WALL AND THEN ON ACROSS THE FIELD. I saw a dog here once! He ran away when he saw me, of course. So did the rest of the fox hunt! People are always doing that. You're not like most of the other humans I meet – you haven't run away screaming and crying yet, not even once. Abigail's going to love you! She's my cousin – the one we're staying with. I should warn you, she *does* like to talk a lot…"

Leonard's voice droned steadily on as they made their way across the landscape, racing across fields sliced up with barbed wire and leaping over stone walls that traced the hills like backbones. The world was deserted: for miles they saw nothing except gun emplacements and flocks of birds that burst from the earth in black handfuls. Every now and then they would spot an occasional sign of life – a stone spire rising out of the treetops, a lone Christmas walker, a barrage balloon strung over a town like a floating

192

whale – and Pendlebury would change her course. At one point a convoy of army trucks rattled down the road towards them, and they had to duck behind a wall until the coast was clear again. Apart from that, it was as if they were the only people left in the world.

They saw signs of the war wherever they went. They passed road signs painted with scrawled messages warning about bomb craters in the road ahead. They saw sandbags piled up along country roads, enormous holes dug for anti-aircraft guns, random watchtowers stretching over the hills. They passed a string of half-built houses in the middle of nowhere, filled with canisters of petrol, designed to light on fire during a raid and confuse enemy planes. The countryside was preparing itself for war, waiting for the moment when tanks would turn paddocks into battlefields and fields into front lines.

Finally, just as the sun was beginning to set, they saw something glimmering in the snow ahead.

"There it is – Leicester!" said Leonard.

Col was amazed. It was an actual city – his first proper sign of civilization in days. He could make out ragged gaps in the rooftops where enemy bombs had chewed the skyline, and back gardens dotted with homemade Anderson shelters. He had almost forgotten cities existed.

"And there's my cousin's place!" said Leonard proudly.

He pointed to a small brick hut with slit windows, jutting out the hillside in front of them.

Col frowned. "That's an army pillbox."

"Yep!" said Leonard. "They built it on a magical sanctuary without realizing!"

"Weren't there soldiers using it?" asked Col.

"Oh, there were loads of them! But they ran away when they saw Abigail and now no one comes here any more. Yoo hoo! Abigail!"

A great spidery monster was curling out of the pillbox, even bigger and hairier than Leonard. Col gave her a wave. He was getting used to bogies now, and like Leonard, Abigail seemed friendly despite her terrifying appearance. Maybe it was her flowery apron.

"Leonard! You've brought friends! I love friends! You know what they say – a friend in need is a friend indeed! And a friend indeed is…"

"I'm not sure I can handle much more of this," said the King of Rogues, his left eye twitching.

"Yes, you can," snapped Pendlebury. "I've been carrying five people on my back all day. I'm exhausted."

"I don't think we're getting *any* sleep with those two around," muttered Mr Noakes.

Col gazed up at the crescent moon. It was thinner than ever before. They still had a hundred miles to go, and only three days to do it … but Col felt hopeful.

Despite everything, they were closer than ever. They had a place of safety for the night. Even the weather seemed less fierce than it had the day before. It was as if knowing they had a chance somehow made everything more bearable.

Abigail ushered the others inside the pillbox, chatting away excitedly. Only Ruth stayed outside, clutching her kitbag.

"Aren't you coming?" asked Col.

"*Must* we?" she begged. "They are so annoying! I think I would rather be attacked by fairies again."

Col smiled. "It's just for one night."

"Can we not stay with those people instead?" she groaned.

She pointed down the hillside. There were dozens of people far below them, huddled in a cluster of tents beneath the trees.

"What are they doing out here?" Col asked, puzzled.

"I suppose they have lost their homes in a raid," said Ruth. "It is safer to stay in the fields than be bombed in the city streets, no?"

Col was shocked. There had been lots of people in Buxton who'd come from the cities to stay with their relatives, or ask a kind stranger to let them stay – no one would have ever needed to sleep outside. In London, people even slept in the Underground stations at night.

To stay outside in a storm like this was unimaginable. Col could see children down there. "But … it's *freezing*. Isn't there somewhere else they can go?"

Ruth shrugged. "For some, yes. But not everyone is so lucky. There are shelters where you can go after your house is hit, but you can stay only for a few days. After this, many people have nowhere else. They must sleep outside or look for new towns where a kind person may take them in." She glowered. "Some places are not so kind. After the raids in London, many went to a town called Windsor, but they said that they will not take in any children. Or Jews."

Col didn't know what to say to that. He gazed down at the people below sleeping out in the cold. He'd been so lost in his own unhappiness these last few months that he hadn't thought once about the others who had lost their homes, their loved ones. He'd been one of the lucky ones – he'd had Aunt Claire to look after him. She might be cold and sometimes thoughtless, but she was a thousand times better than what those people below were going through.

He felt another pang of guilt – Aunt Claire would still have no idea where he was. For all she knew, Col was lying dead in a snowdrift somewhere, or living outside like the people in the field below. It was such a dismal sight. Col wondered how many more would be left homeless after the raid on London – if anyone lived through it at all. And he was just going to let it happen…

He shook his head. He couldn't think like that – he couldn't do anything to stop the raid. All he could think about was saving Rose. This was all for her, wasn't it?

He squashed the feeling of guilt and made his way into the pillbox. It was only a small brick bunker with a doorway and a window, but Abigail had made it comfortable and cosy by filling it with pillows and blankets. She was knitting another one now between her six enormous clawed hands.

"So, this is it?" said Col. "As long as we're inside this bunker, we're safe?"

"That's it!" said Abigail. "The sanctuary is right below us. The Midwinter King can search for you till he's blue in the face, but he won't find you!"

Col felt a weight lift off his shoulders that he hadn't even known was there. For the first time in two days, he felt protected. It felt wrong not to celebrate.

"Well then – what shall we do?" he asked.

Pendlebury frowned. "What do you mean?"

"It's Christmas!" said Col. "We've got to do *something* Christmassy. We might not have presents or decorations or a proper meal…"

"Oh, we have plenty of food!" said Leonard, whipping away a blanket. "See?"

The Guardians eyes bugged out their heads. Underneath the blanket lay box after box of army rations.

"The soldiers left it all behind!" said Abigail. "Go on, help yourselves!"

The Guardians needed no encouragement. They threw themselves at the cardboard boxes and tore their way through them, feasting on tinned meat and oatmeal and biscuits and chocolate and cup after cup of hot, sweet tea. Pendlebury was so hungry she ate the ration boxes whole, cardboard and all. It was the best meal Col had ever had in his life – even the dried eggs tasted good. Soon they were all slumped and groaning on the floor, stuffed to bursting.

"What next?" said Col.

"Let's have a nice long Christmas chat!" said Leonard. "I love chats!"

"Me too!" said Abigail.

The Guardians grit their teeth. Col looked around desperately for an alternative. His eye caught on something in the corner: a large black box with dials.

"Hey – that's a radio!" he cried.

He hadn't listened to one in days. In fact, Col realized, he hadn't heard *any* news since he'd left Buxton. For the first time in months, he had absolutely no idea how the war was going – if Britain was winning or losing, if any more cities had been hit in raids, if President Roosevelt had finally decided to get involved and offer help to the British… It was as if he'd spent the last three days living in another world. Which, in a way, he had.

He switched on the radio. And just like magic, there it was. A string of music, threading out of the speaker and filling the bunker.

Ruth frowned. "What is this?"

Col beamed. "It's 'Children's Hour'! We always listened to this on Christmas Day." He felt a warm glow in his chest. "It was my dad's favourite."

They sat together, huddled under the woollen blankets as the wind raged outside and the narrator read *A Christmas Carol*. For the first time in days, they didn't need to worry about their quest, or about the Midwinter King, or about all the awful things that lay ahead – just for a while, none of it mattered. It was Christmas, and they were safe.

It was strange. Col had spent months imagining a perfect Christmas for himself and Rose … and now here he was, a million miles away from anything he'd imagined, eating army rations in a cold brick bunker with bogies, and it somehow still felt right. He wondered if Rose would be listening to "Children's Hour" too – and felt a sharp stab of guilt. Of course she wouldn't. By now, Aunt Claire would have found a way to tell her that Col was missing. They'd both be worrying themselves sick, with no idea if he was even dead or alive.

Col felt terrible. He'd been so wrapped up saving Rose that he hadn't once thought about anyone's feelings. It wasn't Aunt Claire's fault that she was so uptight – it wasn't Rose's fault for wanting to stay and help people who needed it. He wished there was some way he could reach out to his sister, and explain that all of this was for her ... but of course he couldn't.

Suddenly, the radio began to fade and flicker. The hairs on Col's neck stood on end. The radio signal always died when raids began: no one knew why it happened, it just did. He looked outside – but the skies were empty. There were no planes, no searchlights, no sirens ... it was a raid-free night. The battery was running out, that was all. The sense of relief in his chest was immense.

The radio shut off and the bunker was silent again. Night had fallen completely now: it was pitch black, inside and out.

"Well! Time for that chat, eh?" said Leonard. "That's the nice thing about chats – you don't need a light to chit-chat all night!"

"What a great rhyme!" said Abigail. "Let's make another one!"

There was a noise in the dark that sounded very much like a knight repeatedly banging his helmet against a wall.

"We should light some candles," said Col, looking for a distraction. "My family used to do that on Christmas too. Are there any lamps or…"

"I have something," said Ruth.

She was sat against the wall, holding the canvas kitbag in her lap. Col couldn't see her face in the dark, but he could tell just by her posture that she was nervous. She reached inside the bag and slowly, hesitantly, brought out a cloth bundle. She unwrapped it and carefully placed the object inside on the bunker floor, like she was handling a baby bird. It was a small silver candelabrum, glinting in the last of the moonlight.

"What is it?" Col asked.

Ruth cleared her throat. "It is a chanukiah. My parents gave it to me when I left Berlin. It is for celebrating Chanukah."

"What's—?"

"A Jewish celebration, for eight nights around Christmas time." Her voice was shy and proud in equal measure. "We light a candle for each night. The first night was last night, in fact, but it is no matter – we will catch up now."

Col was surprised. There were lots of Jewish families in Buxton – many of them had evacuated from nearby cities when the raids began. They celebrated different holidays and some had to have their food prepared in a certain way – some even had different clothes that they wore. Ruth didn't seem like any of them.

"I didn't know you were Jewish," he said.

Ruth shrugged. "I did not tell you."

She brought two tiny candles out of the kitbag, each no bigger than birthday candles, and placed them in the holders of the chanukiah. She lit another candle in her hand with a ration-pack of matches, then used it to light the ones in the holders before placing it in another holder in front of her. Col watched the tiny flames beat and glow. He already felt safer and warmer – like they could be OK, the seven of them, tucked in here away from the darkness. It was amazing, the difference that a little light could make.

And then Ruth started singing.

She sang in a language Col didn't recognize – not English, not German – and with a voice that was clear and deep and lovely. He wasn't surprised that her mother was a singer. He felt the words reverberate around the shelter, the candles flickering gently in the dark, until her song faded.

"Lovely!" said Abigail, clapping her six hands.

Ruth smiled. "Thank you. It is a Hebrew prayer."

"What do the words mean?" asked the King of Rogues.

Ruth frowned. "You want me to first make Hebrew

into German, and then make German into English for you. Perhaps I should do this while turning backwards somersaults."

The King of Rogues scowled. "I was just *asking*."

She smiled. "Tomorrow evening we light another candle. And then each day another until the chanukiah is full. We do this every year."

Col gazed at her. He was finally beginning to understand why Ruth had been so secretive over the last few days. He knew a little about what was happening to Jewish people in Germany – that the Nazis were changing laws so they could take their homes and belongings. That must have been why Ruth's family had left Germany and moved to London, he realized. Col wondered how it must have felt for her to hear other children call her a Nazi, when she had reason to hate the Nazis more than anyone. That made him think about the people in Windsor refusing to help evacuees from London – and that made him think about the people in the tents below them. He couldn't imagine what it would be like to sleep out there, in the freezing snow and wind and...

Col stopped.

"Hang on – listen."

They listened.

"I don't hear anything," said Mr Noakes.

Pendlebury's eyes lit up. "Exactly. The wind. It's not there any more."

They looked outside. The night was calm and silent. The storm was gone. For the first time in days, the weather seemed almost … *normal*.

"What's happened?" said Col. "Why has it stopped?"

Abigail gasped with excitement. "Don't you see what it means? The Midwinter King's powers must be growing weaker!"

Col and the Guardians stared at each other in sheer amazement. He could feel it too – a change in the air. Something in the world was shifting.

"Did … *we* do that?" Col asked.

Pendlebury shook her head, her eyes sparkling. "I – I don't know. But if the weather's getting better, then we've got a chance. We might just make it!"

Col's heart pounded. It was true – Pendlebury had covered twenty miles today. If the weather kept improving, she might be able to cover the last hundred miles to London easily.

"This calls for a celebration!" said Leonard. "Let's stay up all night and sing songs! I'll go first…"

Pendlebury's face fell. Mr Noakes put his head in his paws. The King of Rogues started to reach for his sword with trembling hands.

"Actually, there is another part of the Chanukah

ceremony I forgot to mention," said Ruth quickly. "After the last candle is lit, we must all go straight to sleep."

Leonard looked crestfallen. "Really?"

"Yes," said Ruth, nodding sagely. "It is very, very important."

"Oh, what a pity," said Leonard. "Well, if you say so."

The Guardians gazed at Ruth with a look of such intense love that it almost made Col feel jealous.

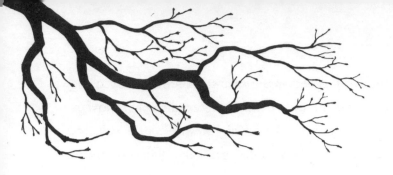

The Turning Tide

THE MIDWINTER KING CAME TO A STOP AT THE crater's edge.

There was nothing left of the fairy fortress in the swamp. The fairies had fled: in fact, they had stopped responding to the King's calls completely. The Midwinter King knew why – they were trying to hide from him. Not that it would do them much good. He would find them, and he would punish them for letting the Guardians slip away.

The Guardians.

The waters of the swamp boiled beneath him. He had set up a nightmare trap for Col, but once again the boy had somehow slipped from his grasp. The Midwinter King had been forced to spend another day hidden in his bone house, waiting for darkness to return so he could search for Col's mind again. And now that midnight was here: nothing. He had searched for hours, and he *still* couldn't find him.

The King gazed at the swamp around him. Losing the boy wasn't his only problem: he could feel his powers growing weaker. He knew why it was happening. He had spent three days away from his throne, living in the world beyond, and it was straining his strength to its limit. His horse did not stand quite as proudly as before, either. The bones were turning pallid and grey, sagging beneath his weight. The Midwinter King had drained the life from it, as he drained life from everything he touched. They would not last for much longer: but that was no matter. He would make as many horses as he needed until he found the Guardians.

That was the beauty of this ancient land. No matter where you stood, you stood on bones...

The movement was almost silent, but not quite. The Midwinter King spun round and fixed the creature in his black gaze, locking it to the ground.

"No! Let me go, please!"

It was King Buttercup, his clothing ragged, his eyes wide and terrified. He had not been able to bring himself to leave his fortress when the others fled: like all fairies, he was proud and vain. The Midwinter King dismounted his horse and leaned over the cowering fairy, like a boy burning ants under a magnifying glass.

You let them get away.

King Buttercup cringed. "I didn't mean to, Your Majesty! They tricked me…"

You saw them yourself? With your own eyes?

"Yes, Your Highness! I'll tell you everything! I—"

You do not need to say a word.

King Buttercup sagged; his eyes turned grey; his arms hung at his sides like a strung puppet. The Midwinter King reached inside his mind and took his thoughts as easily as taking a penny from a table. He saw all King Buttercup's memories spread out before him – everything that had happened in the last two days.

There was Col, standing in the chamber. There were his Guardians, the tiger and the knight and the badger, at his side. There was a girl he did not recognize – Col's sister? No, that was impossible – she was in London, and anyway the King had already seen her in the boy's—

He stopped. There was someone else in the memory – something standing beside the Guardians. He couldn't see who or what it was. It was as if something had been stuck in place, blocking it from his view, a smudge on the lens.

The Midwinter King reached deeper into the fairy's mind – but it was no use. The figure stayed hidden.

Show me.

A weak moan escaped King Buttercup's mouth. He was already beginning to grey and crumble like dust under the Midwinter King's gaze. He was small: he couldn't put up much of a fight.

Show me!

And that was too much. King Buttercup gave a final gasp and disappeared like a handful of smoke in the wind. He was there, then he was gone – there was no in-between.

The Midwinter King stood, his eyes flaring white with anger. Suddenly it all became clear. How Col had been saved from his dreams. How the Guardians had snuck through the barrier. The hidden figure that he could not see.

The Green Man.

He had been with them all along. He had been secretly helping Col and the Guardians on their quest from the very beginning. The Green Man was using the Guardians to show the Spirit World that the Midwinter King was weak, to snatch everything from him at the final moment. There was no other possible explanation for it. But why? Why on earth would—?

The Midwinter King shrieked with agony and reeled back. The edges of his arm were smoking and curling. Dawn was here: a shaft of sunlight had touched his arm.

The Midwinter King was stunned. Daylight wasn't supposed to come for hours yet. But the sun was already touching the horizon. Another day was here.

It was his powers – they were waning. He had to return to his throne at once, and let them grow back to the strength they had before…

No. He could not go back without the Guardians. He could not show failure in front of the Spirit World. That would only give the Green Man exactly what he wanted. He would not let him win when he was so close. He was still a god: the Guardians were nothing. He would not let them make a fool of him.

He held out his arms and his bone horse split apart at once, forming a tight shell around him. The Midwinter King crouched like a foetus in the dark, the air around him filled with the stench of his smouldering arm.

This had gone on long enough. He had been naïve in thinking that he could quickly catch the Guardians – but he would not be naïve any longer. He would not miss another chance. Tomorrow night, he would stop the Guardians, once and for all – and this time, he would not rely on his spies.

He would send something worse after them. Something much, much worse.

The Midwinter King gazed through the portcullis of bones, to the point where the darkness ended on the horizon.

I see you, Col. I see you.

26 December 1940

LOOT GANGS RAID BLITZ TOWNS

Organized looting gangs have appeared in heavily bombed towns.

While raids are going on, these ghouls help themselves from shop windows which have been broken by bombs, or turn up to empty houses when the inhabitants are hiding in nearby shelters. The looters' method is to pose as rescue workers – some have even used women or child accomplices.

Police forces have been warned to be on the guard against them.

The Lair

"WE'RE NOT CLIMBING *THAT*, ARE WE?" GROANED the King of Rogues.

The Guardians stood at the bottom of a hill, its muddy slope bristling with thorny bushes. They'd been travelling all day, and were completely exhausted. The sun was already setting, casting the world in a spectral grey around them. It looked exactly how they felt.

"Just a little further," said Pendlebury wearily. "Leonard said the sanctuary's right at the very top."

They'd left Abigail's bunker at the crack of dawn, with directions to an old stone circle which Leonard had discovered between Leicester and London. It was almost thirty-five miles away, but Leonard assured them it was the closest sanctuary he'd been able to find. Pendlebury had torn across the countryside quickly at first – the fog that had covered the countryside for the last few weeks had all but disappeared – but the good weather came with its own problems. Now there were dozens of people outside, walking the fields again after days of being stuck in their homes. Pendlebury had been forced to fling herself into ditches or under bramble hedges whenever she saw someone coming, which was often.

Now they were running late. Thankfully, the village they'd just passed through was already in blackout, so everyone was tucked inside their homes: the one air raid warden they passed was fast asleep at his post, drunkenly mumbling carols.

Col gazed down the cobbled street behind them. It felt strange, standing on pavements again after days of grass and snow. He could hear people inside the houses lining the street, talking and laughing and eating together. He had missed Dad and Rose more than anything right then, hearing strangers celebrate Christmas. But he felt hopeful too. It had been a difficult day, but they'd covered thirty-five miles: if Pendlebury could keep that pace up, they'd make it to London in time. The news that the Midwinter King's strength was waning felt almost as if a door was opening – like they finally had a chance. Col could even stand how cold he was: after four days of wearing shorts in blizzard conditions, his legs were beginning to turn an alarming shade of purplish-black.

"Let's climb the hill and get it over with," he said. "The sooner we're away from this village, the better."

"Can't we have a break first?" groaned the King of Rogues, throwing down his lance. "We haven't stopped all day! I'm hungry, I'm tired, my legs hurt…"

"Ich habe die nase voll!" Ruth suddenly snapped. "All you do is complain! If you did not waste so much time with complaining, we would be at this sanctuary by now!"

Col bit his lip. Despite everything they'd been through, it still only took the slightest spark to make Ruth and the King of Rogues argue with each other. Col stepped in before it could get any worse.

"Come on! It's been a long day. Let's focus on getting a good night's sleep, and then tomorrow we can worry about…"

"Foooooooooood."

They turned around. Mr Noakes' nose was pointed high in the air, drinking in great breaths as his whiskers twitched.

"Food," he muttered. "In there! Lots of it!"

He pointed to an old pub beside the road. The paint was peeling off the walls and the windows were smeared and dirty. No one had even bothered to put up blackout curtains.

"It's abandoned," said Col. "There won't be any food inside – besides, we haven't got time to—"

"But I can smell it!" said Mr Noakes excitedly. "Please, Col! Can't we just have a little peek?"

"And look what it's called!" said the King of Rogues. "That's got to be a good sign, surely?"

He pointed to the words painted in peeling letters above the door: *THE GREEN MAN*. Beside it was a weather-beaten picture of an old man's face. He had a beard made from leaves and flowers, and vines growing out of his eyes and mouth that wrapped around his neck. Col grimaced. He didn't know what he expected the god of life to look like, but he certainly hadn't expected to see plants growing out of him. "*That's* what the Green Man looks like?"

Mr Noakes snorted. "Pah! Doesn't even come close!"

Pendlebury's stomach growled. "Can we check inside, Col? In case there *is* some food?"

Col sighed. He forgot how much harder the journey was for Pendlebury – she was the one carrying them, after all. "Fine. Mr Noakes – have a quick look and then come straight back."

Mr Noakes saluted, then broke open the cellar doors in the pavement and snuffled his way down into the dark. Ruth and the King of Rogues both turned their backs on each other, muttering under their breaths. Pendlebury stayed where she was, staring at the painting of the Green Man. Col frowned – she looked worried.

"What's the matter?" he asked.

Pendlebury sighed. "I'm thinking about the good

weather we had today – Abigail's right. The Midwinter King must be getting weaker."

Col blinked. "That's a good thing, isn't it?"

Pendlebury nodded. "Perhaps. But if it *is* because of us – because of what Leonard said about our quest making him look foolish – then he's going to come after us even harder now. He won't let us go when he's been so close to winning." She swallowed. "I... I think the next two days are going to be much more difficult. I think we might have to start dealing with worse things than fairies or enchanted trees."

Col swallowed. "Like what?"

"Everyone! Come quick!"

The voice had come from the cellar. Without a word they tore down the steps and found Mr Noakes, eyes gleaming in amazement.

"What is it? What happened?" said Col.

"We hit the flipping jackpot, that's what happened," said Mr Noakes.

Their jaws dropped. The cellar was packed from floor to ceiling with food. There were bags of sugar, pallets of butter, towers of eggs, a dozen pheasants hanging along the wall, jar after jar of sweets, all of it fresh and new. Col had never seen so much food in one place before. His mouth started watering instantly.

"What's it all doing here?" he gasped.

"Who cares?" said the King of Rogues. "Bagsy the sugar!"

"The eggs are mine!" said Mr Noakes.

"SHUT UP AND EAT," cried Pendlebury.

The Guardians launched themselves at the food and tore into it ravenously. Pendlebury slurped the pheasants off the hooks one by one; Mr Noakes stuffed whole eggs into his mouth like they were gobstoppers; the King of Rogues dunked his entire head in a bag of sugar and gave a muffled roar of pleasure. Even Ruth started helping herself to sweets. Only Col stayed where he was, staring at the basement in confusion. Something about this wasn't right. Since rationing came in, all this food was hard to come by – and there wasn't just food, either. There were boxes of cigarettes, cases of beer and whisky, piles of fabric, even some old antiques…

"I don't understand," he muttered. "Why would anyone leave all this stuff in an old abandoned…"

Suddenly it all clicked into place. Col gasped, scandalized.

"These are black market goods! This is a *thieves' den*!" He waved his hands. "Stop! Put everything back!"

"Why?" said Ruth, chewing through two chocolate bars at once.

"It's stealing!"

"So? It is stolen already!"

"That doesn't make it OK!" said Col. "We don't know where any of this has come from – it could have been taken from the needy!"

"*We* are needy," Ruth pointed out. "And we are only taking a little bit, yes?"

It didn't look like the Guardians were taking a little. Mr Noakes had worked his way through half the stack of eggs already. Pendlebury had found a wooden crate of sausages and was writhing inside it, gurgling with pleasure.

"But if the thieves come back…" Col began.

He trailed off. The Guardians looked so happy. It was good to see them having a nice time, after all they'd been through. He sighed. "Fine. But I'm leaving a note."

Crump.

They froze – they'd all felt it. Something had struck the side of the building, hard.

"What was that?" came the King of Rogues' voice from inside his bag of sugar.

They waited – and then it came again, harder this time. *CRUMP.* Dust fell from the rafters. The entire cellar shuddered, right down to the foundations.

"Is this … bombs?" said Ruth.

Col shook his head. It couldn't be – the skies were empty. They hadn't seen a plane in days. "I – I think we should go, before…"

WHAM!

More dust fell down from the rafters, whole handfuls this time. Cracks were spreading across the ceiling like a spider's web – the building was collapsing, it was going to fall on top of them. Col gasped and made to run.

"Everyone out! Quick!"

He was too late. The ceiling wrenched and tore from its moorings: windows shattered, bricks tumbled from the walls, iron pipes tore and twisted, the air flooded with white dust. But when it cleared, Col could see that the ceiling wasn't falling on top of them. In fact, it was … *getting further away from them.*

"I do not think this is bombs," said Ruth bluntly.

Col gasped. The pub was being lifted off the ground above them, like a lid from a pot. He watched, speechless, as a huge shadow appeared in the cloud of white dust. It was almost as big as the cellar itself, and it was getting closer, like a great winged bird swooping down…

Pendlebury's jaw dropped, and a sausage fell from her mouth.

"It's—"

The shadow snatched them before she could finish her sentence, sealing them all in cold stone darkness. By the time Col had worked out that the shadow was a giant hand, they had already been lifted out of the cellar and carried into the night.

Gog and Magog

THEY WERE FLUNG TO THE GROUND, HARD.

Col choked out a breath. They were on top of the hill that they'd been standing at the bottom of just a few minutes before, pressed against a towering rock face. Their only escape was blocked by a huge stone monolith ahead of them. It was the size of a house, covered in moss and lichen … and jumping up and down.

"Gog did it! Gog found Guardians!"

Col's mouth fell open. The monolith was a huge stone man, with arms like boulders and tiny pebble eyes. Whenever it jumped, the ground shuddered like an earthquake.

"Well done, Gog! Magog very pleased with your work ethic."

Col looked up. Sitting on top of the stone man's shoulders was another smaller stone man. He had a set of glasses crudely drawn around his eyes with house paint, and looked like a child being carried by a grown-up – albeit a child that weighed at least twenty tonnes.

"GIANTS!" cried Pendlebury, finally finishing the sentence she'd started earlier.

The smaller giant cackled. "That right! You been captured by Gog and Magog – best bounty hunters in the Spirit World! You can run all you like, but Gog and Magog *always* catch up with you!"

Mr Noakes sat up, rubbing his eyes blearily.

"Giants? Look at the size of you!" He pointed at them. "He's barely twenty feet tall, and you're even smaller!"

"Size not everything!" said Magog, the smaller of the two. "We used to be one enormous giant, called Gogmagog…"

"Very big, lots of smash!" said Gog.

"Then we fall off cliff," said Magog, "and broke into two parts. One big, one small."

"Not so much smash," said Gog sadly.

"But now we even better!" Magog insisted. "We perfect partnership of brain and brawn! That why Midwinter King hire us to track you down."

"Gog got big, smashy hands!" cried Gog.

"Magog got the vocabulary," said Magog.

Pendlebury's face fell. "Wait – does that mean the giants have allied with the Midwinter King?"

Gog shook his head, making a sound like two boulders grinding against each other. "No! Giants still not choose side yet. They too busy hitting each other on head with sticks."

"We *freelance*," said Magog.

The King of Rogues suddenly attacked without warning, somersaulting off the rock wall behind them and landing on Gog's shoulder before swinging his sword at Magog's neck…

"Freelance *this*, pebble brains!"

Ding.

The sword barely chipped Magog's neck. There was an awkward silence, then Gog reached up and effortlessly flicked the King of Rogues off his shoulder with a great stone finger. The knight pinwheeled through the air and hit the rock face with a sickening *thump* before collapsing to the dust like a broken toy.

"Gog hit good!" said Gog.

Col raced to the King of Rogues. "Rogue! Are you OK?"

"*King* of Rogues." He smiled weakly at Col. His armour was dented and his lance was bent, but he refused to be defeated. "J-just a scratch, that's all. If I can just get one good shot at the little one…"

"Ha! That impossible!" said Magog. "There no way you can defeat smashy might of Gog. There no escape for you now! You going to Midwinter King whether you like or not!"

Col flooded with horror. They'd been caught again – and this time, there was no way of fighting their way out of it. He had to escape, fast – maybe they could bargain with the giants. Surely they needed something – he had no idea what being "freelance" meant, but it sounded awful.

"Please – don't hand us to the Midwinter King!" he begged. "Whatever he's offering, we'll give you double if you let us go!"

Magog laughed. "Ha! Fat chance! Midwinter King offer *very* generous reward for capturing Guardians!"

Gog blinked. "He do? Gog not know this."

Magog froze – he'd clearly said more than he meant to. He might have been the cleverer of the two, but that didn't mean much.

"Er, yes! But reward split in two. Magog get stupid, boring gold, and Gog get … this special twig!"

He picked a twig off the ground and handed it to Gog. Gog jumped up and down with delight.

"Special twig! Special twig!"

"Yes, Magog very jealous," said Magog.

Pendlebury used the distraction to whisper to Col.

"That sanctuary must be close. If we can make it there, we'll be protected from the Midwinter King. We have to make a break for it."

Col looked around. There was no way of getting past Gog. "But how? We're trapped!"

"I'm not sure," said Pendlebury. "But if we can get Gog and Magog to turn on each other, we might just have a chance of sneaking away. Giants are always arguing with each other – it's what they do best!"

Meanwhile Magog had jumped from Gog's shoulders and landed on the ground, hitting it like a metal safe.

"Now, Gog stay and watch prisoners. Magog go get rope to tie them up. Then he send good news to Midwinter King!"

Gog's face fell. "Can Gog not tell King?"

Magog shook his head sadly. "No! Gog not know what to say, remember? Gog imbecile. Magog have *glasses*." He tapped the circles he'd painted around his eyes. "He brains of operation! He use extensive vocabulary to express himself fluently."

Gog's shoulders slumped. "Oh, yes. Gog always forget."

Magog marched off, leaving the Guardians alone with Gog. Col and Pendlebury shared a glance – this was their chance to talk to him. The tiger stepped forwards pleadingly.

"Gog, listen to us. You *must* free us before your brother gets back."

Gog shook his head. "No! If Gog let you go, Gog not get special twig."

He held up the twig with triumph.

"It's not a special twig, you nitwit!" said Mr Noakes. "Look around you – there are twigs everywhere!"

Gog frowned, his face creasing up like a stone fist. "But this twig from Midwinter King."

"No it's not – your brother just picked it off the ground!" said the King of Rogues, chiming in. "Can't you see what's going on? Magog's making you do all the work and giving you nothing!"

Gog shook his head. "Magog never lie to Gog. Magog clever. Magog have *glasses*."

"Glasses don't mean anything," said Col. "They're not even glasses – he's just painted them on himself!"

A seed of doubt crept into Gog's expression. Pendlebury took another step forward.

"Gog – you don't have to do what your brother says. Do you want the Midwinter King to keep the Spirit World in darkness for all eternity?"

Gog's tiny pebble eyes grew closer together with the strain of thinking. You could almost hear his brain slotting the pieces into place. "N-no. Gog *not* want this."

"Then let us go, before Magog gets back!" said Pendlebury. "Use your strength for good – find the giants and convince them to join the fight for the Green

Man! With them on side, the Midwinter King might finally be defeated!"

This was too much for Gog. His brain collapsed like a tower of cards.

"No! Gog not think! Gog not *good* at think. Gog do what Magog say and get special twig!"

"But it is not a special twig," said Ruth.

Col groaned. They were going around in circles. "Ruth, we've already tried that…"

"*That* is the special twig!"

She pointed to another twig on the ground. Gog's brow furrowed. "Huh?"

"Do you not see?" said Ruth with a sly smile. "Your brother has tricked you! He has given you an ordinary twig, so that he can keep the special twig for himself!"

The Guardians shared a glance. They knew what Ruth was doing – they just had to play along. Gog looked at the other twig suspiciously.

"Gog not believe you."

"See for yourself!" said Col. "A special twig always has *tiny* writing on it!"

Gog held the two twigs in front of him, squinting.

"Gog not see writing," he muttered.

"Try holding it up to the moonlight," Pendlebury suggested.

Gog turned around so he had his back to them.

"Gog *still* not see writing."

"Look harder," said Mr Noakes as they climbed on Pendlebury's back.

Gog shook his head. "Gog still not see. But then, Gog not know how to read anyway…"

The Guardians took their chance. Pendlebury shot through the gap between Gog's legs and charged across the hillside like a bolt of lightning…

WHAM!

She roared with pain. Magog had returned and thrown himself straight onto her tail, pinning her to the ground.

"*Gog!* What you doing?" he cried. "You letting prisoners escape!"

Gog held up the twigs, confused. "Gog look for little writing on special twig."

Magog shook with rage. "There *is* no writing! It just stupid, ordinary twig!"

Gog's face fell. "But you tell Gog it special…"

"Yes! Because Gog so stupid, he cannot stand still for even two seconds!" Magog bellowed. "This why Magog have to do everything! If it not for Magog, we *never* get job from Midwinter King!"

Gog's face creased into a snarl. "Gog sick of doing what Magog say! Big cat right. Gog want to fight for Green Man!"

Magog laughed heartily. "And why Green Man want Gog? Gog stupid! Gog thick as granite! Gog got rubble for brains!"

Gog trembled, like a volcano about to explode. His teeth ground together like two heaps of bricks. The twigs crumbled to dust in his clenched fists. But Magog kept going.

"Gog a ten-tonne moron! Gog not know his block from his ballast! Gog good for nothing but ornamental garden feature!"

Finally, Gog lost it. He gave a great bellow of rage, raised his fists high above him ... and brought them both down on Magog's head, like two meteors hitting the earth. Magog was still for a moment – then, he crumbled into a thousand tiny pieces. In less than a second, the stone giant was little more than a pile of gravel. Pendlebury pulled her tail free with a yelp.

"You did it, Gog!" said Col, delighted. "You fought back!"

Gog was surprised himself. "Y-yes. Gog did! Now he free! Now he can finally look for *real* special twig!"

The King of Rogues blinked. "Is he serious?"

"Let's just go," muttered Pendlebury. "We need to find this stone circle before..."

She trailed off. The heap of gravel beside her was ... *moving*. Little stones were popping out of the pile one by one, growing tiny arms and tiny legs and tiny, furious faces. Each one was a miniature version of Magog. Soon there was a sprawling crowd of them on the forest floor, squeaking with rage and shaking their tiny fists at Gog.

"Gog, you idiot!"

"What Gog do that for?"

"Midwinter King going to kill us!"

"Now Magogs have to stop Guardians by themselves…"

The crowd of Magogs turned as one – and charged.

Pendlebury gasped. "Hold on, everyone!"

She shot across the hillside as fast as she could, her muscles tensing and heaving like pistons. Col clung to her fur for dear life – Pendlebury was moving faster than ever before, trying to escape from the enormous crowd of stone men. But it was like trying to outrun a landslide: the tiny Magogs were even picking each other up and throwing themselves at the Guardians. They whizzed past Col's ears and pinged off the King of Rogues' helmet like buckshot. The knight swung round and started swiping left and right with his lance, batting the Magogs out of the air as they flew towards him.

"Mr Noakes! Help me!"

Mr Noakes spun round and started swinging his

club, sending the Magogs crashing to the ground ten at a time. It still wasn't enough – the stone men were gaining on them.

Ruth held out a hand to the King of Rogues. "I can help! Give me your sword!"

The King of Rogues laughed. "Ha! Nice try, missy! You might have fooled the others, but not me!"

Ruth looked appalled. "You are *still* saying this?"

"I'm not sure now is the time for this argument," Col whimpered, swatting away another stone man on Pendlebury's back.

"Rogue! Stop being an idiot and give her a weapon!" Mr Noakes bellowed.

The knight clenched his eyes shut with rage. "KING – OF—"

"DUCK!"

Everyone ducked as Pendlebury flew beneath a low hanging branch – except for the King of Rogues, who was struck square in the chest with a colossal *DUNG* and straight off Pendlebury's back, plummeting towards the crowd of tiny stone men. The Magogs screeched with triumph and raised their hands…

"Got you!" Ruth leaped back and miraculously grabbed the King of Rogues at the last second, so he hung trailing in the air behind them. She beamed with triumph. "I have him! He is fine!"

Mr Noakes winced. "He doesn't *look* fine."

"AAAAAAAAAAARGH," said the King of Rogues.

Ruth had grabbed the King of Rogues by his moustache. His face was a frozen mask of pain, his eyes bugging out of his head in agony. The crowd of stone men were mere inches behind him now, jumping up and swiping for his ankles.

"Pendlebury, we have to go faster!" Col cried.

"I see it!" Pendlebury shouted back. "The stone circle, up ahead!"

Sure enough, a ring of stones stood less than a hundred feet away in the moonlight. Col's face fell. It was just a dozen rocks in a patch of grass – they weren't even in a proper circle.

"*That's* going to protect us?" he said.

"Only if we enter through the right stones!" said Pendlebury. "Leonard said we need to go for the ones at the front!"

"Where's the front?" said Col. "It's a circle!"

Pendlebury's face fell. "Um…"

"Wait – is the sanctuary going to protect us from the giants too?"

"I don't know!"

"What if it doesn't?"

"I don't know!"

"Then why are we still doing it?!"

"Do you have any other ideas?!"

Col glanced over his shoulder – the tiny giants would be on them in seconds. They only had one chance to get this right.

"What happens if we don't choose the right stones?" Col asked.

Pendlebury winced. "We're about to find out…"

She charged through the two stones closest to them and raised her head, roaring at the top of her lungs just as the Magogs threw themselves forwards…

"SANCTUARY!"

Sanctuary

THE CHANGE WAS INSTANTANEOUS. THE SOUND OF a thousand screaming Magogs disappeared behind them like a door had been slammed.

"Well! There's no need to *shout*, dear. You just come right in."

Col looked up. At first, he thought he was in pitch darkness – then he realized he'd just screwed his eyes shut. He gazed around in amazement. The world outside the stone circle was now hidden behind a wall of what looked like swirling silver oil. The giants were pummelling it with their tiny fists to get inside, shrieking and cursing, but it was no use.

"Pay them no mind, duckie!" came the voice again. "Those nasty giants can't so much as *breathe* on you while you're in here."

Col looked around. He didn't know where the voice was coming from – there was no one else in the circle.

"You were lucky!" said another voice. "The last time someone correctly guessed the right stones was in 876."

"It was 1876, dear."

"No, it wasn't! You're mixing your millennia again, love, I remember the chain mail."

Col smiled. He'd worked out where the voices were coming from: it was the stones themselves. They each had a mouth and pair of eyes scratched into their surface which moved as they talked.

"Don't worry, you're safe in here until morning!" one of them said. "The Midwinter King won't catch hide nor hair of you."

Col smiled. "Thank you very much. It's awfully kind of you."

The stones all *oooooooohed*.

"What a polite young man!"

"Such lovely manners!"

"It's no bother, dear, we love the company."

"Oooh, yes, love a bit of company!"

"What was that, dear?"

"I WAS JUST SAYING THAT WE LOVE A BIT OF COMPANY."

"Ooh, yes! Haven't had any since 876!"

"What was that?"

"I WAS SAYING ABOUT THE VIKING PILLAGERS, DEAR."

"Oooh, yes, pillagers, lovely."

Col suddenly had a horrible thought. "Hang on – what if the Magogs tell the Midwinter King where we are? He'll be able to find us anyway!"

Pendlebury shook her head. "I don't think they'll be in a hurry to tell him anything. See?"

She nodded outside. Sure enough, the Magogs had already given up trying to get inside and had run away. Col beamed. They had done it again – they were safe for one more night. London was another step closer.

Pendlebury collapsed to the ground and was fast asleep in seconds. The Guardians tumbled from her back and lay panting on the grass beside her. The only one who didn't join them was the King of Rogues. He stayed standing, staring down at Ruth.

"What *now*?" she muttered.

The King of Rogues shifted on his feet. His helmet was busted, he had a black eye, his moustache stuck out of his face at a painful angle, but he seemed to be finding *this* far more painful.

"You … saved my life," he mumbled. "I am eternally grateful to you." He got down on one knee and held out his sword. "I would be honoured if you would take this."

Ruth was shocked. "You are giving me your sword?"

"Just for a bit," he snapped. "Don't get fingermarks on it."

Ruth smiled, but handed it back. "Please, keep it. I am very sorry that I hurt your face."

The King of Rogues snorted. "Ha! It takes much more than *that* to hurt me! But, er ... yes, it was agony." He held out a hand. "Friends?"

Ruth shook it. "Friends."

Col gazed at Ruth with admiration. He would never have expected her to be so kind to the King of Rogues, after how rude he'd been to her – but then, he wouldn't have expected her to successfully trick a giant either. Ruth always seemed to find ways to surprise him.

"Well!" she said. "I think now is the time to light the next candle, no?"

She brought out the chanukiah, placing three in the holder this time and lighting them with a fourth. Once again she sang, her voice drifting out of the circle and over the hillside as the lights flickered and glowed on the stones.

"What does it all mean?" Col asked. "The prayer – the candles?"

"It is to celebrate light in dark times," said Ruth. "*A little light drives out much darkness.* That is what my father always says."

They fell silent. Col glanced across the circle. The Guardians were all fast asleep now – so were the stones. He and Ruth were alone. There was something that had

been on his mind ever since Ruth first lit the chanukiah –
a question he'd been burning to ask her for some time.

"Ruth – can I ask you a question?"

Ruth shifted on the ground. Col sensed somehow
that she knew what was coming.

"Yes. You can."

"Why do you want to go back to London? Is it to
find your parents?"

It was a long time before she answered.

"My parents are still in Germany," she said. "I came
over here on my own, before the war began."

Col was shocked – he'd never been allowed to take
a bus on his own before, let alone travel to another
country. "You left your parents behind?"

Ruth kept her eyes fixed on the candles. He sensed
that finally, she was ready to talk to him.

"Things were very bad in Berlin. They were bad for
a long time, and then they got worse. Hitler does not
want the Jewish people, you see: he made many laws so
we could not live like others. First, we were not allowed
to have servants – our cook and nursemaid had to find
work someplace else. Then, men came to the house and
took our radio, because Jewish people were not allowed
to have one. We could not go to a park or to a theatre.
On the street, people could do whatever they liked to us
and no one would stop them."

Ruth pulled at the grass, not meeting his gaze. Col sensed that if she looked at him, she wouldn't be able to talk.

"When Papa lost his job, he said that our only hope was to leave Germany and go to Britain. That we would all live there together and be safe." She kept pulling at the grass. "We spend many months organizing this, one day thinking we have the correct papers, and the next finding that they are wrong and having to start all over again. We think that any day a new law will come in, and Papa will be arrested and not be able to leave. Finally, Papa found a charity who say they will get us out of Germany and find us a place to live in Britain."

She kept her gaze fixed on the candles. She was focusing all her strength on explaining, on trying to find the right words.

"We go to the train station, and there are lots of children and parents there, all crying. I do not understand why everyone is crying. I do not understand why Mama and Papa have brought no bags with them, either." She paused. "I get on the train, and ... Mama and Papa do not. They say that they are going to stay behind for a few days and they are going to be on the very next train behind me. They say that I am going ahead on my own, and that I must be brave, and that it will only be for a little while and soon we will all be together again." She swallowed. "And this was the last time that I saw them."

Col was silent. So Ruth had been forced to leave her parents behind in Germany. How could she stand it, knowing that they were still stuck inside an enemy country, where anything could happen to them? He had so many questions to ask – but now wasn't the time. He just let her talk.

"We are only children on this train," Ruth explained. "Some have their baby brothers or sisters with them. I do not remember much of the journey, except that it is very long. I remember that when we cross the border into the Netherlands, there are many people at the stations cheering for us, happy that we got out. I did not understand what there was to be happy for." Her face darkened. "We finally get to Holland, and there is a boat to take us to Britain. It is horrible. The boat is huge but the cabins are small, with no windows. Metal doors and metal walls and the ship groaning around us like it is in some terrible pain. Very dark. All I can think about is how much Mama will hate this, when she follows after me. She cannot *stand* boats!"

Her voice faltered, just for a moment – but she kept going.

"Finally we arrive in England. My parents have written to an old friend from Germany who lives in

London, who can pay for me to stay in a boarding school. I do not understand anything at this school. I speak only a little English, and everything is so different – the food, the light switches, the way of making the beds. The teachers say that I am very lucky to be there and that I must be grateful for all the help I am being given – but I do not feel lucky. I cannot talk to anyone. They even put me with the babies, because I speak only German. So all day long I am reading, reading, reading, to try to learn English words. Soon I even begin to dream in English! Mama and Papa are writing to me all the time, saying that they are proud of me, and they will soon be with me again and not to worry…"

She finally looked up at Col, and he saw that her eyes were red.

"And then the war comes. The letters from Mama and Papa stop. Papa's friend is arrested, because he is German, and so there is no more money for my school. I must leave, and then the raids begin, and I am sent away to live on the farm with Mr and Mrs Wilkes. I wait for news about Mama and Papa, but of course it does not come. No one even knows where I am!"

Col understood her fears. Everyone had heard stories about soldiers coming home from war to find that their entire family had been killed in a raid, and no one had been able to tell them. The war had turned everything to chaos.

"I try to find out news about Mama and Papa," said Ruth. "There is a place in London, called Bloomsbury House, where people who have escaped the Nazis can find out about their relatives. I want to write them a letter, to see if Mama and Papa have come to England and are looking for me … but Mr and Mrs Wilkes will not even give me money for a stamp." Her face clouded with hate for a second. "You understand now why I must come to London – yes? I must find out if there is any news from Mama and Papa. If they are looking for me." She started shaking. "If Bloomsbury House is destroyed in this raid, and I never find out where they are … or if Mama and Papa are already in London looking for me, and the bombing starts…"

Col grabbed her hand – he did it without thinking. He felt so ashamed. He had been so wrapped up in himself and the importance of his quest for Rose that he hadn't considered what Ruth might be fighting for – that her pain could be even worse than his. He had spent months wanting to go home – but Ruth had no home to go back to.

"We're going to make it, Ruth. I promise. We'll get there in time. We'll find out about your parents."

He was promising things that he knew he couldn't

keep. He had no idea where Bloomsbury House was, or how on earth they were going to get there *and* find Rose … but how could he listen to Ruth's story and not want to help her?

Ruth wiped her eyes. "I wish only that I had been a better child. Perhaps then Mama and Papa would have let me stay with them. We would still be together."

Col was shocked. "You can't say that. They did it for love – they wanted to protect you. You're lucky you got out when you did."

Ruth sniffed. "Yes. Or perhaps, after everything that has happened, the Nazis are coming here anyway. So it has all been for nothing"

Col made to argue – and stopped. Ruth was right. He knew how it felt to lose everything you loved for your own safety and not be sure it was worth it: but Ruth had it so, so much worse than him. If the Nazis invaded, everything she had escaped from would be right on her doorstep. He thought about all the people he knew who'd come to London to escape the Nazis – how frightened they must be now, knowing the enemy was so close again. What on earth was going to happen to all of them after the raid? And he was doing *nothing* to help them…

"Col."

Col looked up. He was struck, once again, by how

serious Ruth's face was. He had never seen a face look so serious.

"Even if we do not make it to London – I want to say that I am very thankful for everything you have done for me. I am very glad to have met you."

Col smiled. "I'm glad to have met you too."

He meant it. Ruth might not have carried him like Pendlebury, or protected him like Mr Noakes, or fought for him like the King of Rogues – but she'd still helped him, in another way that he couldn't quite define. He didn't know how he would have done any of this without her.

She clapped a hand to her forehead. "*Ach!* I almost forgot!" She reached into her kitbag. "I have a present for you – it is not much, just something I took from the cellar earlier."

Col frowned. "*Ruth!* You stole…"

She handed it over before he could finish. Col stared at it in confusion. It was a pair of green corduroy trousers.

"Instead of the shorts!" said Ruth. "So you are not so cold any more. They are good, yes? They will fit?"

Col was stunned. Despite everything she was going through, Ruth had still found time to think of him. He didn't know what to say.

"Th-they're perfect. Thank you." He cringed. "I haven't got you anything."

Ruth shrugged. "This is no matter. Merry Christmas, Col."

Col smiled. "Merry Christmas." He paused. "Do people say anything at Chanukah?"

"Chag sameach."

He tried to copy the sound of the words. "Hug some air?"

"Yes, like that, but good."

They giggled, and the sound drifted over the hillside, carried into the dark.

The Ravine

THE MIDWINTER KING CLOSED HIS EYES. He searched to the south. He searched to the south-east and the south-west. His black gaze scoured every inch of the land for Col's mind, any scrap of him, any scent…

Nothing. The boy's mind was nowhere to be found. He had lost him.

The Midwinter King was silent for a moment. Then he screamed. The trees shrank and withered in the ground; animals fled in panic; children woke crying in their sleep. His horse twisted in agony beneath him, greying and crumbling by the second, until the bones of its legs suddenly snapped and it buckled forward, shattering to the ground in a great cloud of dust.

The Midwinter King stood in its wake. The giants had failed him – his plan had not worked. The Guardians had slipped from his grasp once again. Another day had passed, and he was growing even weaker. Whatever the

Green Man was doing, it was working. He could not allow it. He could not let it all slip from his grasp when he was so, so close.

He gazed around the desolate ravine he stood in. In front of him stood a jagged boulder, rising from the ground like an altar. He knew what he had to do. It was midnight: it was his time. It was *still* his time. He climbed on top of the stone altar and closed his eyes, and summoned.

It happened in an instant. He did not need to look up to know that it had worked: he always knew when he was alone, and when he was not.

"Your … Your Majesty?"

Barghest stood on the ground before him, her face frozen in horror.

"What – what have you done?"

The ravine was filled with writhing darkness. All the creatures of the King's army stood before him: troops of howling black dogs; eyeless women with fingers that ended in iron claws; haggard men in dried skin clothing, their faces streaked with blood; goblins and trolls by the thousand. The Midwinter King raised his arms across the seething pit.

Armies of the King, I have brought you here for a purpose. Fill the land between here and London. Find the Guardians. Bring them to me.

He was expecting a roar of triumph – but it did not come. The creatures were lost, confused, frightened: many had never been out of the Spirit World before. Now they had been dragged across the barrier without warning, crossing vast distances into a world whose very air burned and withered them.

Barghest stepped forward, trembling with fear. "Master, you cannot do this. The Spirit World is in chaos! Many of the spirits who swore allegiance to you have started fighting back. The resistance is growing! You must return to your throne! To bring all your troops over here, *now*…"

The Midwinter King stared at Barghest.

You dare to defy me?

He reached inside his robes and drew out a handle of darkest black. The metal that made it was burnt and twisted. The mass of creatures instantly recoiled. They knew exactly what it was – they knew what it was capable of. Barghest shrank back in speechless terror.

I am the lord of darkness. I have powers beyond reckoning. I will cut from the world ANYONE who dares to refuse me.

The Midwinter King stepped towards Barghest, his eyes burning fiercer than ever, his edges curling like smoke.

Find me the Guardians. Bring them to me. GO!

He did not need to say it twice. Barghest flew from

the ravine, the army of black dogs howling into the night behind her. The dark mass of monsters fled from the valley, snaking in every direction until the Midwinter King was alone once more.

When he was certain that they were gone, he sank to his knees on the stone. He had pushed himself to his absolute limits. The magic to bring his armies over had been vast, unthinkable. His vision slipped and reeled.

But there was no way he could be defeated now. The Guardians would never win against so many. They would be found, and the Green Man's plans would be stopped, and the dark balance would be restored. The raid would come and the Midwinter King's powers would grow greater than ever, and then he would rule across both worlds for all eternity. He could not be stopped now. It was his time.

And even if the Guardians somehow did get past his armies … he knew where they were heading.

He fixed his eyes on a single point, many miles to the south.

London.

Herne Hill.

Rose.

There you are, said the Midwinter King.

27 December 1940

STRAIN ON ONE MAN KILLS 27 OTHERS

An express train disaster in which twenty-seven people were killed near Taunton was caused by "war strain", it was revealed today.

"The driver was fit and healthy and had forty years of experience," said an inspector for the Ministry of Transport, "but he was suffering from strain as his home had recently been damaged in a raid. His breakdown may also be attributed to the especially difficult operating conditions in the blackout.

"The issue was largely psychological: his inability to concentrate ultimately led to the accident."

A New Day

C OL OPENED HIS EYES FROM THE BEST SLEEP HE'D had in days.

He sat up. Dawn was breaking, the shimmering oil wall had disappeared. The trousers were a revelation. Col promised himself that from now on he would wear trousers every day, maybe even two pairs if he felt like it.

The others were already wide awake. Mr Noakes was packing Ruth's kitbag for her, and Ruth was helping the King of Rogues bash the dents out of his armour. Col's heart glowed to see them all working together.

"Finally! We thought you'd never wake up."

Pendlebury was looking brighter and more alert than she had in days. Col frowned – in fact, *everyone* was looking good. The King of Rogues' cuts and bruises from last night had completely healed.

"What's going on?" said Col, confused. "I feel *fantastic*."

"It's the stones!" said Pendlebury. "Turns out these circles aren't just protective – they're healing too. There's another one about forty miles south of here. If we can make it there before sunset, we'll get to London in time!"

Col's heart lifted. "Are you sure you'll manage forty miles in one day?"

"I feel like I could do a hundred!" said Pendlebury proudly. "And look at this weather – it's even better than yesterday!"

She was right – the sweeping drifts of snow that had covered the land for weeks were finally beginning to melt. The end of their quest was closer in sight than ever before.

"We should leave as soon as possible," said Pendlebury. "The stones are giving me directions to the next sanctuary now."

It didn't sound like the stones were giving her directions – it sounded like they were bickering among themselves.

"No, no, no! *That* mountain used to be over there."

"It was not!"

"I think I'd remember where the mountain was, dear, I'm made from it."

Pendlebury gave him a weary look. "Er … this may take a little while. Why don't you and Mr Noakes see if you can find some food for the journey?"

Col frowned. "Shouldn't we all go together? You won't be protected if I'm so far away from you…"

Pendlebury shook her head. "So long as we stay inside the circle, we're safe. Just make sure you're back before nine o'clock – we've got a lot of ground to cover today. Listen out for the church bells!"

She nodded to an old stone church at the edge of the forest below. It had sandbags piled up at the doors and cheesecloth sheets glued over the stained-glass windows to protect them from bomb blasts.

Col shook his head. "They don't ring church bells any more. Church bells mean Britain's been invaded."

Mr Noakes slapped him on the back. "Don't you worry about that – I'll get us back in good time, Master Col!"

"Just Col."

"What?"

"You called me Master Col again."

"I did?"

"You did."

"Oh! Sorry, Master Col."

"Just Col."

"That's what I said."

With that, the badger marched off. Col smiled. In truth, he didn't find it annoying any more – he'd never felt prouder to be looked after by his Guardians.

He and Mr Noakes strode down the hill towards the forest, side by side, until they came to a black metal gateway circling the trees.

"We probably shouldn't go any further," said Col. "This fence means it's private land. It's against the law to…"

He trailed off. Mr Noakes had already leaped over the gate and was picking mushrooms from the base of the nearest tree, stuffing them into his waistcoat pockets while humming. Col clambered over the fence after him.

"Stop it!" he said. "Remember what happened last time we took food that wasn't ours?"

"I'm only taking a couple!" said Mr Noakes. "A few handfuls of these and an egg or two, and we might just have the makings of an omelette…"

"But what if they're poisonous?"

Mr Noakes chuckled. "For heaven's sake, Col – I can sniff out a poisonous mushroom from a hundred yards!" He shook his head. "Honestly, when did you become such a worrywart? You've been fretting non-stop from the moment we left the cottage! You used to be so adventurous when you were young – all those imaginary quests you'd go on by yourself. What happened to make you so…"

He trailed off, leaving the words unfinished. There was a heavy silence. Mr Noakes shuffled apologetically.

"Ah – of course, Master Col. I wasn't thinking. Of

course you'd want to be careful, after … after what happened to your dad. *Anyone* would."

Col nodded. He didn't want to cry again, but the tears felt very close. "I just don't want anyone else to get hurt. I know what it's like to lose someone you care about. And we're already up against so much. If anything goes wrong now, I'm not just going to lose Rose – I'm going to lose all of you as well."

Mr Noakes placed a paw on his shoulder. "Lad – us Guardians made a promise to serve and protect you until the day you die. That's our duty. And a duty is a duty, even when it's hard."

The wave of guilt rose up inside Col again. "But you wouldn't be risking all this if it weren't for me. If you get cut from existence, it'll be my fault!"

Mr Noakes shook his head. "No, Col, it won't. We knew exactly what we were doing when we broke through the barrier. We didn't come because we had to – we did it because we love you."

"But what if that's not enough?" said Col.

The badger smiled, in a way that Col didn't fully understand. "Oh, you'd be surprised what love can do, Col. It's protected me all this time, hasn't it? Your love for us Guardians has kept us hidden from the god of darkness himself! Think about that. All of his powers, all of his armies, are nothing compared to the love of one boy. Now, doesn't that make you think everything might be OK?"

Col smiled. Mr Noakes had always been the quietest of his Guardians – but it turned out that underneath his shabby waistcoat and gruff exterior, he was an old romantic. Col realized exactly who he reminded him of – it was Dad.

Mr Noakes reached over and rubbed Col's head with a paw, just like Dad used to. "Mark my words, lad – with love on our side we've got something that the Midwinter King can only dream of. Love helped break us over the barrier, and it'll be what sends us home too!"

Col suddenly remembered something from the other day.

"Mr Noakes – how *did* you get over the barrier? Leonard said it was impossible for the three of you to have done it by yourselves…"

Mr Noakes dropped his mushrooms with alarm. "Right – enough chat! This omelette won't make itself, will it? Ha ha, imagine that! An omelette making itself! Ha ha ha!"

Col frowned. Mr Noakes was still trying to hide something – and he was still doing a terrible job of it. Col had no idea what it was, but he wasn't going to get an answer any time soon. "Let's just go back. We're not going to find any eggs around here."

Mr Noakes tapped his nose. "That's where you're wrong, Col! I'll have you know that I can smell a whole *house* nearby that's packed with dozens of—"

"Oi!"

Col nearly leaped out of his skin. He spun round. A man in a flat cap and coat was jumping over the gate behind them – a groundsman, complete with a gundog.

"What do you think you're doing? This is private property!"

Col panicked – they had to make a run for it, now. He turned to grab Mr Noakes – but Mr Noakes had disappeared again. If there was one thing that badger was good at, it was vanishing into thin air.

"Come on, own up!" said the groundsman angrily. "Where did he go? I saw you talking to someone else at the top of the hill!"

"Um…" Col wished he knew. He had absolutely no idea where Mr Noakes had gone – all he could see was the groundsman's dog sniffing around the base of the nearest tree…

Col froze. Mr Noakes was clinging to the lowest branch above the groundsman's head, just out of eyesight. The dog already had his scent – any moment now, it was going to find him. "I … er…"

"Good lord – what are you wearing?"

Col glanced down at his outfit. He must have looked

completely bizarre: his Boys' Brigade uniform was now a patchwork of rips, tears and dried-on sludge. The oversized corduroy trousers didn't help matters.

The groundsman's face suddenly dawned with realization. "Hang on – you're not staying at Havencroft, are you?"

Col blinked. "Havencroft?"

The man nodded through the trees. In the distance, just hidden from sight, was a large stone mansion. Col's heart lifted – this was his chance to get rid of the groundsman before the dog spotted Mr Noakes.

"Yes!" he said. "That's it. I'm staying at Havencroft. Sorry for the confusion."

The groundsman shook his head. "Good grief – I didn't know they were bringing in *children* now." He grabbed Col by the jacket. "Right, come on – I'll take you back. You shouldn't be out here!"

Col panicked. "Wait! I—"

The dog started barking – it had spotted Mr Noakes. The groundsman turned. "What is it, Maisie? What have you found?"

"NO!" Col cried, spinning him back round.

The groundsman was bewildered. "Hey! What are you playing at?"

Col thought fast. He couldn't run away now – the man was already suspicious, and if he called the police then it would all be over. He had to string the groundsman along for as long as possible, and then slip away the first chance he got.

"Did I say no?" said Col. "I meant … yes! Take me to Havencroft, please!"

The groundsman glared at him – but seemed to accept this strange behaviour with a shake of the head. He marched Col away, muttering under his breath, and his dog reluctantly followed. Col snuck a glance over his shoulder. Mr Noakes was still clinging to the branch, watching Col walk away in horror. He made to follow – but Col shook his head. The Guardians had put everything on the line for him: now, it was his turn to help them.

"You're sure there was no one else with you?" said the groundsman.

Col nodded. "Yes. It's just me."

Col took one final glance over his shoulder, and saw Mr Noakes scamper back over the fence and up the hill to the stone circle.

For the first time in six days, Col was on his own.

Havencroft

COL AND THE GROUNDSMAN WALKED TOWARDS THE mansion. With every step, Col's decision to stay seemed more and more reckless. How on earth was he going to get out of this? They were already running out of time and now the Guardians would be trapped inside the circle until he got back, unable to take a step outside without being seen by the Midwinter King. Col could only pray that Mr Noakes would make it back to them safely. And what if he didn't?

The groundsman led him through the doors of the mansion – and Col frowned. Havencroft wasn't what he was expecting at all. He thought it would be filled with posh people and servants, but everyone was wearing pyjamas and dressing gowns. The hall was lined with chairs and hospital beds, and nurses with purple armbands were bringing everyone blankets and cups of tea.

Col finally understood where they were. He'd heard of makeshift hospitals like this in the countryside, where people from the cities came to recuperate for a few days. Wardens, ambulance drivers, rubble clearers... People who'd been pushed to the edge by the relentless bombings. Everywhere he looked, there were signs of damage. Some people had wounds on their faces or bandages around their arms and legs. One man was shaking so violently that a nurse had to help him drink a cup of tea. Now he understood what Rose had meant when she said how bad things were in London. He had been kept away from all this in Buxton.

"There are so many," said Col quietly.

The groundsman glanced at him. "I thought you said you were staying here?"

Col nodded. "I – I am! With my parents – oh look, there they are!"

He pointed over the man's shoulder. The groundsman turned around – Col didn't waste a second. He tore himself free and flew into the crowds.

"Oi! Get back here!"

Col ran as fast as he could – he had to find a way out of here, now. Every second counted. Today was the last chance he and the Guardians had to make up the time they'd lost. He had to get back to the stone circle before...

"Bulb?"

Col screeched to a stop. His way forward was blocked by a table of men playing draughts – and one of them was standing up, pointing at him. It was Gary, the Home Guard soldier who'd tried to shoot Mr Noakes two days ago.

"That's him! That's the boy who was there when the … the *thing* attacked me!"

Col turned pale. People were looking this way, asking what all the commotion was about – soon they were going to start asking questions.

A woman wearing a purple armband patted Gary on the shoulder. "Please, Mr Digby – leave the poor boy alone. You know what the doctor said – no more 'bogie' talk! You've had a terrible shock, but you're safe now."

Gary tore himself away. "For the last time, I didn't make it up! Ask Bulb! Ask him about the monster!"

"That's right!" said the man sitting beside him, who was covered from head to toe in bandages. "And while he's there, he can settle the argument about this invisible badger…"

"SHUT UP, NEV."

Col scurried away before anyone could try to stop him. He had to find a way outside before the groundsman caught up with him, so he could sneak over the fence and get back to his Guardians. He saw a door at the other end of the hall, leading into the grounds, and charged towards it.

This time, he almost made it – but was blocked at the last second by a nurse. She glared at him distastefully. "Good grief – the state of you! What's your name?"

"Co– I mean, Bulb," said Col instantly.

The nurse sighed, and shook her head. "Another one from London." She grabbed his arm. "Right, Bulb – let's get you deloused and into some fresh clothes."

Col's eyes widened. "Deloused?"

The nurse glanced at his clothes in disgust. "Better do it twice."

She threw him into a room filled with steaming metal tubs of water, stripped his clothes, scrubbed him to within an inch of his life, covered his hair with foul smelling paste that blinded him, poked inside his mouth with a stick, shoved him in some starched pyjamas and a huge second-hand pullover that was at least five sizes too big, and threw him back into the hallway with a cup of tea and a corned beef sandwich, trembling like a shaved dog.

"Oof! That's the face of a boy that's just been deloused."

Col looked up. There was a woman sat in a wicker chair in front of him, with her hair in rollers and smoking a pipe. She patted the chair beside her.

"Come on, put your feet up! You can relax by listening to the news."

She cackled and nodded to the room ahead. There were dozens of people crowded round a huge radiogram, listening to the latest headlines. The newsreader was describing the raids from the night before, but as usual he couldn't say any actual place names in case the enemy was listening, so the crowd were all arguing at the top of their voices to piece together what was going on.

"Hear that? The bombings have started again!"

"'A town in the north' – that's got to be Manchester!"

"Nonsense! It'll be Liverpool, after all those raids on the Christmas markets…"

"Turkeys roasting in their stands, they said!"

"*Still* no news from the Americans…"

"So? We don't need any help from the Yanks!"

"Ha! And I suppose *you'd* rather the Nazis bomb us into a new dark age instead?"

"What would you rather do? Surrender?"

"Well, if the Americans don't do *something* soon, we've already lost."

Col gazed at the arguing crowd, his heart sinking. After six days of fighting magical creatures, the reality of the war was suddenly staring him in the face once more. The Guardians were right – the raids didn't just bring bombs. They brought darkness, fear, division; all the things the Midwinter King feasted on. And after London was destroyed, it would only get worse.

Col couldn't stay here – he had to leave and finish his quest, now. He crept towards the nearest door … just as the groundsman barged inside with his dog.

"Anyone seen a boy dressed as a monkey? He was just here!"

Col spun round and quickly sat back beside the woman, trying to look natural. Luckily the groundsman didn't recognize him in his new clothes – and even better, the foul stench of the hair-paste seemed to hide his scent from the dog. The groundsman left the room and started marching around the hall again, looking for him. Col couldn't risk leaving now – he'd have to wait until the coast was clear. Until then, he had to try to look normal. He took a bite of his sandwich – it was unbelievably delicious.

"So! Where are you from, then?"

Col looked up. The woman in rollers was smiling at him.

"Er – London," said Col. "Herne Hill."

The woman smiled. "You don't say! We're practically neighbours. I work the buses in Streatham – you'll have seen me, if you ever use the 133."

Col grinned. "I get on that bus all the time!"

It felt so easy, so natural, to have a conversation about buses. The woman shook his hand. "Ida. Pleased to meet you."

"Col." He didn't feel like he needed to use a fake name – he felt safe around Ida. He kept one eye on the groundsman searching for him in the next room.

"So, what brings you to Havencroft, Col?" said Ida. "Visiting your parents?"

Col didn't know what to say – thankfully, she stopped him before he could attempt to lie.

"No! Don't answer – that was nosy of me. I don't need to know."

Col frowned. "Why are *you* here?"

She laughed. "Fair enough! Well, I was driving during a raid and a bomb landed right by the bus. Hundred kilo, they said! Threw me clear out of the window and took out most of the road too. Luckily there was no one else on it at the time."

Col choked on his sandwich. "You were driving a bus during a raid?"

Ida shrugged. "It's up to the drivers whether we stop or not. It's the only thing that keeps London going, isn't it? Besides, once you've done last bus at closing time on a Friday night, there's not much else that can scare you."

Col looked up. The groundsman was gone – the coast was finally clear. But something kept him on his chair. A question that had been burning inside him for some time.

"Ida … what's it like in a raid?"

She glanced at him. "Don't you know?"

Col fussed the leg of his pyjama trousers. "I got evacuated before they started. I've always wondered what they're like. My sister still lives in London, you see, and she bikes around during the raids, and I…"

He trailed off. Ida sighed.

"Well … it's always different. Sometimes the siren goes and you run to a shelter and wait out the whole night and nothing happens. Other times the bombs are right outside, and your teeth rattle in your head and dust falls down every few seconds and people swear at the ceiling. But the *waiting's* always the worst part. You lie there all night, thinking something awful's going to happen any moment – then the all-clear goes at dawn, and you have to get up and go to work!" She cackled. "That's if you can be bothered to go to a public shelter. Sometimes the siren goes in the middle of the night and I can't even be bothered to get out of bed. I just lie there and let the Nazis get on with it."

Col stared at her in amazement. "That's so brave."

Ida shook her head. "I'm as scared as everyone else. People say you get used to it, but that's nonsense. You're *supposed* to be scared. It would be wrong if you weren't."

She took a puff on her pipe. "Too many brave people are dead."

She looked at him – and paused. Col was spilling tea into his lap. His hands were shaking.

"Good lord – what's the matter?" she asked, concerned.

The last thing Col wanted was to draw attention to himself, but he couldn't help it. Suddenly he was crying again. "I'm sorry, it's just… I've been so frightened for Rose. My sister. We haven't spoken since before Christmas. I haven't been able to stop thinking about all the terrible things that might happen to her…"

Ida looked pained. "Oh, you poor thing! I didn't mean to worry you – I'm sure your sister is absolutely fine." She patted his shoulder. "Tell you what – my son's driving me home the day after tomorrow. He's an army officer, with his own car! He'll be happy to drop you off in London – you can see your sister again."

Col shook his head. The day after tomorrow would be too late – the raid would have happened by then. "That's very kind, Ida, but…"

"Or you could go to the office right now and give her a ring?"

Col paused. "The phone lines are working again?"

Ida nodded. "Ever since the storms stopped. Go on! You go talk to your sister, and I'll bet you feel better afterwards. I'll look after your sandwich."

Col felt his heart beat a little faster. This could be his chance to warn Rose about what was going to happen. She might even believe him when he talked about the raid – Col could get her out of London and finish his quest right now. Not only that – he could hear her voice again. He hadn't heard her voice in six months. He wondered if it sounded the same.

"Thank you, Ida!"

She smiled. "It's nothing. We all have to look after each other, don't we?"

He snuck over to the office – sure enough, the woman behind the desk let him use the phone. He asked the operator to connect him to the party line in Herne Hill – the one they shared with the other houses in his street – and the phone started ringing. Col glanced over his shoulder, heart thundering, praying that he'd get the chance to speak to Rose before he got caught...

"Hello?"

Col gasped. It wasn't Rose on the line – it was Mr Bennet, their neighbour from two doors down.

"Mr Bennet? Please – I don't have much time. Is Rose there?"

Mr Bennet sounded shocked. *"Col! Good grief, where have you—?"*

"There he is!"

Col spun round. He was too late – the groundsman

was striding across the hallway towards him, followed by a fleet of nurses.

"That's the one! I checked the records and there's no mention at all of a child being here!"

Everyone in the hallway was staring at him now. A nurse grabbed the receiver out of his hand and slammed it down. "Right – you're coming with me. Let's get to the bottom of this."

Col gasped. It was all over – he'd risked everything for the chance to talk to Rose, and now he was never going to get back to the Guardians. "Please! You don't understand. I have to go…"

He fell silent. There was a noise carrying through the doors, ringing down the hallway and echoing off the marble floors. Everyone stopped in their tracks. It was a sound no one had heard in a long, long time.

"Church bells," said the groundsman in disbelief. "They're … they're ringing the church bells."

A nurse let a tray of teacups clatter to the floor. A man in bandages leaped up from his bed.

"Don't you know what that means? We've been invaded! *The Nazis are here!*"

The room erupted. Suddenly people were running in every direction, grabbing what they could, stuffing all their belongings into suitcases, while nurses and women in armbands tried to keep order.

"Stay calm! Everyone, stay where you are!"

Col was instantly forgotten. He stood frozen to the spot, his mind reeling. It was the moment that the entire country had been dreading ever since the war began: the Nazis had invaded, and Britain had become a warzone. What did that mean for Ruth, and her parents? For the people sleeping out in the snow? For the people staying here? How on earth was he going to make it to London now? How would Rose—?

Something grabbed him by the scruff of the neck and dragged him out of the doorway. Col suddenly found himself lying in a flowerbed with a hand over his mouth.

A paw, actually.

"From now on," Pendlebury growled into his ear, "you're not going *anywhere* without me."

Col could have cried for joy. They were all crouched in the flowerbed beside him – Pendlebury, the King of Rogues and Ruth. They were all OK. The only one missing was…

"Where's Mr Noakes?" said Col.

"Causing a distraction for us," said Pendlebury. "It's the least he can do, after losing you like that. Honestly, you give that badger *one* job!"

She threw Col onto her back and they tore across the grounds, leaping over the fence in a single bound as church bells boomed through the trees.

"But can't you hear that?" said Col. "They're ringing the bells! We've been invaded!"

"This is, er ... not *strictly* true," said Ruth.

Pendlebury came to a screeching halt at a set of wooden gates beside the path. On the other side lay the church they had seen earlier, the last of the chimes echoing out of its belltower. Two Home Guard soldiers were racing inside just as Mr Noakes was squeezing out of the shutters on the opposite side and pelting towards them.

The penny finally dropped.

"The church bells – that was you?" Col gasped. "We haven't been invaded?"

"Nope," said Mr Noakes, leaping onto Pendlebury's back. "But unless we leave right now, I think we're going to have a very angry vicar to deal with…"

Col frowned – something about this still didn't make sense.

"Hang on – how did you all get here?" he asked. "You said you had to be near me at all times, or else the Midwinter King could find you! In my pocket of love, right?"

Pendlebury coughed. "Er … well, yes, that's right. But it turns out that we could leave the circle in someone *else's* love, instead."

Col blinked. "Who?"

The Guardians turned around. Ruth was blushing bright-red. Col's mouth fell.

"Ruth? You – *love* them?"

Ruth shrugged. "So? This is not so very important."

His Guardians were all embarrassed, avoiding each other's gaze. Col smiled. Sharing his friends had felt weird at first: they had always been his own personal, private companions. But sharing them with Ruth felt like the most natural thing in the world.

"Right!" said the King of Rogues suddenly. "Better go!"

"Yes!" agreed Mr Noakes. "Lots of ground to cover today!"

"No time like the present!" said Pendlebury.

They flew out of the trees as fast as they could, the last tolls echoing through the forest. They were trying to act casual, but Col couldn't help but notice that they all held onto each other tighter now.

The Armies of Darkness

T HEY SAW FEWER AND FEWER SIGNS OF PEOPLE. The roads became sparser, the hills more undulating, the sky wider. After his brief return to reality, it was as if Col had left the world behind again.

"The next stone circle is the last sanctuary before London," Pendlebury reminded him. "If we can make it there today, then we'll only have another thirty miles to cover on the last day."

"Are you sure you can do it?" asked Col.

Pendlebury set her mouth grimly. "We don't have a choice."

She tore across the landscape. True to her word, her strength was greater than ever after a night in the sanctuary – but now the terrain she had to cover was harder than ever before. The snow had burst the riverbanks and turned the earth to sludge, causing terrible floods. They ran for hours across waterlogged fields, scrambling over rock faces worn hard by centuries and past smashed stone walls that sagged in the ground like broken skulls. Soon Col's legs were aching from the strain of riding – he couldn't imagine what it must be like for Pendlebury, carrying all of them on her back for hour after hour. The strain showed on her face with every mile – her pace slackened, her breathing became heavier, but still she kept going.

Finally, just as the sun was beginning to slink towards the horizon, they came to a hill that overlooked a barren brown field, surrounded by a wall of trees.

Pendlebury frowned. "This isn't right. The stones said there's a forest here – a big one."

"There was," said the King of Rogues. He pointed to a jagged stump poking from the earth ahead. There were hundreds of them, covering the field like stubble.

Col's face fell. "They took the trees for the war effort. They cut them all down."

Ruth frowned. "*War effort?* What is this, please?"

"You know – things for the armed forces," said Col. "Wood, fuel, newspaper. Milk bottle tops." He rubbed at his knuckles, worrying the skin. "Metal railings, even."

They gazed at the dead earth in silence. It was a dismal sight. It felt like standing in a graveyard.

"I do not like this place," said Ruth quietly.

"Neither do I," said Col. "Let's—"

"Pendlebury." Mr Noakes had one paw on his club. His fur was bristling. "We're not alone."

Col gasped. He was right. Col could feel it: a taste of rot and malice in the wind. Something bad was coming. Something very bad. The panic rose in his chest, fast. "We have to get to the sanctuary!"

"No." Pendlebury's eyes were wide and frightened. "We don't have time. We have to make camp here, now."

Col looked around in dismay. There was nothing on the hill except a single tree, looming from the top like a dead finger. They were exposed and unprotected. They couldn't be in a worse place if they tried. "We can't stay here!"

"We have to," said Pendlebury. "They'll be here any minute. We have to make a fire. A big one, before they get here."

Col gulped. "Before *who* gets here?"

She didn't answer him. Instead she flew to the place where the wall of trees began and the Guardians gathered branch after branch in taut silence, loading it onto Pendlebury's back and heaving it to the top of the hill. Col joined in, not understanding why they were doing it, too afraid to ask. Before long they had a stack of wood piled taller than Col on the hillside.

"Col – light it quickly," said Pendlebury. "We don't have much time."

Col set to work with the ration-pack matches, trying to stop his hands from shaking. The only thing that kept him from completely panicking was focusing on the fire. He fed it quickly, mechanically, trying not to pile on too much at once and smother it. Soon enough, a small patch of flames was blistering in the ground.

"Rogue, Mr Noakes – go and get more wood, as much as you can carry," said Pendlebury. "We have to keep it burning all night. It's the only thing that will hold them back."

Col's whole body chilled. "Hold *who* back?"

The Guardians ignored him and raced off to the forest. Col watched them leave, the dread building in his chest.

"They can't go alone – they won't be protected!"

Pendlebury shook her head. "That doesn't matter any more, Col."

Col looked around in horror. Night was falling – fast. The moon was barely more than a stitch in the sky now. The fire at his feet was so small in the gathering darkness. Suddenly he couldn't bear it. They had one day left, and here they were in the middle of nowhere, with something dreadful coming for them...

"I'm going to help them!" he cried.

He tore down the hillside after Mr Noakes and the King of Rogues.

"Col, no!" cried Pendlebury.

But he didn't stop. He raced back down the hill and soon he was back in the forest, grabbing every branch he could, shovelling them into his arms until his shoulders were aching with the strain and his hands were pitted with splinters. He had no idea what it was that was coming for them, but he knew it was bad. He could feel it in the pit of his guts. He couldn't let himself panic – he had to focus on getting the job done, on getting as much firewood as possible before…

He stopped.

There was a glow on the edge of his vision. It came from somewhere deep in the forest. A faint ball of yellow light, swaying silently through the trees.

Col watched it, transfixed. The light was beautiful. And it almost seemed if it was … *saying something* to him. Something important.

Collie, are you there? Come quick!

Col gasped – it was Rose. And it sounded like she needed help. It felt so good to finally hear her voice again – he'd forgotten how much he missed it. He dropped the wood and ran towards the light. He was vaguely aware that he had been frightened a few moments ago – but he wasn't worried about the fire any more, or about the raid. He didn't have a care in the world. All he cared about was getting close to the light so he could…

Something wrenched back his shoulder, hard. It felt like being doused in ice water. Col swung around. "Hey…!"

There was no one behind him. The forest was empty.

Col swallowed. He hadn't imagined it – something had pulled him back again, just like when he'd been dragged out of the nightmare. He looked around. He had dropped all the wood he'd been collecting. He frowned – why had he done that? He needed to get back to the others, right now, before…

That was when he saw Mr Noakes.

The badger was a few feet ahead of him. Col hadn't even noticed he was there. All of Mr Noakes' attention was on the floating ball in front of him. It was speaking to him too: but not with Rose's voice.

It was Col's voice.

Save me, Mr Noakes! Please!

Mr Noakes' eyes were pricked with tears. "I'm coming, my lad. I won't let anything hurt you ever again, I swear…"

Col's stomach clenched in horror. Suddenly he saw the light for what it really was – a trap. Mr Noakes stepped closer and the light swung back, revealing a figure crouched in the dark behind it, its breath seething in silent clouds…

"MR NOAKES!"

The badger snapped round just as a hand shot out, missing him by inches. The light reeled up. It was a lantern on the end of a withered branch, and behind it was a man who looked like he had lived in darkness all his life. He had huge pale eyes and sickly white skin and the thin webbed hands of a bat. He shrieked with frustration and lunged again, but Mr Noakes leaped back and swung his club, smashing the lantern to pieces. The pale man howled as if he'd been struck and raced off into the forest. The trees were plunged into blackness once more – and this time, it was even darker than they had realized.

"Mr Noakes!" Col cried. "What was—?"

"A Lantern Man," he said, the words coming fast and scared. "He won't be alone. Oh, we have to go, *we have to go*!"

He grabbed Col and dragged him out of the forest. Pendlebury, Ruth and the King of Rogues were standing beside the bonfire at the top of the hill, their faces alight with terror. The sense of dread was building around them, growing worse and worse by the second: Col could feel it in his chest, in his stomach, at the back of his throat, rising up like a sickness…

The howl came from every direction. It was the most horrible noise Col had ever heard: it rang inside his bones, prickling his skin like cold needles. There was another, and another, and another. It was coming out of the forest on every side.

"The King's army!" cried the King of Rogues. "Oh, we're done for!"

Pendlebury flew to work. "Build the fire! Build it high, build it bright! It's the only thing that can hold them off!"

The Guardians piled everything they could onto the bonfire. The wood spluttered and caught, lighting up the hillside as darkness fell around them like an avalanche…

"Here they come!"

The dogs came out of the trees on all sides, pounding across the bare earth like a flood. Col saw instantly that they were outnumbered, by hundreds. The dogs spiralled around the hillside and surrounded them, howling and barking at the edge of the firelight – but they couldn't come any closer. The light burned them like acid. The Guardians stood facing the wall of baying dogs, blocking them on every side.

One of the dogs pushed their way to the front. She was bigger than the others, but only just: her body was covered in scars and her head was pushed close to the ground by her spine.

"Barghest?" said Pendlebury quietly.

Col was shocked – Pendlebury knew this terrifying creature. And what's more, Barghest seemed to know her too. They stood facing each other on either side of the fire: one in the light, one in the dark.

"You've defied the King long enough, Pendlebury," said Barghest. "Surrender yourselves now."

Pendlebury smiled grimly. If she was frightened, she was hiding it well.

"I always wondered when we'd next see each other – I never thought it would be like this. So you're the King's general now? Was it easy, hiding from him the fact that you knew me? You must have been terrified he'd find out…"

"Enough," spat Barghest. "You're in more trouble than you can possibly imagine. Give yourselves up." She shifted on her paws. "If not … we'll take the boy."

Mr Noakes and the King of Rogues gasped. Even the dogs behind Barghest were shocked – they growled unhappily, snaking and pacing in the darkness.

Pendlebury didn't even blink. "Is that how far you've come, Barghest? You'd break the most sacred law of our kind and harm a human, just to please him?"

Barghest thinned her eyes. "The laws won't matter when the King is on the throne. Hand yourselves over, or we'll take him instead."

Col's heart was pounding. He glanced between Pendlebury and Barghest as they faced each other in silence.

"If you want him," said Pendlebury calmly, "come out of the shadows and take him."

The dogs roared, the sound rising like a sea at storm.

Barghest curled her lip. "As you wish."

The dogs closed in, forming a twisting wall of rising darkness on every side. The firelight kept them back, but only just. There was no way through them, no way over them. The Guardians were trapped, an island of light in a sea of darkness.

"Pendlebury," Col whispered. "There are too many of them."

"I know," she said. "We'll fight anyway."

"But we won't have enough wood to…"

"Col." Pendlebury gave him a look that seemed, at first, like fear: but it wasn't fear at all. "Stay close to the fire. Build it high. Build it bright. Don't let them win."

The fight began. The dogs circled the bonfire, growling and barking, leaping into the light again and again to try to grab Col or Ruth. Each time, the Guardians would beat them back. The King of Rogues thrust left and right with his lance; Mr Noakes took great swings with his club, sending the dogs sprawling to the ground; Pendlebury grew to her greatest size and swiped with her claws, leaping back every time one of the dogs tried to grab her. The dogs could only stay in the light for a few seconds before it burned them, but even so it was like trying to hold back a flood.

"Keep the fire going!" Pendlebury roared to Col and Ruth. "Don't let them get any closer!"

Col and Ruth grabbed branch after branch and stacked them over the fire, until the bonfire was a blazing inferno on the hillside. Soon the flames stretched up higher than they could reach, and the heat was unbearable. It burned Col's face and choked his throat, blinding him, scorching his clothes and melting the hairs on his arms, but still he kept going. The world outside the bonfire was lost to him completely now, the sound of the wind lost to the endless baying of the dogs. Over and over the Guardians beat back the darkness as it surged forwards to grab them…

"That's it, Col!" cried Pendlebury. "Keep going! Keep—"

And then it happened. Barghest flung herself from the darkness and clamped her jaws round one of Pendlebury's legs. Pendlebury howled in agony and tried to pull free, but in an instant the other dogs descended on her and dragged her into the darkness.

"Pendlebury!" Col screamed.

He was doing it before he knew he was doing it. He grabbed a burning branch from the bonfire, the end of it only just far enough from the flames to hold without hurting him, and flew into the darkness after her.

"Master Col! No!" cried Mr Noakes.

Col didn't stop. He couldn't lose Pendlebury: he had to save her. He could see her up ahead in the darkness, fighting off the sea of snarling dogs. Col tore into them, swinging the burning branch left and right, sending them howling from the light.

"Get off! I won't let you have her!"

He cut a path straight to her. She was covered in bites and tears, whole patches of her fur ripped clean away. She gazed at him in horror.

"Col, what are you doing?"

"Saving you." He pulled her up. "Come on! We have to get back!"

But even as he said it, the light in his hands was dying. The wood was burning through, and the dogs knew it. They massed around them, tightening the circle of darkness as the branch's fire ebbed and dulled. Col spun round, swinging the last of the light hopelessly as the dogs moved in. There was no way back to the bonfire now – Col couldn't even see the fire any more.

"COL!"

The burst of white was sudden, blinding. The dogs howled and scattered. Col shielded his face: Ruth and the Guardians had pulled down the dead tree and leaned it directly into the bonfire. The whole nest of branches was ablaze: the tree was a roaring pillar of fire, forcing the dogs back from Col and Pendlebury and clearing the path to safety. Ruth raced to Col and helped him drag Pendlebury back to the fire.

"We can do it – we have to keep going!" Col cried. "We just have to hold them back!"

And they did. They fought for hour after hour, piling log after log against the burning tree until it seemed like the entire hillside was a furnace. They beat back monster after monster, driving back the endless tide of darkness as the night bore down upon them.

No one saw it, of course. The rest of the country were hidden safely inside their homes: those who did glimpse out their curtains that night, to see the distant burning glow in the wilderness, thought it was just another building hit in a raid. No one knew the secret battle that was fought that night, just a hair's breadth away, between the Guardians and the army of darkness, hour after hour after hour…

And then all at once, just as quickly as the battle had started, it was over.

The dogs shrank back, as if scalded. The barking ceased. Col looked up and cried out for joy: the cold grey light of a winter morning was streaking across the landscape towards them. The sun was rising – the day had come again – they had made it.

Barghest's exhausted face sagged with horror. "No –

we cannot stop now! We cannot fail the King! We must not let them get away!"

But the other dogs weren't listening – they were swarming towards the forest, back to the darkness they had come from. Barghest watched them flee in despair. "Come back!"

"It's not too late, Barghest."

Barghest spun round. Pendlebury was facing her again over the smoking ruins of the fire. Her face was matted and burnt, her fur blackened with soot.

"You don't have to follow him. You can join the fight for the Green Man. You can help put a stop to all of this."

Barghest trembled. Col had never seen anything so frightened, so broken, so utterly helpless in all his life. "I – I will not take advice from a creature as doomed as you! I have made my choice…"

"You can unmake it," said Pendlebury calmly. "You can always unmake it."

Barghest stared at the tiger for a moment – then with a howl of anguish, she turned and ran. Col watched her disappear into the forest, and then she was gone. The hillside was empty again. He fell to his knees on the scorched earth. Every part of him sang with exhaustion – but they had done it. They had fought all night against the darkness and won. Tears streamed down his face, cutting lines through the ash that stained his face and clothes. He didn't know if the tears were from the smoke or from sheer, blessed relief, but they wouldn't stop coming.

"We did it – we held them off!" Col cried. "We can still make it!"

No one answered. They were all looking at Pendlebury. She hadn't moved an inch from her spot beside the fire. She was swaying from side to side. Her legs were shaking.

"Pendlebury?"

She tried to turn, and her body failed. She hit the ground, hard.

"Pendlebury!" Col cried.

He scrambled to her side – and gasped. Her fur was caked with blood. The place where Barghest had bitten her was much, much worse than he had realized. She looked up at him, her eyes suddenly dull as stones.

"Col, I'm sorry. I should have been faster, I should have got us to the sanctuary in time…"

Col shook his head. "It – it doesn't matter. The sanctuary's still close – we can get you there and heal you! We can still make it…"

He stopped. Pendlebury was giving him another look that he had never seen before.

"I – I think this is as far as I can take you, Col."

Col blinked. "What do you mean? Pendlebury?"

She didn't reply. Her eyes were focusing on something behind him, something beyond where he could see.

"I'm sorry," she whispered again.

Her head touched the ground, and she fell silent. The only sounds were the fading sparks of the fire on the hillside as the sun rose on a new morning.

28 December 1940

When walking after dark to-night For safety's sake, wear something WHITE!

For the pedestrian:

- Remember that when you can see the motorist, the motorist probably can't see you.
- So wear or carry something white or luminous.

For the motorist:

- Remember you are in charge of a weapon that can kill.
- Be careful – be considerate.

There were 1,146 road deaths last month due to blackout conditions ... most of them avoidable.

Pendlebury

COL GAZED AT THE TIGER LYING ON THE DIRT before him. Her eyes had glazed over and her breathing was heavy and ragged. Suddenly she seemed very small. She had always been strong, even when she was suffering, but he had never seen her like this before: so weak, so helpless, so broken. And it was all his fault. She had pushed herself too hard to help him, and now she was badly, badly hurt.

"Pendlebury, wait! We'll get you to the sanctuary, just hold on…"

"No, lad." Mr Noakes stood behind him. His waist-coat had been torn to shreds. "We have to keep going. We've got one day left to get to London. We can't fall behind now."

Col shook his head in horror. "N-no! We need to find the sanctuary so she can heal! Help me!"

He tried to heave Pendlebury off the ground, but it

was hopeless. She was too heavy, a deadweight.

"Pendlebury – shrink so I can carry you. Quick!"

But it was as if she couldn't hear him – she just lay on the ground, gasping.

Col felt a hand on his shoulder. It was the King of Rogues. His armour was blackened and his eyes were red. "My liege – she would not want to hold us back." He paused. "She would want you to leave her."

Col stared at him, speechless. He had to be joking. There was no way that they could just leave her here, in the middle of nowhere, in this horrible place. She was one of his oldest friends. She had given everything for him.

"We can't," he whispered.

"We must, my liege."

"But…"

"No."

Ruth stepped forward. Her dress was torn and stained, and she had cut her head badly at some point in the night so that blood oozed down her forehead, but her eyes were unwavering.

"Col is right," she said. "She carried us – now we carry her. Come."

Mr Noakes and the King of Rogues looked at each other – and nodded. The four of them heaved Pendlebury from the ground and lifted her onto their shoulders.

Col stroked the patch of fur behind her ears and

leaned close. "Pendlebury – which way to the sanctuary?" he whispered.

She groaned weakly. "Col, no…"

Col was desperate. "No! You're my Guardian – whatever I ask, that's what you'll do, right? So tell me where it is!"

She gazed at him, her eyes grey, her breath whistling. She nodded ahead. "Beyond the trees. We have to go all the way through."

They carried her through the forest. Their journey was slow and laborious: they stumbled down slopes and across freezing streams, slipping on rocks and snagging their skin on branches. After a while carrying Pendlebury began to feel easier, and Col was relieved at first: but then he realized it was because she was getting smaller. She wasn't doing it on purpose: she was shrinking slowly in their arms, like air escaping a balloon. He didn't want to think about what that meant. Soon she had grown so small that Mr Noakes and the King of Rogues could carry her between them.

"Pendlebury, you've got to hold on!" Col begged. "We're almost there. Just a little further."

He didn't know if that was true. He had no idea where he was. But he had to keep looking – for her. There was no way he could fail her now.

The day wore on, and the forest kept going. They

walked deeper into the wilderness, until every direction they turned looked exactly like the one they had last taken. Col's head throbbed and his legs trembled, and the burns on his face and arms stung relentlessly. Soon they were all beyond exhausted, and Pendlebury was so small that Mr Noakes could carry her in his arms like a sleeping child.

Finally they reached the top of a steep slope slick with mud and snow, and the path simply ended. There was nowhere left to go: the forest was darkening around them.

Col spun around frantically. "The sanctuary's got to be here! It has to be!"

"Master Col," said Mr Noakes. "We're running out of time…"

"No!" said Col firmly. "We can still find it. We can still heal Pendlebury and get to London before…"

"That's not what I *mean*, Master Col."

Mr Noakes held out Pendlebury. Col's heart clenched. The tiger was so small that Mr Noakes could hold her between his two paws. She was shrinking faster and faster. Col swallowed down the feeling inside him.

"P-please. Let me carry her."

Mr Noakes handed her over in silence. Col looked down at her, stroking the fur of her face gently. She looked so weak, so fragile. Her bones were frail as matchsticks.

"You have to hold on, Pendlebury. We'll find the sanctuary soon, I promise. Then you'll get better and we'll save Rose, just like we always planned. We've still got time before…"

He looked up at the sky – and trailed off.

He looked from south to north, and from east to west … but he couldn't find the moon. There was no sign of it. The sky was black in every direction.

The realization hit him like a punch to the stomach.

"It's the new moon," said Col in shock.

Ruth stared at him. "What does this mean?"

Col swallowed. It was almost too big, too awful to say out loud.

"In the vision … the sky was moonless," he managed. "That was when the raid was going to happen – the new moon. And it's come." He looked at her. "We're too late. We didn't make it."

Mr Noakes and the King of Rogues opened their mouths – but they had nothing to say. Ruth swayed on her feet, too tired to even cry. The worst had come. They had gone so far, and come so close, but they had failed. It was over. Col sank to the ground, gazing at the tiger in his hands. She was shrinking even as he looked at her, her heartbeat tip-tapping to a stop against the skin of his palm.

"Oh Pendlebury … I'm so sorry."

His eyes filled with tears. She had given up everything to help him. She had fought off an entire army of darkness for a million-to-one chance of saving his sister, and it had all been for nothing. He had failed her. He'd lost Dad, he'd lost Rose, and now he'd lost her too.

"You have her voice – you know that, don't you?" he said, tears pouring out of him. "Rose. I gave you her voice. That's how I always imagined you. And now I've lost both of you."

He felt a hand on his shoulder.

"My liege – we must find this sanctuary before night falls."

"She's dying, Rogue. She's dying and there's nothing we can do about it."

"Master Col, the King's armies will come back for us soon and—"

"It wasn't a bomb that did it, you know."

Col looked up, beyond the trees. There wasn't anything ahead of him – just darkness. But Col wasn't looking at what was in front of him. He was looking at something else, something inside himself, something he'd hidden for the last few months.

"The incident. I know most people think it was a bomb that killed Dad, but it wasn't. He was cycling home in blackout, just like he did every night. There was a piece of brick on the road, but it was too dark for him to see it. He hit it and swerved into a car on the other side of the road and came off his bike and hit his head on some metal railings, and that was it. The doctor said he wouldn't have felt anything." He swallowed. "The railings aren't there any more. They took them out a week later, for the war effort."

The forest darkened around them, grain by grain. Col gazed at the tiny figure in his hands, no bigger than a china mouse, her breath drawing to a close.

"And that's the problem, isn't it? If he'd been bombed, I could hate someone for it. I could join the army when I'm older and fight the Nazis and make them pay for what they did. But *nothing* killed him. It was just … darkness."

The forest ahead was moving, the trunks bending and cracking. Col looked up.

"And how can you fight darkness?"

The Guardians drew their weapons.

"Col, they're here!" cried Mr Noakes. "The King's army – they've found us!"

But Col didn't move. He stayed where he was, gazing at the vast monster advancing through the trees towards them. There was nowhere to run – no way they could fight it. Col wasn't even frightened any more. He had nothing left to be afraid of.

The King of Rogues grabbed Ruth and threw her

beside Col, and he and the badger formed a final wall of protection in front of them.

"This is it," said Mr Noakes, holding his club. "Good luck, Rogue."

"*King* of Rogues."

The knight clutched him warmly by the shoulder.

"Goodbye, old friend," he said.

The monster came lumbering out of the darkness. It was so tall that the top of its head almost cleared the forest. At first, Col thought that it was wearing some kind of crown ... then he realized that its head was covered in branches. Its entire body was carved from wood. Its eyes were deep hollows, its mouth a gash. Long, withered tendrils grew from inside it, trailing down its shoulders and dragging on the floor. Col had never seen anything so twisted, so ancient, so ruined in all his life. It was so broken that it was almost dead.

But not completely.

So you have found me, said the Green Man.

The Green Man

Mʀ Nᴏᴀᴋᴇs ᴀɴᴅ ᴛʜᴇ Kɪɴɢ ᴏғ Rᴏɢᴜᴇs ᴛʜʀᴇᴡ themselves to the ground.

"Get down!" cried the King of Rogues.

Ruth did as she was told – but Col didn't move. He watched the Green Man walk towards them. The god of life looked nothing like the painting they had seen above the pub. He was so dismal, so decrepit. Roots plunged from his feet and burrowed into the ground with every step, holding him steady.

You should not be here, said the Green Man. *You will lead his spies to me. You must leave at once.*

"Forgive us, Lord!" said Mr Noakes, trembling. "We did not mean…"

He trailed off. Col was walking past him, towards the Green Man.

"Col, no!" cried the King of Rogues.

But Col kept walking. He was terrified – but not of

the Green Man. He could only focus on one thing now. He held out Pendlebury.

"My friend is dying," he said. "Please. You have to help her."

The Green Man looked down at the tiny tiger in Col's hands, and shook his head.

There is nothing I can do about this.

"Yes, there is. You're the god of life, aren't you? So save her."

The Green Man glared at him.

I am not your servant, boy. I do not bring back the dead because you ask me to.

"She's not dead, she's dying," said Col, choking back tears. "And I'm not asking you to do anything, I'm *begging* you. Please help her. Please."

The Green Man gazed at Col with pity. He shook his head again, the wooden muscles of his neck twisting and snapping. The very movement sounded painful.

That is not how these things work, child. I know death more than anyone. It is a wheel that only goes in one direction. You cannot turn it back any more than you can turn back a river.

Col snarled. "Don't tell me that. Don't pretend there are rules for who gets to live and who gets to die. If there were, then my dad would still be here and my sister would be safe and Pendlebury would be crowned a queen for what she's done." He held her out again. "You broke the rules by coming into this world, didn't you? So break the rules again. I *know* you can bring her back. Don't lie to me."

The Green Man stared at him, his hollow eyes betraying nothing.

No. I cannot do this now.

"Why not?"

Look at me.

The Green Man held up the withered vines that hung from his hands.

I am weaker than I have ever been. I must save all my strength for spring, when it is my time again. It will be my only chance to retake my throne.

Col finally understood. The Green Man wasn't just using the sanctuary to hide from the Midwinter King – he'd been trying to heal himself so he could fight back.

"But you can't wait until spring," said Col. "There's going to be a raid on London any moment – a big one, the worst yet. And when it happens, it'll make the Midwinter King stronger than ever. You have to fight back now and stop the raid before it happens! This is your only chance!"

But the Green Man just shook his head again. He seemed so defeated, so broken.

I cannot risk this. If I lose, then all will lose. I must wait until I am strong enough.

Col shook with frustration. "Don't you understand – if the raid happens, then the Midwinter King will be undefeatable. If you don't fight now, then there'll never be another chance! Millions of spirits are relying on you – millions of people too!"

No. It is not my time.

"Then make it your time," said Ruth.

She had stood up and was facing the Green Man too.

"While you have been hiding all this time, spirits have been fighting for you," she said. "They have risked everything to find you and bring you back. They did not wait until the right time – they did it because they must."

Col's eyes lit up. "That's right! And it made a difference too – the Midwinter King's been growing weaker, and all because spirits are fighting back!" He held up Pendlebury. "See? She's not a god, but she made a difference. Because she defied the King and broke over his barrier, it made him look weak. It gave others the hope they needed to keep fighting. If *you* fight back now, think of the difference it could make! It could change everything!"

The Green Man nodded thoughtfully. Inside the vast dark hollows of his eyes, Col thought he glimpsed a green shoot of light.

Perhaps. I have felt the change in the world over these last few days. I have felt the shift in the balance of power...

The Green Man gazed at the trees around him, bare and dead and leafless ... and shook his head.

No. I must be patient. The future of two worlds is at stake.

Col was horrified. "You're just ... going to let all those people die?"

The Green Man didn't answer. He turned away and walked back into the forest.

Col ran after him, his anger boiling over. "Fine! If you're not even going to try – if you're just going to turn away and let them all die – then save her!" He held up Pendlebury. "If she's so unimportant, it won't take much magic to help her, will it?"

The Green Man glared at him. *I will not risk my powers to help one person.*

"Why not? It's better than doing nothing!"

One life makes no difference.

"Rubbish," said Col. "If it wasn't for Pendlebury then I wouldn't be here, would I? I'd still be in Buxton. Instead I'm here, fighting for both of them. That's more than you're doing!"

The Green Man gazed at him, unmoving. Col kept going.

"What about my dad? He wasn't just one life, was he?

He might not have done much, but he meant everything to me and Rose. And because of what he taught us, Rose went on to help other people. Think of all the lives she could have saved. Every single one could have gone on to save hundreds more. So don't tell me one life doesn't matter. Everything matters."

Something about the Green Man was changing: it was as if every word Col said was making him grow. Wildflowers burst from his eyes. Waves of bugs were swarming from cracks in his body, making his skin ripple and sway. New shoots were growing in place of the withered vines, curling and twisting around Col's legs, blossom sprouting from the ends.

"See?" said Col. "Look at you! You still have strength! You can fight back!"

The Green Man shook his head – but it was as if something had been lit inside him, something that couldn't be stopped.

Perhaps. Perhaps. If the six of you have come so far, with so little hope...

Col frowned. "There are five of us."

The Green Man paused. Then he looked over Col's shoulder.

I see.

He kept his gaze fixed over Col's shoulder for a moment longer – and then he flung back with a cry of pain, his root feet tearing up soil in chunks as he stumbled away into the dark. A cluster of snowdrops burst from the earth after him, leaving a trail of white puddles in his wake. Col ran after him.

"No! Don't go!"

But the Green Man wasn't leaving. He was steadying himself between two trees, hunched over in agony. His shoulder blades were cracking and breaking apart: new vines were exploding out of him like a waterfall, spreading across the forest in every direction. Col watched in horror and amazement. The Green Man was changing – and he couldn't stop. The dead earth where he stood blossomed and plumed with flowers, growing and spreading across the forest floor. The trees were trembling with the force of life exploding from them, every branch shuddering and bursting into leaf. The air filled with pollen until it was thick enough to drink.

Something was happening inside Col too – his blood was fizzing, his insides were on fire, his brain felt like it was pouring smoke. He had never felt so awake, so alive – it was almost too much. And it didn't stop. A kaleidoscope of life was erupting inside him and around him, getting bigger and stronger and wilder and brighter...

"Ruth! Mr Noakes! King of Rogues! What's happening?"

He clutched his head and turned to his Guardians, but he couldn't see them any more. The light was too bright: life was rippling out the forest in shockwaves, into the darkness and the land beyond. The world turned on its axis, and Col hit the ground. Grass wrapped around him like a green hand, lifting him up into a universe of light, towards a centre where a great flame always shone and never died, towards…

Rose?

The Midnight Guardians

"Rose?"

"Mmmmm?"

"The candle's gone out."

It was midnight. Col was four years old: Rose was nine. The attic bedroom at the top of the cottage in Darkwell End was pitch dark.

Rose groaned, half-asleep. "It has to go out *sometimes*, Collie."

"But it's dark!"

"Midnight *is* dark."

"What if there are bogies?"

There was a squeak on the staircase, and a head poked through the hatch. It was Dad, his face glowing in the light of a gas lamp. Col could just make out his moustache, his thinning hair, his tired gentle eyes.

"Christmas won't come any sooner if you're awake, you know," he said.

"Col's going on about bogies again," Rose grumbled.

"No, I wasn't!" said Col.

The idea of being scared in front of his father was mortifying, but Dad didn't seem to mind. He never did. He climbed into the attic and sat beside Col's bed. It wasn't a proper bedroom; it was where they stored all the tat that wouldn't fit downstairs, with a couple of camp beds set up in the middle. Dad relit the candle, one light making another, and the room glowed into life again.

"There you go. Right as rain."

Col squirmed. "What if it goes out again?"

Dad smiled. "Bogies don't exist, Collie. And even if they *did*, your sister and I would protect you from them."

Col thought about that.

"How?"

Dad frowned. "What do you mean, how?"

"You'd never get up here in time," said Col. "And she sleeps through *anything*."

Rose gave a moan of protest into her pillow, then immediately started snoring again.

Col looked at his father, wide-eyed. "Who protects me when you're not here?"

Dad looked at him, half-shadowed in the candlelight. Col could see the lines twitching around his eyes. Col knew, right away, that he had thought of something good.

"Why," he said, "your Guardians, of course."

Col blinked. "My Guardians?"

Dad nodded. "Oh, yes. Kind, brave, gentle creatures who watch over you while you sleep. This cottage is filled with them!" Dad looked around the attic. "Like ... *him.*"

He pointed to a dusty old toy in the corner: a stuffed badger on a chair, wearing a moth-eaten waistcoat and carrying a gnarled wooden stick. Dad held his candle close to the badger, so a flame shone in its amber eyes.

"This is Mr Noakes. He can smell bogies a mile off! And when he sees them – bop! He whacks them on the head and sends them running."

Col giggled. "Really?"

"Really," said Dad. "And he's not the only one looking after you. See?"

He pointed to a tattered painting on the far wall: a gallant knight, with boggling eyes and a big moustache. The artist had mucked up the proportions, so he only looked about four feet tall.

"He looks rubbish," said Col.

"You wouldn't say that to his face," Dad warned. "He's the King of Rogues. He's the most daring knight in all of England! He'll fight monsters, slay dragons, attack whole troops if he has to. But his sworn duty, above all, is to protect you. The bogies don't stand a chance."

Col had never heard Dad talk like this before. He was usually so quiet, so steady and calm. Yet here he was, making up silly stories, just for him. It warmed Col from the toes up.

"Mr Noakes and the King of Rogues argue so much about who's going to look after you, they spend most of their time fighting each other!" said Dad. He picked up an ornament from the chest of drawers beside him. "They're lucky they have Pendlebury to keep them under control."

Dad held up the ornament: a china tiger, no bigger than a mouse.

"He can't be leader," said Col. "He's tiny."

Dad smiled. "*She's* a girl. And she can grow to any size whenever she likes! Big or small, short or tall, she's the strongest, fastest, cleverest Guardian of all, and she's sworn to protect you too. They all are."

"Why?" said Col

"Because they love you," said Dad. "And because it's their job."

He kissed Col on the forehead, so the stubble scratched his nose. Col loved it when Dad did that.

"Whenever it's dark, Col, your Guardians are always watching over you. They'll take care of you, no matter what happens." He tucked him in. "Just like you and Rose will take care of each other after I'm gone. Promise me you will, Col. I know she's older than you, but Rose needs looking after too. Everyone does."

Col didn't understand, but he nodded anyway. "I promise."

"That's my boy," said Dad.

Col listened to Dad's footsteps creak down the stairs, back down to his own bedroom on the floor below. It was smaller than the attic room, and colder too. Dad had given the best room to his children.

Col lay awake for a moment longer. He felt like something important had just happened – something more than just a story, something he didn't quite understand. He felt like there had been some kind of shift in the world. He gazed at the figures glowing in the candlelight around him: the badger, the knight, the tiger.

His Guardians.

"Here to protect me," Col whispered. "No matter what happens."

29 December 1940

RAID FIRES: BE SAFE!

Have you taken every precaution to guard your home against incendiary bomb fires during this short Christmas holiday? Here are some safety tips:

- If you are spending Christmas away, see that your blackout curtains are down, all lights out, gas-meter turned off, and the bath is full of water.
- See that sand, earth, and water buckets outside are full and easily accessible, to help others put out any fires started by incendiary bombs.
- Tell your local Warden you are going away, and where you can be found.

The Earth Moves

C OL OPENED HIS EYES.

The darkness was gone. The sun was shining. He was warm where he had been cold, and awake where he had been tired, and alive where he had felt almost dead.

He was no longer in the forest. He was lying beside a great rocky hillside, the sky stretching out wide and blue in every direction. He had no idea where he was, or how he had got here. His torn pyjamas and pullover were gone. Instead – somehow – he was wearing his old Boys' Brigade uniform. But it wasn't old any more. It had never looked better. The mud had been cleaned off. The buttons sparkled like brand new.

"Col?"

Ruth sat beside him, dazed. Her dress was spotless. The cut on her forehead was gone.

"What – what happened? Where are we?"

Col sat up and looked around. The Guardians were waking up too. The King of Rogues' armour shone like polished glass. Mr Noakes had never looked so *undusty* before.

And pushing herself to her paws beside them...

"Pendlebury!"

Col could hardly believe his eyes. She was alive. The wound on her leg was completely healed. She had been within a hair's breadth of death, and yet here she was, back to her old self again, her colours burning brighter than ever. It was a miracle.

"Is it really you?" Col whispered.

"Yes, Col," she said. "And I'm not *lion*."

Everyone stared at her.

"Lion," she said. "Lying. I'm a tiger."

There was a long silence. She looked at them pointedly.

"See? I *told* you I could make jokes."

The others bundled on top of her, yelling and cheering. Only Col stayed where he was. A part of him wanted to cry with happiness – after all, Pendlebury was alive. The impossible had happened.

And yet...

Ruth caught sight of Col's face. She knew instantly that something was wrong. "Col? Col, what is it?"

He looked at his Guardians, lit in front of him by a glorious ray of sunshine. The day couldn't have been more beautiful. It was strange to think that something so terrible could have happened in a world like this. His eyes welled up. "Don't you remember? The new moon. The raid's already happened. We're too late to save Rose."

Pendlebury gasped. "Oh, Col…"

Col shook his head. "We – we were so close. One more day would have been enough. There's nothing we can do now but—"

"Gog did it! Gog found Guardians!"

They spun round. Someone was running down the rocky hill towards them – someone very big and very loud and very, very heavy.

"Gog?" said Col in disbelief.

It was him all right. The giant was racing towards them like an excited puppy – if a puppy weighed eighty tonnes and left inch-deep footprints in the ground with every step. The Guardians leaped back and drew their weapons.

"No, no! Gog not *fight*," he said, waving his arms. "Gog here for help!"

Mr Noakes frowned. "Help? What are you on about?"

Gog smiled proudly. "Gog been through many important changes since he meet Guardians. He turn from life of seedy, directionless crime and get glasses! See?"

He poked his face with the force of a sledgehammer

pounding a brick wall. He had painted on his own pair of glasses, upside down, several feet above his eyes.

"Gog use *newfound intelligence* and *extensive vocabulary* to do good!" he said proudly. "He find other giants and convince them to join fight against the Midwinter King. Gog's words *mellifluous* and *most persuasive*. Now all giants fighting for Green Man, thanks to Gog! He never do it, if not for advice of nice big kitty." He patted Pendlebury on the head, lightly concussing her.

Col was speechless. No wonder the world had started to feel so different over the last few days – behind the scenes, the war in the Spirit World had been shifting. And just as he'd said to the Green Man, one person was enough to make all the difference.

"And that not all," said Gog excitedly. "Can't you feel it? Green Man come back! All Spirit World feel his return!"

It was true – it was more like a spring morning than a winter's day. The sense of despair and fear and darkness that had covered the land for weeks had disappeared.

"He's right, my liege!" laughed the King of Rogues. "Whatever you and Ruth said to the Green Man, it's changed everything! Can't you feel it in the air? The tides have turned!"

Pendlebury gawped. "Hang on – you met the Green Man?!"

"Yes!" said Gog. "He return to Spirit World and take back his throne! Even goblins and fairies turn against Midwinter King now. All Spirit World searching for him, so Green Man can imprison him before raid happens!"

Col frowned. "Wait – what do you mean, before the raid happens? The raid was last night!"

Gog shook his head. "On contrary! Col *gravely mistaken*. Vision not happen yet! There still time to stop Midwinter King!"

Col was confused. "But … the new moon was last night. I saw it with my own eyes!"

Pendlebury's eyes lit up. "But the new moon doesn't just last for one day, does it? It lasts for two or three. The vision could be showing what's going to happen *tonight* – or even tomorrow night! We still have time to get to London and save Rose!"

A surge of hope shot through Col like electricity. She was right – they could still make it. He looked at the sky – the sun was already setting. No wonder so much had happened since their encounter with the Green Man: they had been asleep for almost an entire day. Darkness would fall in a matter of hours.

"But how can we make it to London in time?" he cried. "Once blackout starts, the raid can begin!"

"Ha! Why you think Gog here?!" said Gog. "He help you on your quest! If not for Guardians, Gog never turn new leaf and meet brand-new girlfriend. He take you to London with her now!"

Col blinked. "Girlfriend?"

Gog pointed at the empty space beside him.

"Her name Gargantua!"

Col glanced sideways at the Guardians.

"Er… Is Gargantua always invisible?"

He stopped. Gog wasn't pointing at thin air – he was pointing to the hill beside them. The one that was standing up.

It took a long time for Gargantua to reach her full height – after all, she was over a hundred feet tall – but when she did, the top of her head seemed to scrape the clouds. Birds roosted in her ears; mountain goats skipped across her shoulders. She jammed a finger the size of Stonehenge into her nose and sent down an avalanche of shale bogies.

"GAAAARGAAAANTUUUUUAAAA HEEEEEEEEEELP," she roared.

"Now *that*," said the King of Rogues, "is a giant."

Col had never been so close to the sky before.

The wind ripped past him as he clung to Gargantua's head, the landscape tilting and rolling beneath them. It felt like clutching a cliff edge in a sea storm: with each step, the giant crossed entire valleys. The Guardians held on beside him, and at the back sat Gog, perched high on Gargantua's shoulders just as Magog had sat on his.

"Gargantua and Gog been together almost six hours now!" Gog explained. "We *soulmates*. She get you to London in no time, and she do it careful too! She *subtle*."

"Biggest fish *I've* ever seen," muttered Mr Noakes.

The sun was already beginning to set, making it impossible to tell how fast they were travelling, but they must have been moving at an incredible speed. Col could see roads winding below them like dropped thread, clusters of factories, train tracks converging from all corners of the country into a single point. Soon they would be in London. After all they had been through, the end was finally in sight. They'd come so far. It couldn't end any other way.

"Can you believe it, Ruth?" he cried. "We can get you to Bloomsbury House and find out about your parents after all!"

Ruth didn't reply.

"Ruth?"

She looked up. She had spent the last two hours pressed face-down like a starfish to Gargantua's head and was extremely pale.

"Yes," she squeaked. "It is very good. Now if you don't mind, I would rather not talk or look at anything."

Gargantua came to a slow, rumbling stop. Gog pointed ahead. "There it is! London!"

Col peered through the darkness … and gasped. There, in the far distance, lay a whole city, lit up in pinks and reds.

"We made it!" His face fell. "But … why are the lights on? It's after sunset. It's supposed to be blackout!"

The sound of the howling wind fell for a moment – and hidden beneath it was a noise that Col recognized instantly. A low buzz, slowly building to a roar. He understood at once. He'd heard that noise almost every night over the rooftops of Buxton, and had never once got used to it.

It was the sound of plane engines.

The clouds over London parted. There they were – a silver swarm of bombers, their undersides scored with spotlights. And then more sounds: the distant *thump* of exploding mortar, the rattle of gunfire, the wail of sirens.

Col gasped. Those weren't clouds over London – it was smoke. The pools of light weren't streetlamps – they were fires.

The raid had begun.

They were too late.

The Raid

COL GASPED. LONDON WAS ON FIRE, THE WHOLE city lit with a blood-red glow in front of them. It wasn't as bad as what he had seen in the vision, but he guessed that would only be a matter of time. Rose could be out in the streets right now, cycling messages between posts, with no idea that soon the entire city would be burned to the ground.

"The raid's started! We have to get to Rose, now!"

Gog looked nervous. "Gargantua cannot take you any closer. Too many people. She might step on them!"

Col was desperate. "But we're miles away! How can we get to Herne Hill in time?"

"Look!"

Ruth pointed below. There was a set of headlights winding down a dark road towards them. It was a car – the first one Col had seen in months. And clearly, the driver couldn't see magic: they were heading straight for Gargantua's foot.

"Gargantua! Put us down – quick!"

The giant bent over, and the Guardians raced down her arm and leaped onto the road. Col managed to wave down the car just in time – it screeched to a halt, mere inches in front of Gargantua's ankle. The woman in the passenger seat leaned out of her window.

"You idiots! What the hell are you doing, standing in the middle of the—?"

"*Ida!*"

It was her – the woman from Havencroft. The man wearing the army officer's uniform and shaking his fist in the driver's seat must have been her son.

"You're damn lucky I didn't run both of you over!" he shouted.

Col glanced at the others. So Ida and her son could only see Ruth and Col – that made *one* thing easier, at least.

He raced to her window. "Ida – are you still going back to London?"

She stared at him in disbelief. "Of course not! Haven't you seen? The whole city's on fire! We're going to spend a night at my son's barracks."

"You have to take us there," he said breathlessly. "Please. It's my sister – the one I told you about. She's still in London! I have to save her!"

Ida shook her head. "Col, you'll get yourself killed!"

Col grabbed Ida's arm. "Remember what you told me, about how we all need to look after each other? You're right. Rose needs my help. She's all I have. If I lose her, I lose everything."

Ida took a good long look at Col, then rolled her eyes. She got out the car.

"Move over, Alan. I'm driving."

Ida's son stared at her in confusion. "Mum? What are you doing?"

"Col's right – the emergency services are going to need as much help as they can get tonight. I've had enough time off – I'm dropping these two off at Herne Hill, and then I'm going to help the ambulance drivers."

Alan stared at her incredulously. "Mum, we won't get anywhere near London – the roads are going to be closed!"

"Then use those flipping officer privileges you keep going on about!" snapped Ida. "Now, for the last time, move over. I've kept my mouth shut for as long as I can, but you drive even worse than your father."

Alan glared at her, but he moved over.

"You're lucky I love you," he muttered.

Col's heart pounded. It felt like everything was finally clicking into place – as if somehow, the world was shifting back to centre. "Thank you, Ida!"

"Thank me later," said Ida. "Now stop stalling and get in!"

Col and Ruth leaped into the back of the car, and the Guardians piled in beside them. It was a tight squeeze, especially with the King of Rogues' lance poking Col in the ribs, but they just about managed to look normal. Ida slammed her foot on the accelerator and they tore down the road.

"Slow down!" cried Alan.

"Keep your hat on," muttered Ida. "London's on fire, no one's going to stop me for speeding."

They shot through the darkness, watching the distant fires of the city grow closer between the trees. Soon the fields and forests gave way to houses, and the smell of burning carried on the wind towards them: the air even *felt* warmer as they grew closer. Alan wound down the windows, and the roar of wind was just loud enough to cover their voices.

"What is the plan?" said Ruth.

"We head to Herne Hill – that's where Rose will be," said Col. "Maybe Brixton or Stockwell, if she's doing her despatch duties." He swallowed. "That's if she hasn't been hurt already…"

"Don't worry, Master Col," said Mr Noakes. "I'll track her down, wherever she is."

"And if anyone tries to stop us, I'll make them regret it!" said the King of Rogues.

"We'll get her out the city," said Pendlebury. "We've come this far, Col – we're not going to lose her."

Col's heart swelled. He loved his Guardians so much right then. They hadn't just protected him and fought for him. They had reminded him what it meant to have friends.

He turned to Ruth. She needed friends too – and she had her own quest to finish.

"Ruth, listen to me. Once I've found Rose and we're leaving the city, I'm going to give the Guardians to you. They'll help you get to Bloomsbury House and find what you need."

Ruth gawped at him. "You are serious?"

Col looked at the Guardians – they nodded back.

"You're going to need all the help you can get – and so do they. Until the Midwinter King has been defeated, they're still in danger. They need one of us with them to stay protected." He squeezed her hand. "I never did get you a present, did I? Well this is it. To thank you for everything you've done for me. Now they're your Guardians too."

Ruth squeezed back. "You are welcome, Col."

The burning silhouette of London was growing closer, and the sounds of the raid were getting louder too: the roar of plane engines, the ear-splitting crack of anti-aircraft fire, the endless *thump, thump, thump* of bombs. Col had never heard anything so loud in his life. So *this* was what people all over the country had been living through, night after night. He watched the transformed city as it flew past him: the heat was stifling, the air unbreathable, the windows of the buildings lit up in firework flashes. It already felt another step closer to the hell of the vision, to the desolate world he had seen in his nightmares…

And then the car screeched to a stop. Ida gazed out the windscreen in shock.

"My god," she said.

There was a roadblock in front, manned by soldiers – and beyond it, the city was unrecognizable. A whole square mile of London was on fire, the sky lit by a glow you could read by. Smoke poured from the rooftops, catching on the bellies of enemy bombers as they dropped trails of bombs onto the streets below. The thump of explosions was constant, deafening.

"It's no use!" Ida shouted. "We'll have to drive back out of the city and find another way into Herne Hill!"

Col shook his head. "We don't have time!"

Ida pointed to the inferno ahead of them. "Go through that and we'll all get killed! What good will you be to your sister then?"

Col looked to where she was pointing – and gasped. There was the dome of St Paul's Cathedral, cut out in silhouette above the forked flames of the rooftops. London Bridge lay on the other side of it – the fastest way to get to the south of the river. Col looked at his Guardians.

"We keep going," he said. "It's the only way."

"*Through* the fire?" said Ruth weakly.

Col clutched their hands. "Whatever happens, we stick together. The way it's always been. All of us – right to the very end. OK?"

There was a sudden reel of gunfire above them. RAF planes were spinning and circling around the bombers, trying to stop them from flying low. Shrapnel rained down onto the streets around them, rattling and pinging off the cobblestones. The soldiers at the roadblock scrambled for cover – Ida started fumbling the car into reverse. It was the perfect distraction.

"Go!" cried Col.

He and the Guardians jumped out of the car. Within seconds, Pendlebury had grown to her regular size and they leaped on her back, tearing down the road and leaping over the army roadblock while the soldiers were still turned away.

"Col!"

Col turned around … just in time to see Ida and Alan staring out their car in stunned amazement. Judging by the expression on their faces, it was clear that they were looking at two children magically floating down the street in mid-air.

"Thank you, Ida! Thank you, Alan!" Col cried. "I promise one day I'll find you and explain everything!"

If there's still a city left, he thought. *If there's still a tomorrow.*

And with that the Guardians disappeared down the street, into the raging fire.

Inferno

THE STREETS WERE FILLED WITH AMBULANCES AND fire engines, all careering towards the city centre. No one tried to stop the Guardians: no one even seemed to notice they were there. Those who could have seen them were too busy searching for fires, racing for cover every time a plane flew over ... or, perhaps, they simply didn't believe their eyes.

"Which way?" shouted Pendlebury.

Col pointed ahead. "London Bridge! We need to get south of the river before—"

"Look out below!"

There was a sound like sudden rainfall, and the street ahead filled with a cluster of blinding lights. They were incendiary bombs, designed to burn at two thousand degrees and set fire to anything they touched. They clattered and bounced on the cobbles like footballs before bursting into white-green fire, spluttering into molten masses on the pavement.

"Quick! Another one, down there!"

Col looked up. The rooftops were filled with spotters, calling down to the streets below. At once a dozen people flew from the darkness on every side, laden with buckets of sand and water pumps, covering up the fires as fast as they could.

"That's it! Keep going! Get the one by the telephone pole before…"

He was too late. The wooden pole caught in the heat of the bombs and the telephone wires exploded, raining down sparks on the people below. Col gasped – it was horrible to watch, and yet there was nothing they could do to help. Rose could be out there in this, right now. They were running out of time. Pendlebury tore across the cobbles, dodging more incendiaries as they burst into fountains of white fire on every side, and skidded around the corner…

She reeled back. The road ahead was completely on fire, the buildings ablaze on either side. Red-hot embers flew down the streets, caught in plumes of yellow-black smoke that choked the throat like acid. Fire fighters raced back and forth with fire hoses, sending white poles of water hissing off buildings in every direction. The heat was blinding, like opening an oven door. Orders were being shouted from all sides, fire engines were screeching over craters, gas mains were flaming up through the cracks in the road. A boy on a bicycle flew past them, both his wheels on fire. It was chaos.

"*Aiiii!*"

Pendlebury reared up in agony. The pavement was like standing on hot coals: her paws were already black and blistered.

Col jumped off her back, and the leather of his shoes started smoking on the cobbles instantly. "Quick! Pendlebury, on my shoulders!"

Pendlebury shrank to the size of a mouse and clutched his shoulder. Mr Noakes clambered onto the King of Rogues' back, who yelped and scampered down the road on his metal shoes. Col grabbed Ruth's hand and they tore ahead, searching for a way out through the smoke – and suddenly there it was. The dome of St Paul's Cathedral, silhouetted against the blood-red sky.

"That way!" cried Col.

They ran down the street, past abandoned fire engines whose tyres had melted, past jewellery shops whose windows were warping in the heat, their trays of wedding rings melting into pools of bubbling gold on the pavement. They ran against the swarms of city rats and clouds of pigeons racing to escape the flames, past a church whose spire was lit up like a Christmas tree, its stone statues blackening inside. The heat was indescribable, constant, worsening every second: Col could feel the soles of his feet baking through his shoes.

"We're almost there – keep going!" he cried. "Just past this corner and—"

There was a sudden vicious roar, and a whistle twisting to a scream. A plane had swooped low above them and they felt the ground shudder, like the footsteps of a giant running towards them, *crump, CRUMP ... BOOM!*

The end of the road heaved – Col felt his eyes being sucked from his head. He was wrenched towards the explosion and instantly flung back, pinwheeling through the air and landing hard on the ground. He felt the shock of cold instantly and sat up spluttering: he had landed in a crater filled with freezing water. A water pipe had burst inside it, dousing him from head to toe and steaming off the cobbles.

"Look out!" cried Pendlebury on his shoulder.

The building beside them was collapsing. Col scrambled out of the crater just as the entire wall sheared off, burying the ground where he had only just been and sending up a great cloud of red-hot dust. He looked around, choked, half-blinded. Ruth and Mr Noakes and the King of Rogues were up ahead, helping each other to their feet – but the rest of the road was empty. The fire fighters who had been beside them moments before were no longer there.

Col shook his head in mute horror. How could Rose possibly survive this? How could *anyone* survive this? He couldn't even recognize where he was any more. His ears were filled with the roar of burning wood and the relentless drone of planes and the constant explosions... The Guardians raced towards him and grabbed his hands, dragging him down the road.

"There it is!" cried Ruth. "St Paul's!"

Col looked up – and through a crack in the wall of smoke, he saw the rising dome. It was right beside them all along, closer than he had realized. He shook himself back to reality – they had to keep moving. "Pendlebury – that way! Across the bridge!"

She leaped off his shoulder and within moments they were sat on her back again, racing over the river. Col could see for himself how far the fires had spread. The entire Thames was burning on both banks, cranes buckling and crashing into the water in the distance, boats floating downriver entirely aflame. The worst of the fires were behind them now – but even here, on the other side of the river, the devastation of the raid was clear. They flew past a giant hospital that was completely on fire, nurses leading patients out in their hundreds, a flotilla of stretchers weaving down the streets. London Bridge Station was on fire too, smoke billowing out of a hole in the roof as fire fighters raced around on all sides. The streets were packed with people – and some of them were gawping straight at Col and his Guardians in disbelief, trying to understand what they were looking at.

Col pointed down the road. "Quick! This way! This road leads all the way to Herne Hill!"

They tore through the shadows and away from the crowds, past collapsed houses, craters in the road, barking dogs and streets carpeted with hose-pipes. They passed shops and houses that were already being looted by robbers. They passed a tarmac playground that was completely alight, swings and slides melting inside a perfect square of fire. Col had never seen anything like it.

Just hold on, Rose, he prayed. *Please be safe. I'm coming.*

And then Pendlebury came screeching to a halt, almost throwing them off her back.

"The road's blocked," she cried. "Look!"

Col looked up – and knew where they were at once. They were in Brixton, barely ten minutes from his house. The road was blocked by a huge heap of rubble, and all around it was chaos.

Pendlebury leaped back into the shadows before anyone had a chance to spot them. "We'll have to take the back roads," said Pendlebury. "Col – which way to Herne Hill?"

Col didn't answer. He was watching the people

racing around the rubble, shouting orders to each other, and knew deep in his heart that something terrible had happened: he felt it the way you felt bad weather coming. He leaped from Pendlebury's back and raced to the nearest warden, who was sending boys on bicycles in four different directions at once. He stared at Col in disbelief.

"What on earth are you doing out here? Go find another shelter, right now!"

Col grabbed the warden's sleeve. "Please – I'm looking for my sister! It's an emergency! She's a despatch rider and…"

The warden pushed him away.

"It's all an emergency, mate! We don't have enough people and communications are down, so for heaven's sake, let us help them!"

"What happened?" said Col.

The warden pointed to the mountain of broken masonry behind him. "There's a public shelter buried under that. The building beside it had a direct hit. We've got who knows how many people trapped inside there – it could be filling up with gas or water as we speak! Now get out of here and find somewhere safe, right now!"

Col stared at the shelter in horror. That was what killed most people in a raid: not being hit by bombs, but being crushed by bricks, choked by dust, drowned by burst water pipes or leaking gas. Dozens of people were scrambling over the rubble, trying to clear a path to the shelter doorway as fast as they could, but a huge steel girder had collapsed onto the entrance, sealing it shut. They were in a race against time. There could be whole families trapped inside, waiting to be saved from the darkness. What if Rose was in there, trying to escape?

"Col! Come on!" Ruth dragged him back, away from the chaos and into the shadows at the side of the road.

"Master Col – I can smell Rose!" said Mr Noakes excitedly. "She's in this direction!"

He pointed down a road beside them – the road that led to Herne Hill. Rose must still be at home.

"We have to go!" said Pendlebury. "We're running out of time!"

Col didn't reply. He stared at the rubble, his heart pounding. He thought about all the people trapped inside. He thought about Ruth and her parents, and Ida and her son, and all the people he had met on the way to get here. He thought of all the people who might wake up tomorrow and discover they had lost someone they loved. Was he really going to turn his back on them now?

What would Dad have done?

"No." He shook his head. "We can't leave them. We have to save those people!"

The King of Rogues looked horrified. "But my liege, Rose is waiting!"

"No." Col turned around. "We *can't* just save Rose. She was right – there are millions of people in this city who need help. They all matter. And if we *can* help them, then we have to. It's what she would do – and it's what Dad would have wanted."

Pendlebury shook her head. "Col, there are too many people – if someone sees us…"

She caught sight of Col's face – and sighed.

"As you wish." She turned to Mr Noakes. "Are there people in there?"

He sniffed the air. "Fifty, at least – but there's gas coming in. We don't have long."

Col didn't need any more convincing. He pushed through the crowds, back to the warden shouting orders beside the rubble. His face fell when he saw Col coming back.

"Stand back," said Col calmly. "I can't explain what's about to happen. If you want to save those people—"

The warden lost his patience. "Son, go home before…"

He trailed off. Ruth had stepped up beside them – as had Mr Noakes and the King of Rogues. The warden's eyes boggled.

"Is … is that badger wearing a waistcoat?"

Pendlebury rose from the darkness and stood behind them, the firelight sparkling in her eyes.

"Do what he says," she growled.

The warden stepped away in speechless amazement. Col could see other people in the crowd, stopping what they were doing and dropping their shovels, not able to believe their eyes. They had to act fast.

"Pendlebury, the doorway! Quick!"

Ruth started pushing back the crowds, clearing a path for Pendlebury. The tiger tore up the rubble and leaped to the shelter doorway. It was still blocked by the collapsed girder, held shut by tens of tonnes of bricks and mortar. She dug her shoulders under the girder, steeled herself – and grew.

Her whole body trembled with effort. Her claws scraped and slid on the bricks: her back arched and strained – then finally, the girder lifted above the doorway, shedding tonnes of rubble on either side. The crowds watched in stunned disbelief. Some were able to see the tiger that was growing in front of their very eyes: but most of them were watching a collapsed building lift itself from the ground. Either way, it was a miracle.

"Make way!"

The King of Rogues lowered his lance and charged, and the doorway gave in with one swift blow. Mr Noakes ran inside, sniffing the air.

"They're all fine – we're just in time! This way!"

He and the King of Rogues disappeared into the shelter while Pendlebury held the girder … and finally, dozens of people came pouring out. Men and women, children and babies, all choking for breath and so covered in dust they looked like stone statues. The stunned crowds finally came to their senses and flew to work, bathing eyes and tending wounds. Col watched in shock: just a few more minutes and they would have been too late. The emergency services would never have got them out in time.

"COL!"

He snapped awake. Ruth was shaking him.

"We can take it from here! For heaven's sake, go home and find your sister!"

Col didn't need telling twice. He turned and fled, racing against the waves of helpers and ambulances that were heading towards the shelter. He ran without stopping on melted shoes, down roads he had known all his life but no longer recognized, against the endless roar of planes overhead, following the white lines painted along the pavements to the one place that was left to go.

Home.

Please be safe, he begged. *Please be home. Please don't let me be too late…*

And finally, there he was: the corner to his street. He skidded around it, his heart in his throat, and there was his house. A thin needle of light was poking between the blackout curtains. Rose was home: she was inside, she was alive, she was safe. Col could have screamed for joy. He tore down the street towards the front door, clearing the final footsteps to his front gate…

And then it came. The roar of a diving plane: the scream of dropped bombs. The pounding beneath his feet, like a monster's footsteps.

Crump. Crump.

Col turned to the darkness that lay at the end of the road. A line of explosions was flying towards him, one after the other, headed right for the house.

"No!"

BOOM!

The noise was vast, unimaginable. The flash of light was brighter and more blinding than anything Col had seen. He was thrown back in a blaze of burning air, and felt himself lift off the ground, up and up and up…

And then the world was dark.

The Last Battle

COL STOOD IN THE DARKNESS.

He was alone. Everything was rubble and dust and silence. This was a world where the sun never shone, and the sky was always black, and everything was dead.

There you are.

Col turned around. He knew instantly who the figure at the end of the road was. He stood out, even here in the darkness. His edges curled and drifted like smoke.

I thought I might find you here, said the Midwinter King.

He walked towards Col, his feet leaving no tracks in the dust. Col felt his approach as one feels a cold wind.

You have caused me so much trouble, said the Midwinter King. *I have fought so hard and lost so much to catch up with you.*

Col swallowed, trying to hide how terrified he was. "How – how did you find me?"

I saw this place in your memories.

Col looked around – and his heart lurched. He finally realized where he was standing. It was his street. There was nothing left of it – nothing of his house, or any of the others on the streets beyond them. The desolate place he was standing in was London. The entire city was gone.

The Midwinter King raised his arms. *You were too late, Col. The raid in the vision came to pass. Your city is destroyed. Your sister is gone.*

Pain rose up inside Col like a wave, engulfing him. "N-no!"

He fell to his knees in the dust and buried his face in his hands. He had failed. He had tried to move heaven and earth to save Rose, and he had come so close … but it had all been for nothing. For the first time in his life, he was truly alone.

Yes, Col, said the Midwinter King, clearing the last of the space between them. *You tried to meddle in things that were greater than you understood, and it was not enough. Now she is dead. Soon I will be at my greatest strength: the Green Man's return will be nothing compared to my new powers. I will cut him from existence, and the Spirit World will be mine for all eternity.*

Col howled with misery. All was lost. The fate of both worlds was doomed to darkness, for ever and ever and ever. He wanted to cry out, to disappear, to lie down and never get up again, to let the darkness do its worst. After all, what did it matter without Rose? What did anything matter? There was nothing left to fight for.

The Midwinter King stood before him.

Now let this end. Give me your Guardians.

Col begged. "No, please, not that too..."

Yes, Col. You cannot protect them any more. Tell me where they are hiding.

Something suddenly sparked in Col's mind.

"You don't know where they are."

The Midwinter King still couldn't see them. That meant they were still protected – and that meant that whatever else had happened, however much the city had been destroyed, Ruth was still alive. And if she was alive, others could be too.

It was only a small mercy – but it was enough to fight for. Col pushed himself from the dust, and took a deep breath, and stood against the dark figure looming over him.

"No. I'm not going to give them to you."

The King's eyes flared. *Do not be foolish, boy. I can reach in your mind and take their whereabouts as easily as I like.*

Col gasped. He felt a freezing tendril enter his body and snake up through his guts, crawling towards his mind. He tried to push against it, but it was impossible. The strength of the Midwinter King was too great. It slid through the cracks of his defences, prising between the gaps left by his fear, rising up into his mind. Col felt it touch his brain, and the sickening terror from his nightmares instantly filled him from head to toe. He was entirely in the Midwinter's King grip, powerless in the face of his darkness.

It will be much easier if you simply tell me where they are.

Col gritted his teeth. He couldn't give him his Guardians – he had to fight for them. So long as he didn't show where he had left them, they were still safe. He might not be able to save them – but he could still buy them time. He pushed hard against the tendril from his mind – and found to his surprise that he could do it. It was hard – he lifted onto his toes with the strain – but it was possible.

"N-no," he said again, his voice trembling. "I won't let you have them."

The King looked surprised for a moment – then he swelled with anger.

Give them to me, boy.

Col laughed. "You're not used to that, are you? You're

not used to people fighting back. You're used to people giving you whatever you want."

A moment of silence pressed between them. Col could feel the cold rage emanating from the Midwinter King, bristling on his skin like a draught beneath a door. He sensed that something was about to happen – some kind of battle of wills, a tug of war. He was terrified – but he had to stay strong. He had to fight for Ruth and the Guardians. He had to protect them. He steeled himself.

"If you want them," said Col, "come out the shadows and take them."

The Midwinter King smiled, in his way.

As you wish.

He drove the tendril into Col's mind, hard and fast. Col cried out. The Midwinter King was inside his head and ripping through his memories, pulling them out one by one and staining them in front of his eyes. Col saw the cottage at Darkwell End, drowned in a sea of blackness. Abigail's bunker, blown apart by bombs. The stones of the sanctuary shattered to rubble, the ground between them salted so that nothing would ever grow again. The Green Man torn apart and scattered.

Show me where they are, said the Midwinter King, *and I will stop.*

Col screamed and tried to fight it, but it was like fighting a rip tide. As each step of his journey flew before him, he saw how pointless it had all been. He had failed – all the pain, all the fight, had been for nothing. The raid had come after all – the Green Man was doomed – the Spirit World was lost. His Guardians were going to be cut from existence no matter how much he suffered. What was the point of protecting them, when everything was already lost? The pain, the grief, were more than Col could bear. He opened his mouth to say the words...

And then another memory flashed in front of him. Pendlebury on the hillside as the dogs swarmed around them.

Build it high. Build it bright. Don't let them win.

Col gritted his teeth. He had to keep fighting. For Pendlebury – for his friend. He heaved the tendril out of his head with all his might and pushed it down. He could still feel it in his gut, crouched and waiting to strike again.

"N-no!" Col cried, sweat pouring down his face. "I already told you. You can't have them!"

The Midwinter King was stunned. His eyes flared with anger.

Don't be a fool. I am a god of darkness. You are one boy and his made-up friends.

Col laughed again. "That's why you hate me, isn't it? All you can do is destroy. No matter how much you hurt me, you'll never know what it means to love something!"

The Midwinter King's eyes gleamed.

I do not need to hurt you, Col. You have hurt yourself. You stopped to save a handful of miserable strangers, and because of that your sister is dead and you will never see her again.

The words cut deep, and Col's strength slipped for just a moment – but it was enough. The Midwinter King drove the tendril back into his brain, not just one this time, dozens of them. It felt like a thousand needles driving different poisons inside him. Col howled with pain. Everything he feared flew at him at once, blinding his eyes and choking his throat. Bombs, darkness, fire, ice, smoke, acid, blood. The Midwinter King used everything he had to break Col down and find the memories he needed.

She's dead and it's all your fault.

Col's mind was scrambled and his whole body was flooded with terror. But he had to keep fighting. "Y-you're wrong! Rose would be proud of what I did. Dad too. You can't understand that. All you know is darkness and misery!"

The Midwinter King laughed. *Look around and tell me what else you see.*

Col caught sight of the destroyed city, and his mind slipped again. The tendrils bore further into him, deeper, harder, crushing his every thought and feeling like an avalanche of thorns, creeping into his bones like winter cold, burning through every happy memory he had ever had as the failings of his journey flew in front of his eyes again and again…

And then he saw the Guardians, huddled under blankets in the bunker on Christmas Day.

Build it high. Build it bright. Don't let them win.

It was enough. The warmth, the friendship, the light, the love, was enough. Col reached deep inside himself and found his love and held it up like a shield. Rose's letters. The King of Rogues holding his hand. Pendlebury's jokes. Mr Noakes rubbing his head. Ruth laughing in the sanctuary. Dad, Dad, Dad, Dad, Dad, Dad, Dad. He fought back with everything he had. It was agonizing, it was exhausting, it was unbearable, it was hopeless, it was impossible, it was more than anyone could possibly stand. And still he kept fighting.

You stupid boy, said the Midwinter King. *You're fighting when you've already lost. Your family is dead and your city is destroyed.*

"I haven't lost a thing," said Col through gritted teeth. "They're all still here, all inside me. And I'll never let you have them!"

Give them to me! the Midwinter King roared.

Col held his ground. "That's how you work, isn't it? Your power is all lies. All you can do is try to frighten me into giving you what you want, when really…"

And it was like a match had been struck.

Col gazed at the destroyed city – the whole of London, wiped to a desert around him. He pushed the tendrils from his mind like they were so many pieces of string.

"This isn't real," he said.

The Midwinter King was knocked off-balance. Col held out his arms.

"This is all a lie. This is just something you've put in my head. This is another nightmare you've made, to try to trick me into giving up. To fool me into giving the Guardians to you."

The Midwinter King sneered. *You can convince yourself of anything you like, boy.*

Col shook his head. "No – I see through you now. You're lying."

And just like that, the vision began to flicker and fade. It was like a veil had been pulled back. The city came to life around them. His street was still there: damaged and burning, still standing, almost dead – but not completely. Col faced the Midwinter King.

"The raid isn't over. It was supposed to give you strength, but it hasn't worked. You're still weak – and you're getting weaker. You're losing."

The Midwinter King roared with anger and

redoubled his efforts, the tendrils flailing and grappling to get inside Col's mind.

Give them to me!

But Col's heart was a raging furnace now, a burning bright light. He held against the darkness with everything he had.

"No. You have no power over me."

Give them to me!

"I'm not afraid of you."

GIVE THEM TO ME!

The Midwinter King seemed to grow somehow, bearing over him like a mountain of darkness, impossible to fight against. Col's strength slipped for a moment, and he stepped back in fear…

And suddenly he felt a pair of hands pressing down on his shoulders, and he felt safer than he ever had in his life, and he flung out the tendrils with the strength of a hundred men. The Midwinter King fell sprawling to the ground.

"I told you. You can't have them."

The Midwinter King looked up … and his face was dreadful to see. Something inside him had finally broken. His eyes were bright red. When his voice came, it was the shriek of an animal.

If I cannot have them, then I will take you!

The Midwinter King reached into his robe and

brought out a handle of darkest metal.

I will cut you from the world. You will not even be with your dead father again.

He drew out the handle, and Col saw what had been hidden in the darkness of his robes all this time. It was a sword, longer than the Midwinter King was tall, sharpening to a point that he could not see the end of. Col's heart failed, in spite of himself. He realized what it was. He understood what the Guardians had said about it being worse than death. It was inhuman, vile, beyond imagination. He felt it in the air like ice against his skin. He tried to step back – but he couldn't. The King had locked him in place. He could only watch as the Midwinter King flew towards him like a tsunami, the sword held high above his head, his mouth wide-open in a ragged maw…

And the light came.

The Midwinter King reeled back. It came from the end of the road, faint at first, but growing brighter and brighter with every second. The King dropped the sword and fell to his knees. The light burned him like acid, dissolving him into smoke and vapor. His face and hands were smouldering and warping, the layers of his darkness bubbling away onto the pavement.

No! No, no, no! It is my time…

"It was," said Col.

The Midwinter King shrank and withered in front of

him, until all that was left was a tiny, dismal, shrieking thing on the ground. He wasn't dead – not completely. But what was left of him was so pitiful, so wounded, that Col almost felt sorry for it.

The hands squeezed at his shoulders.

"You did so well," said the voice behind him. "I knew you would. I'm so proud of you."

Col's heart clenched. He knew the voice – he would know it anywhere. It warmed him from the toes up. Until that moment, he hadn't realized how cold he had been.

He turned... And standing on the road behind him was Dad. His thinning hair, his moustache, his tired gentle eyes. He was just as Col remembered.

But his *colours*...

"You came back," Col whispered.

Dad just smiled, and started turning him towards the light.

"No," said Col. "I want to come with you."

"Not yet, Col," said Dad kindly.

"Why?"

But Dad didn't reply. He just kept turning him, until all Col could see was the light that was glowing brighter and brighter at the end of the road.

It was orange and violet, where it had been stained with rainbows.

Rose

COL WAS LYING ON THE GROUND, LOOKING UP AT the night sky. He could just about make out the stars through a gap in the clouds.

"COL? COL! COL, WHERE ARE YOU?"

There were voices all around him, sirens and shouts and footsteps and crackling wood. He knew they had to be close, but they felt as if they were all coming from somewhere further away. Someone was calling his name.

"COL!"

"Hang on, we've got another one…"

Then hands were lifting him up. Col looked around. He wasn't in front of his house any more – he was lying in someone's garden on the other side of the road. Lots of people were staring at him.

"Jesus! He's alive!"

"What?!"

"There's hardly a scratch on him!"

"Can you hear me, sonny? What's your name?"

"COL!"

The shout came from down the road – from the orange and violet light floating out of the darkness. Col watched it swerve and fall to the ground with a clatter. It was a bike lamp. The person who had been riding it was running towards him, shoving through the crowds of people, tearing off her helmet. Her face was black with soot and her hair was shorter than when he had last seen her, but none of that mattered because Col knew exactly who it was.

"Hey!" one of the men shouted at her. "You're a despatch rider, right? Get to central office and tell them there's been an incident..."

"He's not an incident," said Rose. "He's my brother."

And there she was. She threw herself at him and held him tight, and finally the only thing that mattered was right where he was. Col could hear people talking around him, and the warden sending out calls for ambulances and fire engines, but they felt even further away than they'd been before.

"Oh, Collie, what are you doing here? I thought you were dead! I thought..."

"I fought the Midwinter King," said Col.

She stared at him in confusion. "What?"

"The Guardians brought me," said Col blearily.

"Because of the vision. I met a bogie too, but he had a Christmas hat."

Two men appeared with a stretcher. "How's he doing, miss?"

Rose shook her head. "I – I don't know. I think he's hit his head, he's not making any sense."

Col was lifted onto a stretcher and carried into an ambulance. It wasn't a proper ambulance – it was a greengrocer's van with bunks in the back. Rose climbed in beside him and the car rattled off down the road, rumbling over rubble and hosepipes. The night was filled with wailing sirens and shouts and pounding footsteps and crackling fires – but that was it. There were no more planes, no more explosions.

"Where's the raid?" asked Col.

Rose squeezed his hand. "The planes stopped half an hour ago. We're going to go to a hospital, and then it's all going to be fine."

"That's good," said Col.

"No it's not good!" snapped Rose, suddenly furious. "Oh, Col, how could you do it? I've been going out of my mind! To hear from Aunt Claire that you'd gone missing, and then to get a phone call from a hospital in the middle of nowhere, and then to find out you'd run away from *there* too… How could you do that to me? After *everything* that's happened! How could you?"

She was hitting him while hugging him, her eyes filled with tears. And suddenly Col couldn't hold it in any more. The words that he had held in for days, weeks, months, spilled out of him.

"You promised we'd be together. You always said that it would be just the three of us, and then you sent me away. I've missed you so much."

Rose's face creased up like a ball of paper. She was openly crying now.

"Oh, Col ... don't you understand? That house – I couldn't leave it. It's the only thing of his I have left. It's the only place I feel close to Dad. I had to stay and make sure it was all there for us!"

"I could have helped you," said Col. "We could have done it together."

"But I had to send you away!" said Rose, tears streaking through the soot on her face. "I couldn't lose you too! I couldn't, I couldn't, I couldn't!"

Col finally understood what had happened. Rose had tried to protect everyone. She had tried to carry them all, and it was too much.

"When I got the letter from Aunt Claire, saying you were missing... Oh, Col! I've been like a ghost these last few days. I haven't even left the house. I told myself that if you came home, I'd be here waiting for you ... but then a despatch rider came by just now, saying there'd been an incident at a shelter in Brixton and they needed help, and I felt something – like a hand at my shoulder. Something that made me go." She shuddered. "If I hadn't gone, I'd have been inside the house when that bomb hit. How you ever managed to survive it, Col…"

Col frowned. The world was slipping away again. "Incident? Shelter?"

"A public shelter got buried in Brixton," Rose explained. "Everyone got out safely, thank goodness. Right at the last minute too – there was a gas leak inside. A few more minutes and they'd all have died. Children, babies – every single one of them." She laughed. "You won't believe what some people there were saying – they said that a tiger and a badger and a knight had saved them! Can you believe that? Just like your Guardians! They must have all been off their heads on gas…"

Col let her words wash over him. He wasn't afraid any more. A hundred planes could have dropped a thousand bombs and whatever happened, he was right where he needed to be.

He slipped into darkness and slept as the fires raged around him.

The Second
Great Fire of London

THE ALL-CLEAR BLEW AT MIDNIGHT. IT WAS ONE
of the worst raids of the Blitz. In just three hours,
ten thousand bombs fell across a few square miles. The
flames caught fast in the wind and the attack came when
the tide was low, so fire engines couldn't get water from
the river in time. Two hundred people died, many of
them fire fighters trying to stop the blaze. Hundreds of
buildings were lost: twenty million books were destroyed.

It should have been much, much worse. Another fleet
of bombers was supposed to descend on the city after the
first wave, blowing apart what was left of the burning
buildings and spreading the fire even further. Some
thought it was even meant to lead to an invasion in the
New Year. But an unexpected storm blew up suddenly
over the Channel, and the second wave of planes had to
be cancelled. No one had seen it coming: it was almost
as if, halfway through the evening, something changed.

The fires burned for two days, stripping away the layers of London one by one. Churches that had stood for hundreds of years were razed to the ground, their bells plummeting from burning rafters and striking their last on the stones below. Red-hot air was sucked through organ pipes, playing strange final songs that no one heard. Roman temples buried for centuries underground were revealed again, perfectly preserved, as if waiting to be rediscovered.

At dawn the following day, a newspaper photographer standing on a rooftop saw St Paul's Cathedral looming through the smoke: it had somehow managed to survive, despite every other building around it being destroyed. He took a photograph of it, and the newspapers published it the very same day. Even the *Telegraph* went to press, despite the fact that their offices were on fire.

The raid made the front pages, and several pages after that. The original front-page stories – about an abandoned pub being lifted off the ground in Northamptonshire, and earthquake tremors felt across the countryside the previous evening, and how some had claimed they were caused by a giant they had seen walking the countryside – were moved to the second page, and then back several more pages, until finally they were forgotten and dropped altogether.

30 December 1940

ROOSEVELT'S RALLYING CALL TO AMERICANS

Following the heaviest raids on London yet, President Roosevelt uttered a rallying call to his fellow Americans to offer every ounce of help to Britain.

In a voice that rang with passionate belief, Mr Roosevelt declared, "Not for 300 years has American civilization stood in such danger.

"The Nazi masters of Europe have made it clear that they intend to enslave all Europe and then use its resources to dominate the rest of the world. The evil forces which have crushed, undermined and corrupted so many others are already within our own gates.

"If Britain loses this war, the U.S. would be living at the point of a gun."

President Roosevelt's broadcast evoked an immediate and enthusiastic response from all over the United States. The President's private secretary said that the address had brought a greater response than any previous Roosevelt talk.

Mr Arthur Purvis, head of the British Purchasing Commission, said, "President Roosevelt's plan to loan and lease war material to Britain opens up a new chapter for our country."

The Aftermath

COL WOKE UP.

He knew instantly that he was in a hospital. He could tell because everything hurt, and the bedsheets were awful.

"Ah, finally! We thought you'd be asleep until New Year's Eve."

He looked up. A nurse was at the end of his bed, glancing over his notes and shaking her head.

"Amazing," she said. "Blown across a road and hardly a scratch on you! You must have a guardian angel."

Col groaned. "Where's Rose?"

"Your sister? She popped out a second ago – but don't worry, your cousin's just arrived too."

"Cousin?" said Col.

A girl stepped into the room. Col gawped.

"Ruth! You're—"

"Hello, cousin!" She strode over and hugged him

before he could say anything else. "You are looking very well!"

The nurse left, apparently content. Col sat up in shock.

"What are you doing here?"

"Waiting to see you!" said Ruth. "Rose was with you all night – she has left to help with some new patients who are arriving. Come! She will be back soon. We must be quick." She threw a pair of melted shoes at him. "Put on, please."

Col thought about asking where they were going, but decided against it. He had a feeling he already knew. "How did you find me?"

"It is easy," said Ruth. "I go to every hospital, asking if they have seen a boy dressed as monkey at a funeral."

Outside, the air reeked of charred timber and cordite, and was as warm as a spring day. A veil of smoke hung between the buildings like mist, and the sound of scraping shovels came from every street. People were going to work as if nothing had happened last night. No one even noticed two children walking around, covered from head to toe in brick dust. It was how everyone looked.

"It's all still here," said Col in amazement.

London was still standing – the raid hadn't destroyed it. And that wasn't all. Col could feel the change in the air too – the sense that something had shifted.

"The bombs finished earlier than anyone was expecting," said Ruth. "I was even able to find Bloomsbury House! It has not been hit, thank goodness – but it is closed until the New Year." She bit her lip. "I will have to wait until it opens again before I can find out about Mama and Papa."

Col frowned. He finally asked the question. "And – the Guardians?"

She smiled and took his hand. "Come. I show you."

They caught a bus and made their way through London. It took much longer than normal: there were unexploded bombs stuck in buildings, and burst water mains spraying into the road, forming icicles on the statues. They passed a store that had lost every single window in its shopfront, covering the pavement in snowdrifts of broken glass. The staff inside were wrapped in big coats, next to a sign saying: *More Open Than Usual.*

It was like a dream-version of London, where nothing made sense. The fountains were off in Trafalgar Square and there were no pigeons. Theatres and cinemas had been opened up like tin cans so you could see the stages from the street, their red curtains shifting in the breeze. There were shattered tombstones in the road that had been blasted from churchyards on the other side of the city. Col saw a postman pull a handful of burning letters out of a post box. He didn't know how long he'd been asleep for; there wasn't a single public clock that told the right time any more.

They finally came to the city centre, where fire fighters were still putting out blazes. Buildings that had stood for centuries were now ragged skeletons, their pillars holding up nothing but sky. The streets were filled with businessmen with nothing to do, standing around with their shirttails out and scratching their heads. Children had turned the wreckage into a playground. In the middle of a huge water-filled crater that had once been a bank, two teams of five year olds floated on wooden doors and threw sticks at each other.

"Here!" said Ruth.

They stepped off the bus and made their way down a side street. There, tucked at the end of the road, was a tiny stone church. The windows had been blasted out, and a rope was tied over the doorway to stop anyone from walking in. Ruth stepped over it without breaking a stride.

"It took much time to find this place," she explained. "The Guardians wished to come and find you, but by then it was getting light again. We thought that here is a good hideout – no one will want to come in if it is already bombed, no?"

The church was empty. The pews had all been cleared, or burned. A pulpit sat in the centre on a pile of rubble, lit up by sunbeams that streamed through a hole in the ceiling.

Three figures were sitting on the rubble. They had been waiting for some time.

"Master Col!"

The Guardians leaped to their feet. There they were: his oldest friends and protectors, singed and bruised and exhausted but here and alive. Col was delighted beyond words to see them. He charged over the rubble and held them tight. They had done it – they had been through so much, fought against so many odds, risked everything and almost died, but finally their quest was over.

There was something different about the Guardians, though – Col couldn't quite put his finger on what it was. But he was too excited to think about that. He had so much to tell them.

"You won't believe what happened – I found Rose! She's alive! The house was hit by a bomb, and then I fought the Midwinter King…"

Mr Noakes chuckled. "We know, Master Col – *everyone* knows! The Spirit World's talking about nothing else!"

Pendlebury's eyes shone with pride. "The Midwinter King used the last of his powers trying to fight you, Col. He's finally been imprisoned, and the balance has been restored. And it's all thanks to you."

Col was speechless. He'd seen the Midwinter King shrink and wither in front of his eyes, but he still found it hard to believe that he'd helped win the war in the Spirit World.

"What about all his armies?" he asked. "All those evil creatures that were loyal to him? Barghest and his dogs…?"

"They all turned on him in the end," said the King of Rogues. "It didn't help that he'd weakened them by bringing them over here!"

"And Barghest helped too," said Pendlebury. "She betrayed the King and reopened the barriers, so the Green Man could re-enter the Spirit World. It turned the tides at the last moment. It was very brave of her. If the raid had happened as planned and the Midwinter King had returned, her punishment would have been unimaginable."

Col shook his head. "So … she's not going to be punished for what she did? *None* of the Midwinter King's followers are?"

Pendlebury shook her head. "The war in the Spirit World is over, Col. We have to put aside what happened and find a way to make sure it never happens again."

"But it *can't* happen again," said Col. "The Midwinter King's been defeated."

"For now, Master Col," said Mr Noakes. "But he will

be back again next year. And the year after that – and the year after that. Beings like him are part of life. You can't destroy them. You can't have light without darkness."

"That was his biggest mistake," said Pendlebury. "He tried to destroy something which can't be destroyed. We must make sure that he never grows as powerful ever again. His sword has been taken from him and hidden inside one of the stone sanctuaries. He will never again be able to cut anyone from existence."

Col beamed. "Does that mean you're safe? When the Midwinter King comes back next year, he won't try to take his revenge?"

Pendlebury shook her head. "If he does, the whole Spirit World will rise against him. We've shown each other that together, we can do it."

Col's heart flooded with relief. The sense of guilt that he had carried with him for days melted like fog in sunlight. "That's amazing!"

Then they fell silent. There was something unspoken passing between them – something none of them wanted to say. Only this time, Col knew what it was.

"Does this mean you'll go back?" he said quietly.

Pendlebury smiled. "There is nothing left for us to do, Col. Rose is safe, isn't she?"

"The rest is up to you," said the King of Rogues, squeezing his shoulder. "The hardest part of all. Carrying on. Fighting darkness is one thing, but keeping it away is harder."

"And we can't help you with that, Master Col," said Mr Noakes sadly. "Not any more."

Col gazed at the Guardians and something caught in his throat. He realized what was different about them: their colours were fading. They were drifting away, right in front of his eyes.

"Wait – right now?" he said.

Pendlebury nodded. "I am afraid so, Col."

The Guardians were already half-in and half-out of the world. Col could see right through them now, to the rubble behind.

"But – but I'm not ready," said Col. "I don't want you to go!"

Pendlebury smiled. "We're closer than you realize, Col. We're just a hair's breadth away. We'll always be listening."

"That's right," said Mr Noakes. "Whenever you think of us, lad, we'll hear it. Like we always have."

"And always will," said the King of Rogues quietly.

Col gasped. The Guardians were still fading ... and he could see now that they weren't alone. The barriers between their worlds were opening in front of him: he could see the entire Spirit World spread out ahead, a whole world of light, filled with thousands of creatures waiting to welcome back the Guardians. There were enchanted trees and fairies and bogies and goblins and brownies and giants by the dozen. There was Leonard, and Abigail, and Gog and Gargantua, and Barghest and the dogs, and a thousand things that Col hadn't even seen yet, things he didn't understand. A million years of magic and history and fables, all in one place, bowing down to his Guardians.

"Master Col."

"My liege."

"Col."

He faced his Guardians for the last time. There was the King of Rogues: so courageous, so undaunted, his kindness just visible beneath his armour. There was Mr Noakes, so steady and loyal, his paws resting at his waistcoat pockets. And then there was Pendlebury, a creature woven from stars and midnight, the bravest, strongest, cleverest Guardian of them all. They had given him so much and asked for nothing.

"Wait!" said Col suddenly. "Before you go, I… I have to…"

He grabbed Pendlebury's paw. He had so much to say, so many things to thank them for that he didn't know where to begin. But there was one thing, standing clear above everything else. A question burning at the centre of everything.

"When I fought against the Midwinter King, I wasn't alone. There was someone with me the whole time. Someone I didn't realize was there until I needed him most." He swallowed. "It – it was Dad, wasn't it? He came back to help me, right at the very end."

Pendlebury's eyes shone with tears, even as they faded.

"Oh, Col," she said. "He's been with us the whole time."

Col felt a hand on his shoulder – and there, standing beside him, was Dad. Col understood the truth now: he had been with him on every step of their journey. It was he who had sent Rose out of the house at the last moment and saved her life; he who had given Col the strength to stand against the Midwinter King; he who had protected him at the final second from the Lantern Man; he who had woken him from his nightmares; he who had helped the Guardians break over the barrier in the first place. He had come back to protect his children, just like he always had in life, silent and unseen and unnoticed.

"Dad," said Col.

Dad rubbed his hair. It felt just like it always did. Col had missed it, so, so much.

"I've done all I can," he said gently. "The rest is up to you. Take care of yourself. Take care of Rose. And Aunt

Claire too. You all need looking after."

Col's heart burned so much that it hurt – but it was good pain, the right kind of pain. "I promise."

"That's my boy," said Dad. "I love you, Col."

"I love you too, Dad."

The Guardians stood shoulder to shoulder with his father and waved – and with that they slipped away, as easily as a breeze passing from one room into another, and the church was empty.

Col stood for some time, gazing at the empty space where his father had been. He understood that he would never see him again – not in life, at least. He wouldn't see his Guardians, either. But none of them were gone, not really. They were all just a hair's breadth away, in their own worlds, beyond where he could see.

"Col? Are you OK?"

He felt another hand on his shoulder. Ruth had been beside him the whole time – Ruth, his friend. Col smiled, even as the tears fell.

"Yes. I'm OK."

And he meant it.

The Armistice

THEY ARRIVED BACK AT THE HOSPITAL JUST in time. The nurse was so rushed off her feet she didn't seem to have the slightest idea that Col had even left. When Rose came back, she was in the same clothes as last night. She was so tired that she didn't even blink when she saw Ruth. Instead, she just kissed Col on the forehead and held him. Being in her arms felt as warm and familiar as an old coat.

"Come on," she said. "Let's go."

Col frowned. "Go where?"

"Home, silly."

The three of them made their way back to Herne Hill. Brixton was slowly pulling itself together after the bombings. They passed houses patched with cardboard windows and tarpaulin doors. Others were roofless, windowless, still on fire, being pulled down even as they burned. One had ten untouched milk bottles lined up outside the door, the colours running from white to yellow. They saw a bathroom opened out to the road like a stage set, high above the street. There was a bathtub and a blue towel on a hook, and a cross-stitch reminding you to wash your hands. A young girl was rooting through the rubble beneath it, gathering toys, her face pitted with slithers of glass.

Col's house was a smoking heap. The front door had been blasted from the hinges and thrown across the road: the window shutters lay in fragments on the lawn. Col could see the corner of a rug flapping over a shattered bannister, and the legs of a dining-room chair poking from the rubble like broken bones.

"We'll go through it and gather what we can find later," said Rose, rubbing his shoulder.

Col shook his head. The wreckage was unspeakable. He had spent months longing to return home – and now he had no home left to go to.

"But … it's gone. You said it was the only thing that made you feel close to Dad, and now there's nothing left…"

Rose grabbed him and turned him round. "Col, look at me."

Col fell silent. She was giving him The Look. Col had never been given The Look before. It was like Rose had grown ten sizes without anyone realizing quite how she'd done it.

"I don't *care* about the stupid house. I thought I'd lost you. I thought you were dead. I could spend the rest of my life eating nettles in a ditch and I'd thank my lucky stars every single day because I still had you." She held him tight, angrily. "From now on, we're doing everything the way we said we would. Sticking together, no matter what happens. Understand?"

Col laughed. "But where are we going to live?"

Rose sighed. "Yes, well, I've been working on that…"

"COL!"

Col turned around – and gawped. There was someone standing at the end of the road that he hadn't expected.

"Aunt Claire?"

She looked indescribable. Even from the end of the road, Col could see that her face was actually trembling with anger. She marched towards him like a rampaging tank. Col winced, preparing himself for the ear-clipping to end all ear-clippings … but instead, Aunt Claire fell to her knees and hugged him.

"Oh, you're OK! Oh, Col, Col, Col, I've been so worried! I haven't slept, I haven't *eaten*… How could you do it to me, Col? I *promised* your father I'd look after you – I promised him! Oh, if something had happened to you, if I had let him down… *Oh, Col!*"

She just held him and cried. Col was speechless.

Of all the surprises of the last few days, this was easily the strangest. So Aunt Claire really was like the King of Rogues: underneath all that armour, she was more vulnerable than anyone. Col hugged her back. Dad was right – she needed looking after too. Everyone did.

"I'm really sorry, Aunt Claire. I didn't mean to upset you. It was… It was something I had to do."

Aunt Claire wiped her eyes. "Yes! And it was a *stupid*, selfish thing to do!" She sighed. "But I've been stupid too. I should have understood how much it meant for you two to be together. I should have helped. I just wanted to keep you safe, Col – but I got it all wrong. I'm sorry." She blew her nose. "I'm going to be a better guardian to you from now on. To *both* of you."

She cleared her throat and stood up, facing Rose. Aunt Claire steeled herself.

"I owe you an apology as well, Rose. If you'll accept it."

Rose shook her head. "No – I owe *you* an apology. I'm sorry I wasn't very nice to you after Dad died."

Aunt Claire was shocked – she clearly hadn't been expecting that. "It's OK, Rose. I understand." She touched her face. "Oh, my poor girl."

Col took Aunt Claire's other hand and the three of them stood together, staring at the wreckage of the house. It was a good silence – the nice kind.

"It'll be blackout soon," said Aunt Claire nervously. "Oh, goodness – I only just arrived, and there are no more trains today, and I don't have *any* money for a hotel…"

"Ahem."

They turned around. Ruth had been waiting patiently on the pavement, flicking through a charred copy of *The Swiss Family Robinson* that she had found in the branches of a tree.

"I know a place we can go."

Queues for the underground station started at mid-morning, long before blackout began. After last night, no one was taking their chances. Col stood behind people loaded with blankets, eiderdowns, deckchairs and hot water bottles. A slightly exhausted porter was trying to send them all away, and failing.

"NO! You know the rules: no sheltering in the tube! Travellers only!"

"We *are* travelling!"

"With pillows? Pull the other one, mate."

It was no use. The crowds just pushed past him and made their way into the dark, and Col's group joined them. The ticket office and stairwells were already packed with people settling in for the night. Aunt Claire stepped onto the platform and wrinkled her nose. "Oh, my…"

Every inch of the platform was rammed. The air stank of wet clothes and hot grease. There were families cooking dinner over gas stoves, old men playing cards, mothers knitting in deckchairs, babies in suitcases, homeless people snoring in foot-muffs made of newspaper, rich old dowagers clutching handbags of jewellery, children playing gramophones, all shouting and laughing and crying and arguing at the same time. Weirdest of all, the trains were still running – passengers had to clamber over everyone to get out.

Col found a porter and tapped him on the shoulder. "Excuse me, sir – do you have a second? We're looking for space and—"

"Second's up – hahahahaha!"

Col blinked. The porter wiped away a tear and sighed.

"Might as well have a laugh, eh?" He pointed over his shoulder. "Try over there, by the library."

The "library" was a stack of books at the end of the platform, beside a poster advertising a play-reading on the southbound line at eight p.m., and a request for more sopranos in the station chamber choir. Col, Aunt Claire, Rose and Ruth squeezed themselves in beside a grumpy-looking man who glared at them as they shuffled past.

"Mind where you're sitting! And don't try anything funny – I know where all my stuff is!"

Aunt Claire looked appalled. "How *rude*!"

A man on the other side of them laughed. "Never you mind Bernard, miss – he's a miserable old sod! Nothing makes him happy!"

Bernard glowered at him. "What's there to be happy about? Food rations lower than ever, bombs getting worse…"

"But look at today's news!" The man held up a paper, slapping it like a prize-winning fish. There was a photo of St Paul's Cathedral on the front, looming out of a cloud of black smoke. "Looks like that raid last night finally changed Roosevelt's mind – he's talking about sending help to Britain! Who knows – America might even join the war soon. Think about that! With them on our side, we might have half a chance of winning!"

Bernard grumbled. "What a load of rubbish. We don't need some Yanks telling us what to do."

"Oh, yes, Bernard, we're just fine. That's why we're all sleeping in a tube station."

They kept arguing as a train pulled in. This train was different to the others: all the carriages were labelled, *T.R.*, and were filled with women holding trays of tea and cake.

"Train Refreshments! About time!" said the man next to them, clapping his hands.

The women started walking up and down the platforms, selling tea and cocoa and buns. Aunt Claire perked up instantly – she got each of them a slice of cake and a cup of cocoa, and even treated Bernard, who grunted a begrudging thanks before turning away.

Col gazed at the station around him in amazement. It was uncomfortable, unclean, completely unsustainable, absolute chaos – but it was a miracle too. No matter what people said, the worst way to experience a raid was alone.

"I could get used to this," said Col through a mouthful of cake.

Aunt Claire sighed. "Well, *I* couldn't. Forgive me, but my idea of happiness isn't using a drop toilet next to a ticket office." She coughed. "I've a few ideas about what we do next, actually. I know this might sound funny, but I was thinking—"

A voice suddenly carried over the noise of the station. A man was standing on a wooden box at the far end of the platform reciting over the crowds.

Ruth gasped. "Look – he is lighting the next candle for Chanukah! It will be the seventh night tonight!"

Col turned to Aunt Claire. "Can we go and see?"

Aunt Claire nodded, and Col and Ruth leaped up. Bernard shot them a filthy look as they ran past.

"Ha! Of course. I should have known."

Col stopped. "Known what?"

Bernard nodded at the crowds around the chanukiah.

"You're one of them, aren't you? Makes sense – your lot are always grabbing the best places in the shelters. It's bad enough listening to your services down here – you can do it up on the streets if you're all so desperate!"

Aunt Claire stared at Bernard in disgust. "There is *absolutely* no need for that. There's enough room for everyone down here."

Bernard gestured at the packed platform. "You call this room? We can barely look after our own, let alone help people coming here from other countries with their hands out. If you ask me, Hitler had the right idea chucking them out in the first place!"

Col stared at Bernard in disbelief. Even here, hiding from the enemy, he still wanted to hate. Col wanted to shout at him, to tell him how vile everything he had just said was, but he only had to take one look at his face to know that he would never listen. He was beyond listening. You could offer him all the miracles of the world, show him the whole, great blazing truth of it, and he would choose to live in darkness. That's just the way it is. Some people can see magic, some people can't.

Ruth gave Bernard a disgusted look, and took Col's arm. "Come," she said, leading him away. "Let's look at the lights."

They made their way down the platform, where a crowd was watching the man light the next candle in the chanukiah, filling the platform with light. The glow of the candles flickered over the faces as they waited out the night, sheltering in the tunnels beneath London, standing together against the darkness.

31 December 1940

BAN ON ALL "JERRY" BUILDING IN NEW BRITAIN

Plans for rebuilding Britain's bomb-scarred cities and towns after the war were announced today.

There will be, "no haphazard rebuilding with slums, black fogs, dirty railway stations and rolling stock, rubbish dumps, ugly highways, and many other evils which can only bring about a desperation of the spirit."

The new Britain, they say, will be a beautiful Britain.

A New Path Home

"R EADY?"
"Ready!"

It didn't take long to sift through the rubble of the house – there wasn't much left that they could get to. They found some photos and Dad's favourite books, and that was all they needed.

Now they stood on the pavement, gazing at the remains of their home. It had snowed sometime in the night, and everything was covered in a layer of fine white. It was nice to be reminded of how pretty winter could be, after the worst storms in living memory. No one had ever known a winter like it.

"Remember what I told you all," said Aunt Claire, resting a hand on their shoulders. "This will *always* be your home – we'll come back and rebuild it one day. For now, I think it's only right that we get started on our new plan."

Col turned to his sister with a grin. "What do you say, Rose? Are you ready to live in Darkwell End?"

Rose smiled. "Collie, I can think of *nothing* better."

"You won't be sad to leave home?" he asked.

"I *am* home," said Rose, squeezing his hand.

Col smiled. Rose had already started talking about turning the cottage into a small hospice, a miniature version of Havencroft where people from nearby cities could come to recuperate. Within seconds, she and Aunt Claire had already started bickering about it.

"We've got more than enough to do as it is!" said Aunt Claire. "That cottage needs a good clean – honestly, the amount of rubbish in that attic is unbelievable. All Grandma's china animals, that filthy old badger toy of your father's … although I believe there's a painting of a knight I once did that's still up there, I seem to remember it was really quite good…"

Col turned to Ruth. She had stuck with them all day, helping them to clear the rubble. As the day wore on, she had become quieter and quieter. Now she stood alone on the street, fumbling at her dress pockets.

"Well," she said, "I suppose this is goodbye. I will have to stay in London until Bloomsbury House is open again. Perhaps I will write to you and tell you if I find…"

"Ahem."

Aunt Claire stepped forward. She looked decidedly uncomfortable – Col was beginning to realize that this was how Aunt Claire looked when she was about to do something kind.

"Ruth, I've been thinking a lot about your, um … situation. To be honest, the attic is going to be pretty full, and I'm not sure we can afford it, and I can't exactly let you…"

She trailed off, sighed, and tried again.

"Look – I'd like to invite you to stay with us at Darkwell End. I know it's a long way from London, but we'll help you find out about your parents. I'll help you write letters, and we can find a phone you can use, and I'll bring you down to London whenever you need. I really *should* ask permission from someone before simply taking you, but … well, who am I going to ask? I certainly can't let you stay down here on your own." She looked at her. "What I'm saying is, I owe you more than I can ever repay you. I don't know how you did it, but you kept my nephew safe. I'd be very happy to become your guardian."

Col gasped with delight. Aunt Claire was surprising him more by the minute. It was amazing how much people could surprise you, if you gave them the chance. "Will you, Ruth? Will you come and live with us?"

Ruth nodded immediately. "Yes, thank you. I would be so pleased."

Col lifted her over his shoulders and spun round, whooping and cheering.

Rose put a hand on Aunt Claire's shoulder. "This is really good of you, Claire. Thank you."

Aunt Claire blushed and waved her quiet. "No! Don't thank me. No point in it, really. Now we really *must* get going. There's only one more train to Buxton today, and it's going to take for ever to get there."

With that she hurried away before Rose could say any more nice things to her.

The journey took much longer than normal. The streets were filled with drunken soldiers, Brits and Canadians and West Indians and Irish, starting their New Year's Eve celebrations as early as possible. The fires from the raid were dying out, one by one, and the city was already moving on from the destruction. There were makeshift signs on destroyed shops advertising new premises. People had covered the rubble in little Union Jack flags. Wildflowers were already beginning to grow in the masonry: willow herb, buddleia, conch grass, brambles. A homeless woman huddled inside what had once been a cinema, gathering snow to make tea. The trains at London Bridge were running, even though it was still on fire.

Col watched it all pass by the bus window in silence. In the vision, he had only seen the city burn: he hadn't been able to see any of the people who were trying to help each other. Maybe that made all the difference.

"Look at all of this," he said quietly. "One day, no one will believe it really happened. Everyone will just forget it. It'll just become some legend and it will stop meaning anything."

Ruth shrugged. "Maybe. But you never forgot your Guardians, did you?"

Col frowned. "What do you mean?"

Ruth sighed. "To be honest, I do not know. I have slept on a wooden pallet all night next to a horrible old man, and before that I spent seven days running across the countryside and almost died many times and now I have not the foggiest. But I suppose what I mean is: nothing ever really goes away. Even when everything seems lost, the answer is still there, where it cannot be easily found. It is always there."

They finally reached Euston Station and waited on the platform for the last train back up north. It was packed with soldiers with kitbags and children being evacuated again after their holidays, holding their parents and crying. They piled inside the train and, miraculously, managed to find a compartment to themselves. The train set off with a whistle, while lines of parents stood outside the windows, trying not to cry themselves. Col and Rose sat together, hand in hand, as the train pulled out of London.

Col watched the buildings disappear, and the trees and fields and rivers and valleys and hills that had been his home for the last few weeks slip past him. After the few days of early spring weather, it seemed like winter was settling back in. Col understood why. The world had swung to darkness, then hard back to light. The Green Man was making sure that the world settled back to the way it was meant to be: a mixture of lightness and darkness. You couldn't have one without the other. Col thought of the Guardians, and knew that meant they were thinking of him too.

The countryside was still flooded, and the train had to stop constantly on its way up north. Hours passed: soon the sun set, and the train's blackout bulbs flickered on, filling the carriage with a faint blue light. Col gazed out of the hole cut in the lace that was glued over the windows. The moon was back, a waxing crescent cradling the stars above it, shining brighter than ever before. That was the nice thing about darkness, Col supposed. It let you see the stars.

"Good grief! It's a minute to midnight," Aunt Claire tutted. "It'll be 1941 by the time we get to Darkwell End…"

Ruth's eyes lit up. "Just in time! It is still the last night of Chanukah. Shall we?"

She took out the chanukiah and lit each candle one

by one, until the holders were full and the compartment filled with light around them. A crowd formed outside their cabin, watching and pointing as Ruth sang the song for the final time. A train porter tried to push his way inside, hammering on the window of their compartment, but it was no use.

"Oi! What do you think you're doing? Put those out! It's blackout!"

They ignored him. Someone had worked out it was midnight, and the whole carriage was singing *Auld Lang Syne* at the tops of their voices, and the porter tried to get them to stop but then eventually gave up and joined in. Col held his family close as the train slowly carried them on through the night towards Darkwell End, protected in a pocket of love.

None of them knew the challenges that lay ahead. There would be more raids to come, more damage and darkness and death. There would be years until the war was finally over, and it would get worse before it got better. But in that moment, carrying the candle towards a future that lay unmapped, waiting to be written, they knew that no matter what happened to them they would at least face it together. In some ways, it was the only hope they had.

But sometimes that's the only hope you need.

HISTORICAL NOTES

Whenever I need a new idea for a book (or whenever I'm avoiding doing my work) I go for a wander around London. The city still bears the marks of the Second World War, over seventy-five years later: there are gaps in rows of terraced houses where bombs landed, and shrapnel scars in the walls of the Victoria and Albert Museum. Fences around housing estates in Brixton and Peckham are made from old metal stretchers used during the raids; concrete blocks that used to house anti-aircraft guns now house pigs and goats in Mudchute Farm. It's amazing to think that these things *really happened*: that they're not just stories.

When I started writing *The Midnight Guardians*, I wanted to make Col's story as close as possible to what really happened during the war. The newspaper articles at the beginning of each chapter, as unbelievable as they sound, are all based on real newspaper articles and government information leaflets from the time. The raids you hear about are all real too. I needed to invent a few details to make the story work – for example, there were no terrible storms during the winter of 1940 – but for the most part, everything else is based on truth.

I did make up the bit about fairies.

THE BLITZ AND BLACKOUT

Between September 1940 and May 1941, around 43,000 people were killed and another 139,000 wounded by night raids on factories, docks, and cities like London, Liverpool, Manchester and Coventry. The attacks were spread throughout the country and came almost every single night: London was bombed for sixty-seven nights in a row. They finally stopped after eight months, though heavy bombing started again in 1944 when the Nazis developed V-weapons – flying bombs which could be fired from bases without the need for pilots.

During night raids, it was vital that towns and cities were hidden from enemy planes. As a result, all street-lights had to be turned out after sunset, and all windows and doors covered with blackout curtains so no light escaped. They even sprayed ink on the chalk footpaths along the White Cliffs of Dover so they couldn't be seen at night. Accidents were common when people tried to make their way through pitch black streets: one in five people suffered an injury during blackout.

THE EVACUATION

When war was first declared in 1939, millions of British children were evacuated from cities and sent to live in rural areas for their own safety. They either went to live with relatives or with complete strangers who'd volunteered to take them in. Sometimes brothers and sisters were split up without warning; sometimes entire families were taken in, including the parents. There were even cases of entire schools that were sent away together, teachers and all! While lots of children had wonderful experiences living in their new homes, others had a horrible time. There were some children who didn't see their parents at all during the war – nearly six whole years.

THE RAID OF 29 DECEMBER

The raid that Col witnesses at the climax of the book is based on a real occurrence. On 29 December 1940, London experienced the worst raid of the war so far. But worse was to come. On the very last day of the Blitz, 10 May 1941, Nazi planes dropped a final flurry of bombs that killed 1,364 people – the highest death toll in a single night of the raids.

The street where Col lives – Herne Place in Herne Hill, just in case you're wondering – really existed, and was completely destroyed by a stick of bombs on the night of 29 December. It's right around the corner from where I used to live in Brixton: there's a school there now, and a series of high-rise flats. Whole areas of London were rebuilt after the raids.

It is very important to remember that while all this was happening, British planes were also bombing German cities. Hundreds of thousands of German civilians died as a result of bombing raids throughout the war.

Countries all over the world were involved in the war, from Jamaica to India, Iraq to Japan, Kenya to South Africa – many suffered terrible losses.

RUTH AND THE KINDERTRANSPORT

On 21 November 1938 – twelve days after the Nazi party led a series of particularly terrible attacks against Jewish people in Germany – British Parliament agreed to allow Jewish children to come to Britain for their own safety, without the need for passports or documents.

Over the following nine months, 10,000 Jewish children were evacuated from countries such as Germany, Austria, Poland and Czechoslovakia, in what is now referred to as the Kindertransport. A huge amount of work was done by different organizations joining together to bring over as many children as possible. Some went to live with relatives, others went to live with complete strangers – many spoke no English, and their parents weren't allowed to come with them. There were even adult volunteers who travelled with the children to Britain, and then returned to their home countries afterwards, knowing that they would not be safe. Without this amazing work, who knows what might have happened to those children: many never saw their families again.

The Nazis continued to attack, imprison and kill Jewish people throughout the war: between 1941 and 1945, six million Jewish people were murdered in what is now known as the Holocaust. They were not the only ones targeted: other groups included people with disabilities, Roma, Sinti, Slavs, and gay men and women. People with different political beliefs, and those who spoke out against the actions of the Nazi party, were also imprisoned.

Knowing these facts can be upsetting: but facts empower us. It is vital that we talk about these things, even if they happened a long time ago. Ask questions: talk to your teachers about it, ask family members and librarians where you can find out more information. These are not just stories: these are things that really happened, and that can never be allowed to happen again. We must recognize darkness in all its forms in order to stand against it. Take your candle and hold it high.

ACKNOWLEDGEMENTS

"I know!" I said. "I'll write a story set during the Second World War! That sounds like fun."

And it was! But I'd be lying through my teeth if I said that making this book wasn't also really, really hard, and that I didn't require shedloads of help from hundreds of different people.

First of all: Claire Wilson, agent extraordinaire, who always had faith that this story could fly even when it was just a cardboard box with planks for wings. Also to my amazing editors – Annalie Grainger, Megan Middleton, and Denise Johnstone-Burt – for all their time and patience with me while I fumbled my way through this. They say that editors help you write the story you thought you'd already written, and that couldn't be truer of this book – thank you. Thanks also to David Dean for his incredible front cover! I cannot tell you how happy it makes me every time I see that chubby badger.

I'd also like to thank the people to whom this book is dedicated: my nan Doreen Montgomery, who'd always tell me stories about the war, like when her dad left his shelter during a raid and got blasted into a neighbour's garden;

and John Muckley, for telling me about his childhood in East London during the Blitz. Their stories were the seeds of what eventually became Col's story. Thanks also to Ngaire Bushell at the Imperial War Museum, who put me in touch with Alan Francis and Kitty Baxter, two amazing volunteers who give up their free time to talk to schoolchildren about their experiences of being evacuated during the war. Their knowledge and stories and suggestions (and frank criticism!) helped send me down the right path. HUGE thanks to Lissa Evans for her kind help with fact-checking during the coronavirus outbreak!

This book is also dedicated to Eve Willman, Vera Schaufeld and Elsa Shamash – three original Kinder-transport refugees who so kindly let me into their homes and shared their stories with me. I still can't believe that my job allows me to meet people like them, to sit in their living rooms and ask questions while they give me biscuits. I am particularly indebted to the Association of Jewish Refugees, and especially Carol Hart, for putting me in touch with them in the first place, and all her support in helping me write Ruth's story – thanks also to Tony Grenville for his invaluable fact-checking. Huge thanks also to James Ingram, for all the early proofreads, suggestions and corrections while I was creating Ruth (even though you don't like fiction!), and to Anne-Marie and Barbara Greenland for helping me with Ruth's voice and providing some fantastic German idioms – *ich grinse wie ein Honigkuchen pferd!*

Thanks also to Jem Roberts, who was so kind in answering all my questions on British folklore – what this man don't know about knuckers ain't worth knowing! Jem's compendium of folktales for children, *Tales of Britain* (Unbound, 2019), is brilliant – how had I never heard about the Lambton Worm?! Find yourself a copy, or even better go and see him perform it live as Brother Bernard.

Thank you to all the patient friends and listeners and supporters, of which there are too many to mention here, but to scratch the surface: my mum, Lian, Julien Godfrey, George Murray, David Isaacs, Helen, Helen, Helen, Helen, Helen, Helen, and also Helen.

Finally, thank you to all the children's authors, librarians, publishers, booksellers and passionate teachers that I've gotten to know over the last few years: your friendship and support makes doing this much easier. I honestly can't think of a time when our job felt like it mattered more: when telling children stories about the world that they will one day inherit feels more important. There are far too many of you to mention by name, and Walker are going to kill me if I make these acknowledgements any longer, so if you're reading this and thinking, "He'd better mean me when he says that", then I did.

ROSS MONTGOMERY started writing stories as a teenager, when he should have been doing homework, and continued doing so at university. His debut novel, *Alex, the Dog and the Unopenable Door*, was nominated for the Costa Children's Book of the Year and the Branford Boase Award. It was also selected as one of the *Sunday Times'* "Top 100 Modern Children's Classics". His books have also been nominated for the CILIP Carnegie Award, while his picture book *Space Tortoise* was nominated for the Kate Greenaway Award and included in the *Guardian*'s Best New Children's Books of 2018. He lives in London with his girlfriend and their cat, called Fun Bobby.